EVERYTHING
BEAUTIFUL BEGAN
AFTER

ALSO BY SIMON VAN BOOY

FICTION

The Secret Lives of People in Love

Love Begins in Winter

EDITOR

Why We Fight

Why We Need Love

Why Our Decisions Don't Matter

EVERYTHING BEAUTIFUL BEGAN AFTER

A NOVEL

Simon Van Booy

HARPER PERENNIAL

NEW YORK • LONDON • TORONTO • SYDNEY • NEW DELHI • AUCKLAND

HARPER ● PERENNIAL

HarperCollins books may be purchased for educational, business, or sales promotional use. For information please write: Special Markets Department, HarperCollins Publishers, 10 East 53rd Street, New York, NY 10022.

FIRST EDITION

Designed by Justin Dodd

Library of Congress Cataloging-in-Publication Data is available upon request.

ISBN 978-0-06-166148-8

11 12 13 14 15 OV/RRD 10 9 8 7 6 5 4 3 2

For C

Les vrais paradis sont les paradis qu'on a perdus.

—Marcel Proust

I am not I: thou art not he or she: they are not they.

—Evelyn Waugh

PROLOGUE

Everything was already here and I am the last to be born.

Small questions fill her mind like birds circling. Skeleton trees, stripped of their flesh by frost, are changing again. Green tips harden at last year's final moments.

She waits at the wild end of the garden, leaning on a gate in her coat—the one she wouldn't wear. But now everything about it seems beautiful—especially the buttons; small tusks discolored by a thousand meals. The mystery of pockets.

At the farthest end of the wood, where no one comes, is where her life begins and ends.

A sea of new grass will soon flood the fields beyond the gate.

It's her birthday too. Ten years old; suddenly allowed to venture to the far gate alone; old enough to lie awake in her bed, listening to the applause of rain on the window. Even her dreams are older: hair cascading, she digs with her father for treasure in faraway countries; then fleeing the storm of growing knowledge, she escapes into morning and forgets.

Her father is in the woods looking for her. Dinner is ready and waits in the pot to be eaten.

Her mother is lighting candles with a single flame conjured by her eyes.

Her father is out calling the name she's been given.

But her real name is known only by the change in light that comes without sound, and by worms pushing up through the soaked crust of soil; they glisten and swing their heads in blind agreement. Her father raises them by tapping the ground with a stick. They think it's rain.

Her father used to pretend he'd found *her* in the garden— that she wasn't his daughter, but some creature of nature— that she appeared in the wake of a few early daffodils—that he pulled her from the ground the way he finds all ancient ruins, with luck and enthusiasm.

Her mother has long hair. She ties it up behind her head in a soft nest. Her neck bears the silence and freshness of dawn. Years have spun lines around her eyes. Her mouth is small and moves with the promise of kindness.

Her father said this morning that snow is coming.

But in her mind it's falling fast. She can't stop it. Soon, everything she thinks will be covered by what she hopes will happen. And at midnight she will peep through lifted corners and marvel at the glowing shroud.

Sometimes when she cries out in the night, her father comes in. He holds her hand and rubs it until her eyes begin to soak and slowly she sinks, leaving behind small questions that float on the surface of her life until morning.

She knows she came from them.

She knows she was held aloft—a hot, screaming ball, with tiny arms flapping.

There was blood.

She knows she grew inside. She knows that people grow each other.

Once there was a tree upon which she found something growing. Something shuffling inside a small, silken belly webbed to the rough bark. A white sack spun from fairy thread. She visited her magic child with devotion. She spoke quietly and hummed songs from school.

Words at their finest moments dissolve to sentiment.

She couldn't be sure, but her child in its white womb was growing, and sometimes turned its body when she warmed it with breath.

She imagined one day, a surprised face peering at her from inside. She would peel her glowing baby from the tree, give it milk and a matchbox crib until it was big enough to sleep in her room, and like all children—confess everything with questions. She imagined its tiny body wriggling in her hand. The black dot of an open mouth.

But then one evening after supper, she went to her child on the tree and found the chrysalis empty.

The dreamlike skin, the gossamer veil ripped open in her absence. She waited until dusk, until crows barked solemnly at that distant fire beyond their understanding. Her eyes were red too. She walked slowly through the garden to the house.

Just as she was too afraid to tell anyone she had borne a child, she was now too proud to share her grief.

One day in summer, as she lay against the tree, her heart full of emptiness—a butterfly landed on her bare knee.

Its wings rose and fell—two eyes staring at her in their blindness. Her eyes staring blindly back. Nature's victory is seamless.

She can hear her father now.

His voice is clear and sharp. It rings through the damp trees.

There was a time before he met her mother.

It was before she began.

It was a shadow world with no significance. A world that was breathing but without form.

She hadn't even been thought of. She was dead without having died.

As her father calls out to her now at the edge of night, she wonders how he found her mother. Did he call her name in the dark woods? Did it echo through him before he knew, like some lost science of attraction?

She will ask tonight over dinner for the story of what happened.

Do we love before we love.

She knows her mother fell—not from the sky like threads of lightning silently over hills, but in a place called Paris. Her camera in pieces. Spots of blood on the steps.

Her father is very close now.

She considers falling to the earth, but instead remembers her name—a hook upon which she is carried through the world.

On the walk back home through the dusk, she's going to ask her father for the story of how he met her mother.

All she knows is that someone fell, and that everything beautiful began after.

BOOK ONE

THE GREEK AFFAIR

ONE

For those who are lost, there will always be cities that feel like home.

Places where lonely people can live in exile of their own lives—far from anything that was ever imagined for them.

Athens has long been a place where lonely people go. A city doomed to forever impersonate itself, a city wrapped by cruel bands of road, where the thunder of traffic is a sound so constant it's like silence. Those who live within the city itself live within a cloud of smoke and dust—for like the wild dogs who riddle the back streets with hanging mouths, the fumes linger, dispersed only for a moment by a breath of wind or the aromatic burst from a pot when the lid is raised.

To stare Athens in the face is to peer into the skull of a temple. Set high above the city on a rock, tourists thread the crumbling passageways, shuffle across shrinking cakes of marble worn by centuries of curiosity.

Outside imagination, the Parthenon is nothing more than stacked rubble. And such is the secret to life in a city ravaged by the enthusiasm for its childhood. Athens lives in the shadow of what it cannot remember, of what it could never be again.

And there are people like that too. And some of them live in Athens.

You can see them on Sunday mornings with bags of fruit, walking slowly through the rising maze of concrete, adrift in private thoughts, anchored to the world by unfamiliar shadows.

Most of the apartments in Athens have balconies. On very hot days, the city closes its million eyes as awnings fall, drowning the figures below in dreams of shade.

From a distance, the white plaster and stone of the buildings glow, and those approaching from the sea on hulking boats witness only a rising plain of glistening white—details guarded by the canopy of sharp sunlight that sits over the city until evening, when the city slows—and then a quick blush that deepens into purple veils the sea and becomes night.

In this city of a thousand villages, families huddle on balconies with their bare feet on stools. Lonely men dot the cafés, hunched over backgammon, they stare at the ends of their cigarettes—lost in the glow of remembering. It is a city where people worship and despise one another in the same breath.

For the lost souls of this world, Athens is a place not to find themselves, but to find others like them.

In Athens, you will never age.

Time is viewed in terms of what has been, not what is to come.

Everything has already happened and cannot happen again, even though it does.

Modern Athens buzzes around truth that everyone believes but no one can remember. As a visitor, you must simply find your own way through the foul, dry streets, where dogs follow at a distance close enough to be menacing and walls still gape where smashed by missiles of ancient wars.

And the lingering smoke and bustle, the strange music of the laturna machine, the forever pushing of strangers.

The museums are crammed with moments that went missing from history, that are impossible to put back, that were discovered by the thump of a plough, or hoisted up from wells, or dragged in tangled fishing nets along the sea-bed: mossy heads, stone hands teeming with barnacles, rotten oars rowed by the current in the dream of where they were going.

The beauty of artifacts is in how they reassure us we're not the first to die.

But those who seek only reassurance from life will never be more than tourists—seeing everything and trying to possess what can only be felt. Beauty is the shadow of imperfection.

Before Rebecca moved to Greece to develop as a painter, she flew around the world serving meals and drinks to people who found her beauty soothing.

Thousands possess the memory of her neckline, the deep blue of her uniform, the smooth edges of her navy heels, a tight bouquet of crimson hair.

She moved in straight lines, always smiling, a mechanical swan wrapped in blue cotton. In the mornings before work, she tied up her hair in a mirror. It was soft and always falling. She held bobby pins in her mouth, and then applied each one like a sentence she would never say. Her hair was dark red, as though perpetually ashamed.

It was an effort for her to talk, and so like many shy people, Rebecca found a face in the mirror and a voice that went with it. She used them like tools, to make sure it was tea that was desired and not coffee—or whether monsieur or madame might like another pillow. The real Rebecca lay beneath, smuggled onboard each flight inside her uniform, waiting for the moment to reveal herself.

But such a moment never happened, and her true self, by virtue of neglect, turned from the world and slipped away without anyone noticing.

Though her work did have its moments of salvation. She paid particular attention to children traveling alone. She often sat with them on her breaks, holding their hands, folding soft ropes of hair into braids, watching a piece of paper come alive in lines. Her dream was to become an artist—to be loved for moments beyond her own life.

She had spent her own childhood with her grandfather and twin sister, waiting for someone to come home, but who never did. And then suddenly it was too late. And the person she waited for became a stranger she would no longer recognize.

During the first seasons of Rebecca's femininity, she sensed there was a world outside her disappointment. Her twin felt it too, and they watched each other in the bath in the dull afternoon like porcelain dolls, their lives a story within a story.

They seldom talked about their absent mother, and never ever mentioned their father—who, they were told, was killed in a car accident before they were born. When something on the television alluded to motherhood, both girls froze until the moment passed. For even the most subtle movement would have been read by the other as an acknowledgment of a feeling they shared in silence—a failure forced upon them.

Then came the idea of another sort of love. In bed alone, aged sixteen, Rebecca gripped the sheets and conjured the strangeness of something inside her body, something living, spiraling deeper and deeper into the swirling pool of who she was, almost reaching back into the past to look for her.

For such a quiet girl, who walked to school every day across soft fields, her red hair as wild as blowing leaves—to love without fear would be to drown in another person. A first mouthful of water; a face disappearing; the sun changing shape, a bright rim, like the edge of a bottle into which she had fallen. Then her body would fill, go limp with gentle heaviness, and drift with the current.

Her supervisor at Air France was forty-five and divorced. Her ex-husband lived in Brussels and worked for the government. Her face was very thin. She possessed an elegance that made her seem taller when she walked. She was the sort of woman Rebecca imagined her mother could have been.

When Rebecca first arrived for training, she watched videos of flight attendants at sea, paddling octagonal orange rafts as small heads (presumably passengers) peered out through clear plastic windows. She was asked if she felt capable of daring rescues.

At a six-week training camp she learned to put out fires, kick through windows, and free helpless passengers trapped upside down in their seats. And she learned to do all this in a skirt and high heels.

She was taught to disarm a terrorist with the heel of a Dior pump and disable a live grenade with a bobby pin. But if at any point she ripped her tights, a whistle would blow and she would have to start the exercise again.

The training took place in large, unmarked warehouses outside Paris. Rebecca was always reminded how lucky she was to be chosen for her profession. After a while, she just bit her lip. Most of the training, she thought, is completely useless.

The majority of airline crashes are fatal to everyone on board.

Her real job (for which she received considerably less training) was to serve food and straddle the line between authoritative and sexy. In the 1960s, mandatory retirement age for flight attendants was thirty-five, but it was expected that they use their position wisely to secure a husband before then.

She kept her small Renault Clio at a staff parking facility near Charles De Gaulle International Airport. The window washer smelled like shampoo. The seats were gray fabric. The Muslim man who ran the garage had a small office, where he drank tea all day and fed stray cats.

·   ·   ·

After two years, she left Air France and moved home to her grandfather's house. Many of his friends had gone to nursing homes in Paris or Tours to be closer to their children. Her sister was living in the south, close to Auch, with an older man who sometimes hit her.

Away from her twin sister for the years she spent flying, Rebecca had become her own person. No longer one of a pair, and no longer responsible for her sister's strange outbursts, which, growing up, had scared and repelled her.

If anyone asked whether she had siblings, honesty compelled her to admit the presence of a sister. She veiled the subject by turning away. It was her life after all—and it was all she had.

Rebecca found her grandfather's house as she had left it: the same pictures on the walls; the same things in the refrigerator; the same noises coming from the television; birds nesting in trees; the cough of a distant tractor; cool soundless nights, then morning's cheek against the curtains; the sound of water rushing from a faucet; her grandfather whistling in the kitchen as he snipped pieces of mint leaf into a cup.

She drew either in the morning or in the late afternoon. Her grandfather watched from the kitchen window if she was in the garden. Sometimes he'd come out with coffee and a Madeleine cake. It was very quiet. Sometimes a small airplane would pass overhead. Sometimes just wind and the chatter of clothes-pegs on a swaying line.

Most of Rebecca's friends from school had moved to larger towns in search of work and adventure. Some had enrolled at universities in small cities.

Occasionally, Rebecca would venture into the dark shed at the end of the garden. Inside was a black bicycle with flat tires, oil cans, rotting window frames, cobwebs, and a tea chest of watercolor paintings, signed by Rebecca's mother with two initials.

Her sister knew about them, but by fifteen she had shed any artistic ambition and took very little interest.

They made Rebecca feel an immediate intimacy with someone far away. They all depicted the lake that was a short walk from their cottage. In the paintings the water was calm, with two figures on a grassy bank—as though waiting for something to break the surface of the water. The sky stuffed with cloud. Tiny specks for wildflowers, and always the same two initials in the bottom right corner in red.

After a quiet year in the cottage—a year spent in the relief of not flying, of not being pretty; a year of gathering strength, painting, mustering bravery—Rebecca decided to use the last of her savings and move to Athens. She knew nobody there. She would take her sketchbooks, her oils, and a few other things from home that she thought might inspire something.

She would live in exile with her desires. She would live as she imagined them on canvas, like faint patches of starlight: hopeful, but so far away; compelling, yet dispossessed of change.

TWO

Not long after settling into her own, small corner of the city, Rebecca met a young man called George. He was very lost and lived alone. She had seen him strolling through the square outside Monastiraki Station—close to the narrow entrance to the flea markets, where she liked to sit and watch people.

He was always overdressed, not only for the climate but for his age.

Street children followed him in cheap clogs playing toy accordions, pulling at his jacket and jumping in front of him. He was perturbed by them, but never unkind—like some uncle with a great many nephews and nieces whom he loves but hardly knows.

He looked the sort of man who had read all of Marcel Proust in bed. The sort who wanted to get up early but chronically overslept. And he walked slowly, hunched into a cigarette.

One day, he unknowingly sat next to Rebecca on the low marble wall where the locals sit and close their eyes. She sat still without saying anything. His shoes were deep brown. And then the street children recognized George and raced over, their clogs echoing through the square.

They eyed Rebecca with suspicion.

"Is she your girlfriend?" one of the children said in English.

George flushed with embarrassment. Rebecca noticed lines at the edge of his mouth quiver, like parentheses around what he felt but couldn't say.

"She's not my girlfriend," George said, blushing.

"She is pretty," one of the Romany girls added.

"That's probably why she's not my girlfriend," George said.

The children stared at him, mulling over the idea. Then one of them yawned.

"Got any sweets for us, Mr. George?"

George removed a bag of sweets from his briefcase and handed it to one of the children. They skipped off laughing.

"Did you buy those especially for them?" Rebecca said.

He seemed surprised she had spoken to him. He said he couldn't eat sugar, so they were doing him a favor. Then they chatted a little about the weather, then the Greeks, and the flea markets that managed to draw them both in from time to time. It was better on Sundays, they agreed, when things were spread out on blankets and people had the time to stand around.

Each blanket was a sea of lost things, George said. The relationship between the objects was what the passerby cared to make of them.

He was American. From the South. Rebecca told him she had read *Gone With the Wind*, but a long time ago, and in French. George said that his grandfather was in it somewhere—in the background, a minor character riding by on a lazy horse. Rebecca thought that was funny. His voice was slow, and his mouth held on to the words for as long as they could.

They continued talking. One conversation led to the next. Hours passed. Rebecca admitted she had noticed George before. She thought he looked friendly. George admitted that he was a bit shy.

"I'm shy too," she said.

After some time, George had to get going and abruptly stood. Instead of kissing her on each cheek, he simply raised his hand and then bolted—looking back once to wave again.

Some weeks later, neither would remember exactly how long, they spotted one another on the fringe of a café, and like before they exchanged a few words. As their impromptu chat deepened into conversation, Rebecca sat down. A waitress wandered over with two glasses of water, thinking they were customers—and slightly annoyed they had chosen the farthest table.

And so their first meal together was an accident.

An unplanned ritual began to take place where they would meet close to Monastiraki Station, eat supper, drink too much, and then George would walk her home, sometimes putting his arm across her shoulders.

Two months after their initial meeting, their friendship consisted of long flowing conversations, smoking, late-night drinks, and then slow walks home. He was always smartly dressed, and always likable, despite a tendency to get very drunk. When they arrived at her apartment, Rebecca would always stand outside her building with him for longer than she wanted, lingering somewhere between fatigue and awkwardness.

One night, he leaned in and kissed her on the cheek.

She bowed her head slightly, as if in prayer. When he dragged his lips toward her mouth, she drew back. He pulled back too with a jerk, as though his body had been acting independently of what he wanted. He fixed his gaze on some low steps, upon a tangle of plants that climbed the outer walls of her building—absorbing all they could from the dry soil below.

"Sorry," he said. "It was too forward."

"No, no," she said. "It's fine."

Rebecca lost her virginity in Moscow, at the hotel where the Air France team is kept overnight. It wasn't far from the Kremlin. She was twenty-two.

They drank vodka on the bed and laughed. He had white socks. It was very cold outside. They started talking on the bus that ferries staff between the airport and the hotel. He was from Holland. Afterward, he kissed her forehead and then rose to open a window. Freezing air poured in. He smoked and nodded at everything she said. Then they took showers and dressed. He watched as she waved the hairdryer around. His wife was Dutch too. They had no children. He was the sort of man she could never love, but she allowed her body to want him.

Her body did not change when George was close. She did not feel the calm violence of attraction she had felt with the

Dutch pilot in Moscow. *That* was something outside of themselves, something to which they had mutually conceded—like a particular hunger, brought on and satisfied only by one another. Rebecca did not feel that sort of visceral intensity with George, but his arms on her shoulders made her feel safe. And his torso was soft. George was a calm sea upon which she could have floated forever without ever going anywhere. And she would have to tell him sooner or later so that his feelings wouldn't be hurt.

"Do you always wear a tie?" she said.

The city around them disappearing under nets of evening.

The streetlights had not yet come on.

People carried out garbage in small bags tied at the top.

He was more drunk than usual and had trouble standing still. "Oh, I just like to, that's all."

"Actually, it suits you."

George looked down at his pale orange tie—raising the bottom of it with his hand. Printed on the fabric were little hands clapping.

"They're applauding." He smirked. Then he turned away. Rebecca wondered if he might cry. She tried to imagine it.

That evening in Athens was very quiet. Only the hollow clunk of backgammon pieces thrown across a board from a nearby balcony.

A barking dog somewhere else.

A scooter, then footfall.

"Hug me, George."

Stiff arms wrapped about her waist, then rested lightly on the climb of her hips. He was barely touching her.

"Don't hate me," she whispered.

"I hate myself," he said. She could tell he was very drunk.

"For wanting me?"

"Yes," he said.

Then he withdrew his arms as if untying something from around her waist. His shoes made noises on the stone, rearranging themselves, anxious to leave and begin walking away.

"I've spent my childhood learning to be alone," she said.

"Me too."

"Then you can't hate either of us," she countered with sudden grace.

Rebecca continued chatting as a way to dispel the awkwardness that threatened to linger until their next meeting. Then she kissed George on the cheek, again and again, until her kisses, like empty words, carried only the weight of consolation.

She could feel the heat on his forehead, the faint aroma of salt.

A car slowed as it approached them. When they didn't turn around, it sped up again. The heat of an approaching summer was something they would have to endure, for better or worse.

Rebecca stared past George at a kitten sleeping under the wheel of a parked car.

"If you need a can opened or something stirred, or to borrow a hairdryer, I'm not too far away."

"Thank you, George."

"Actually, I don't have a hairdryer, but I have some sublime recordings of the Bach partitas."

Rebecca shrugged.

She did not know when she would wish to see him again. In some ways he was an easy escape from her old life: he knew her simply as a French painter in Athens. She had come to Greece to paint enough work for an exhibition, which she hoped to have in Paris, to great acclaim.

Maybe her mother would stumble into the gallery by accident, unaware of her unofficial biography on the walls—the narrative of absence.

Before climbing the steps to her crumbling apartment, Rebecca turned in time to see George scoop out the kitten she had forgotten about. He set it down beside a bush and turned to walk away.

Then suddenly she felt the weight of emptiness upstairs. Her things still and heavy, as if underwater. She was in a city where she knew only one person.

"George!" she shouted. He turned to face her.

"Why don't you come and see my place?" she said, then smiled weakly and motioned with her hand. He followed her up the stairs to her apartment.

Her shoes made gentle claps on the marble steps.

They drank coffee on the balcony. Rebecca's limbs were already half-asleep. George reached over and began to massage her neck and shoulders. She closed her eyes and sighed deeply.

George got up and stood behind her. She could feel his breath on the back of her head, and the city was suddenly quiet then, somehow emptier than it had ever been.

"Stay," she said.

The hands on her shoulders stopped.

"Tonight?"

Later it was very hot.

George caressed her bare back with his fingertips.

"That's nice," she said. Streetlight fell across the bedsheets.

He moved closer. She felt him press against her. Half asleep, she shifted her body to accommodate his intent. Then she closed her eyes for a few minutes. He kissed her back with deliberate slowness. It was sweltering, despite the open shutters.

She saw that his eyes were wide open, drawing what little light there was in the room. The weight of his body drew forth her physical desire, and she opened her legs. Then, barely inside, George fell back with a gasp.

For a few minutes he didn't move. Then he pulled the sheet over her slowly, as if covering something delicate he wouldn't see for a long time. He kissed her once on the lips and lay down without saying anything.

She was very thirsty, but too tired to reach for anything. Morning was only a few hours away.

THREE

Whilst vacuuming, Rebecca once found a shoebox under her grandfather's bed. Inside were photographs from 1957 of a vacation in Cannes. His handsomeness startled her.

It was amazing to think that once, her grandfather had been young. In many of the pictures he was wearing a black tie and dinner jacket. In another picture he was putting the top down on an old Porsche with a cigarette in his mouth. The Porsche was matte silver. It had a Swiss license plate and thin wheels.

Each photo caught him in the middle of something: unfurling a sail, uncorking champagne, changing a wheel on the car, taking suitcases from the trunk, petting a dog.

Some photographs featured the woman who would become his wife, Rebecca's grandmother. Rebecca's life was the history of missing people. She didn't even know her own father's name. The one her mother had written on the birth certificate was made up, named after a French pop star killed in a crash.

Inside the shoebox, she found all that remained of her grandparents' happiness.

Her grandmother had been very beautiful, but her eyes carried the haunted look Rebecca had seen in her sister. In one photograph, she descended the steps of a small airplane. A man behind with black spectacles carried two suitcases. It was the only photograph Rebecca took from the box. A year later, she wrote away to Air France. It was the closest she could get to her grandparents' early life without money or education.

She wondered who would discover *her* shoebox. In the village of Linières-Bouton, the only glamorous men were the ones who sometimes appeared in summer from Paris on vacation with their wives and children—or visiting elderly relatives who otherwise annoyed them.

Rebecca dwelled on how everything had changed for her grandfather after her grandmother drowned and left him with a single daughter to raise that was her mother.

Did he consider the second half of his life a failure? He was unable to travel because of the burden of child care, and so worked with local businesses, rather than the bigger sales contracts in Paris, Tours, and Nantes that he'd been so successful with. He had also lost the woman he loved to a freak accident.

Rebecca felt it was too harsh to think about. Did he remember the moment that everything changed, like a subtle shift in light? Morning, and then a long afternoon of darkness.

She wondered how much of it was still with him. Was *that* man trapped inside the slow, sighing grandfather with unsteady hands?

Rebecca was too young to understand the conditions and the feelings that come with age. "The Quiet Story of a Sleeping Man" was the title of a sketch Rebecca had made of her grandfather one afternoon. When she showed it to him, he nodded and patted her head gently. Then he went into the bathroom and closed the door. The hollow clank of his belt hit the floor. Then a long sigh. A newspaper rustling.

Later that afternoon, during a game show on the television, he mentioned that Rebecca might like to hang her sketch in the hallway.

"Use nails from a jar in the shed," he said. "There are plenty, and they're all the same."

FOUR

Bands of wasteland skirt the city of Athens. Sometimes people wander there, looking for things of value to sell in the flea markets of Monastiraki. Bend down and brush away dry soil to reveal a single tile, laid two thousand years ago.

About four hundred years later as the Roman Empire crumbles—cheering as a baby takes his first steps across the very old tiled floor. Centuries on, stories of a new world fill the house, as honey spills from a jug and is lapped up by a hungry dog.

There were more trees then.

The air heavy with dry grass.

Birds came and went.

Now, just yellow rocks, a couch, and a mattress abandoned in the dead of night. Broken glass blinks in the sun. The only shade is from a low crumbling wall—pieces spat out like rotten teeth. The wall was once smooth. An architect fingered the seams then blew the dust from his hands. His horse was outside, drinking loudly from a deep bucket.

Athens is a world of despair and sudden beauty.

And it was from these two conflicting moods that Rebecca found her way as a woman.

It wasn't long before she loved the city.

And the ability to love Athens, like all love, lies not in the city but in the visitor.

The city matched Rebecca at every turn. Her moods reflected in the things that took place around her—things that she noticed: a cigarette vendor giving bits of fish to cats, a sudden shower of rain, deformed children sitting calmly on the steps of churches as their mothers shook their fists at God and then opened them to passing tourists.

Rebecca felt a physical part of the city, and sensing such blind devotion, it embraced her as its own.

When she opened her eyes, George was already awake. He turned and smiled at her, then offered another massage.

"I must start drawing soon," she said. "But let's have some coffee."

George offered to go out for fresh bread, but Rebecca said it would take too long.

He seemed dreamy and light. She even heard him laughing in the shower.

George stared at things in her kitchen, drinking his coffee slowly.

Rebecca held the front door open and wished him luck with his day. He waved again and stepped out backward. Then she took a long shower.

She spent the day making sketches and drinking chamomile tea. In the afternoon, she slipped from her clothes and worked in her underwear. When it became too hot, she turned the squeaking taps of the shower and waited a few moments before stepping in. There were cracks in the yellow wall, and water found and filled each one quickly—soaking the exposed cement that had dried in the darkness.

She slowly made everything cold.

Pellets of water broke the film of sweat on her body.

She let her mouth fill.

Rebecca's grandmother had drowned one afternoon at the end of summer.

The lake wasn't far from their house.

Rebecca's mother had watched. She was only a child herself. She ran home and told her father. The back door swung open. His daughter couldn't keep up and soon found herself all alone in the forest. She slowed to a walk. She was afraid. She started crying and then peed. Her legs stung. When she arrived at the lake, all she could see was a cool expanse of water. Then on the other side of the lake, perched on the grass—two bodies, one moving frantically—the other very still.

It was 1964. Rebecca's mother was almost six years old.

A policeman sat with them at the kitchen table. He kept touching his belt. They drank tea.

His hat was on the table next to a currant cake.

"What will you do with her clothes?" the young gendarme asked. The clock in the hall ticked loudly as if trying to answer.

Then the policeman nodded at the little girl on the couch with her doll. "What are you going to do with her?"

Her father looked at his empty cup without saying anything. He hardly said anything ever again.

The policeman finished his tea and went home.

Rebecca's hair was wet and heavy from the shower. Evening was falling over Athens.

Her drawings came to life in the dusk.

The city was cooling and traffic had thinned along the main avenue. Her neighbors hit spoons against pots. Someone was setting out plates. Children called in by a voice on the verge of anger.

She thought of George and their single night together.

She tried to imagine what he was thinking. The love of a man is like a drop of color into something clear.

When Rebecca worked for Air France, an old man once died in his seat.

Most of the other passengers were asleep. She noticed him because his eyes were open. She flipped through his passport. He wasn't married. His shoes were nice. He also had a mole on his face. His watch was heavy and light gold. Its hands shone in the dark. There were people on the ground who thought he was alive.

Rebecca lived mostly in hotels. Sometimes she would lie in bed and look at her uniform laid out on the chair.

That's me, she would think.

That's who I am.

FIVE

George's father ran away when George was about seven.

George had inherited his large jaw, which gave him the appearance of being more athletic than he was. Deep-set green eyes lingered in places where other eyes passed without feeling.

In the paradise of daydreams, George liked to think he was a reincarnation of Johann Sebastian Bach, who, like George, was famously unappreciated in his own lifetime, especially by his family.

George liked to stay up all night in the cafés of fashionable Kolonaki and read international newspapers. He sipped grainy Greek coffee and ate sticky baklava with a knife and fork. When no one was looking, he poured liquor into his coffee.

His chronic drinking began when he was fourteen, and inspired long walks through Portsmouth, New Hampshire, where he attended boarding school. It was a stark, gray town, with lingering fog at the windows of houses on the dock, the tall white nose of a town church illuminated against a white froth of sky.

Drinking gave George a sense of quiet happiness. It was something to look forward to. It allowed him to focus on the moment and think wild things he never would have thought while sober. When he was drunk, the past was a smoking ruin far away—something he could shrug off.

George attended the famous Exmouth Academy. The floors were always shiny. There were many other boys like him. They got along quite well. Anything edible sent from home was shared. They also loaned each other cushions and phone cards and had long group discussions after lights-out.

On Sunday, whole lines of boys could be seen trudging up the hill to church from the grounds of the school, like specters in their black capes. In summer they wore white button-down shirts, striped orange ties, brown blazers with white piping, brown shorts with brown socks. Chestnut oxford shoes were suggested but not required.

In the evening, they were free to watch television in the common area and eat a limited amount of candy.

Every Sunday, each boy had to write home. Here is a letter that George wrote home to his mother:

Pas Sans Nous

George Cavendish
Exmouth Academy
Portsmouth
New Hampshire
08801

Dear Mrs Cavendish:

How are you? Alix has given me a breakdance tape I can now body pop. The caterpillar is next. Did you enjoy the firework display on July 4th? We did it. I need a new fountain pen. The nail clippers you sent me great. If you do send a fountain pen — could you send it to me this week? ~~ If you can't don't worry to much.

Mrs. ~~Coleman~~ called me a southern gentleman because of my accent from Kentucky! There's a bug going around. Everyone in the dorm has it except me and now it's left the dorm and I still don't have it.

We have a new fencing team
But I'm not in it.

Instead, we fight with sticks at lunch time

At the moment my leg is in a bandage because I slipped going to Church.

PPS
Can I have come half term for half ~~term~~

💗 LOVE

George

P. Smile in ,,,!
Porters here...!
✗✗✗
XXX
✗✗✗
Ɫ ✗ ✗

As George aged, his enthusiasm for the rigorous life at school began to wane. The other boys became mechanized versions of themselves. One boy jumped off the roof. The headmaster said he died on the way to hospital.

Unlike many of the boys whose teenage years drained them of the sweetness upon which they'd shared early happiness, George simply failed to harden to the idea that life is disappointing because:

i.   People are motivated by vanity
ii. Life is over before you get to understand anything and so is probably meaningless

Instead, George became messy, emotional, careless, and weepy. His teachers in the upper school always seemed tired when they looked at him, and on several occasions they made sure the house staff confiscated his liquor without actually writing it up formally. When he threw up, younger boys could smell it in the hallway, and talked about it loudly at breakfast. Eventually one of the groundskeepers told George not to eat before or during his drinking sessions—at least as a way to control the odor.

Another way George escaped the circumstances of his loneliness was through music. He especially loved J. S. Bach. It was formal tenderness—love confined to structure. George played his music nonstop. There was so much to hear and he was never disappointed. George often bragged that Bach wrote so much in his own lifetime that if someone were employed full-time to copy out his entire library of work, it would take sixty-three years of labor just to copy the music from one page to another.

Bach also raised children. That was another reason George liked him. Unlike George's own father, Johann Sebastian Bach didn't run away from his son—even if he could only afford to give him two meals a day and a bed made of straw.

And then at fifteen, while other boys were swapping pictures of girls ripped from photography books in the library, or smoking in the orchard, George developed an obsessive love for language and classical history. His teachers' faith in him was renewed, and their sudden avuncular affection somehow cemented his natural sweetness for good.

By his sixteenth birthday (which his mother forgot) George spent Sundays translating whole chapters of Latin into modern English. He also loved the old Greek stories of myths and gods. He liked to imagine all the characters dancing together on stage to some eighteenth-century organ piece by Bach. He even tried to make a small theater from cardboard, but abandoned the project when he glued his fingers together and had to spend a day with the school matron, who was once in the army and didn't like classical music.

George was attracted to the Greek gods because no one believed in them anymore.

When Matron asked what he liked to do for fun, he went on about language. He told her that language owes its existence and identity to what it can never be, to what it can only point at. For the sound of language is the very embodiment of desire. And despite its greatest efforts, language is destined only to fail. Matron nodded and asked if he had been drinking.

"I won't lie to you, Matron," he said. "I have been."

She shook her head in reproach. "Well, don't let the masters catch you or I'll be bandaging more than your hands."

George loved every aspect of language. He loved to see it written, to hear it used, to feel its sounds in his mouth. What couldn't be felt in real life *could* be felt through language—through the experience of another by the setting of marks upon a page. It was unthinkable, yet it worked.

"We have found a way to record . . ."

George had once begun one of his term papers.

" . . . And for the past 5,000 years there has been a thread running through humanity keeping it together, so that we may know a person's innermost feelings without ever having known them personally . . ."

Considering himself something of an expert, George liked to analyze the few letters his mother had written to him at the academy. They required careful examination, for in them (George had convinced himself) there was veiled love.

George's parents were like a jigsaw puzzle that came without the parts he wanted most.

George sometimes took the afternoon off school. There was a churchyard overlooking the sea that he liked to sit in. His boarding school was set high on the edge of town, with fields that sloped to an apple orchard. Beyond the far wall of the orchard, where the older boys met local girls and lied to them, lay the churchyard and then the town of Portsmouth. Beyond that, unknown valleys and fields.

George loved sprinting through the orchard toward the far wall. In early autumn, sunlight fell golden through the trees.

Once across the wall and through the field, he came upon the churchyard.

Even when George could see his own breath, the bright sun warmed the tops of graves, as if anointing each silent dweller. The flat graves were the oldest. Children's headstones made the best seats. George liked to sit on them and smoke cigarettes. Sometimes he would chat to the child, and say things like, "Well, if you came to my school, you should take Miss Corday for French . . ."

The longer George sat on each headstone, the closer he felt to the child beneath him. His "best" friend in the churchyard had died in 1782. His gravestone read:

1778–1782
HERE LIES OUR SON,
TOM COPTHORNE
WHO DIED AGED FOUR YEARS,
EIGHT MONTHS, TWO WEEKS,
THREE DAYS, AND FOURTEEN HOURS.
EVERY MOMENT WITH HIM
WAS OUR HEAVEN ON EARTH.

George wondered if one day, somebody might count the minutes of his life.

Sometimes he stole a small carton of chocolate milk from the cafeteria and poured some into the ground for Tom.

Some of the flat tombstones had been split by weather. On another, time had erased whole sections of lettering. One gravestone was completely blank. George imagined it was his.

In summer, he lay in the dry grass without moving. The sun on his face like the hot cheek of a lover. His eyes closed to a glowing curtain of warm blood.

He wondered what his father was doing and blamed himself for his father's departure when he was seven years old. He felt bonded to his mother by deficiency. Somehow, in a way he couldn't understand, they had all failed as a family.

George once considered that his father was dead, and that his secret life overseas was a cover-up because George was somehow responsible for his death in a way he couldn't remember. But the reality was probably that his father was happier without them, and if he had a son in Saudi Arabia where his oil company was based, then he was probably more intelligent, more handsome, and a bit taller than George. The truth about his father would have to wait until he showed up several years later.

George decided on Athens long before he actually went. It was a city he felt he knew intimately through the many texts he had translated.

As he neared graduation from Exmouth, George told his mother in a letter home how he planned to do his college degree in two years and then move to Athens to embark upon life as an archaeological linguist. George argued that archaeologists help modern cultures through what they expose with their excavations. He gave examples. Israel's unwelcoming Negev Desert—a place where archaeologists uncovered the method by which the ancient Nabataean people had irrigated the land for crops two thousand years ago using the rain from cloudbursts through a system of irrigation channels and water cisterns. After this technology was relearned, life quickly returned to a place modern residents had found was beyond any type of cultivation.

Even more miraculous, George wrote in another letter, was how—after years of failed agricultural efforts four thousand meters up, in a lake region of Peru and Bolivia—archaeologists uncovered a technique that ancients had used to grow crops successfully on about two hundred thousand acres.

In the few letters his mother wrote back, she never once mentioned any of his historical stories. Instead she told him what she had eaten for breakfast, how the weather had ruined her plans, the state of the house, their lack of money, and that she dreaded her birthday. Once she said she was having minor surgery, and would be unable to write for three months and not to worry about her.

Between Exmouth and Athens, George went to a small liberal arts college, not far from his school. He lived in the dormitory known as Foxhole. He had a bed, a desk, a chair, a lamp, and a small bookshelf, which was stacked precariously with too many volumes.

He had a roommate from an island off Maine called Joshua, who wore a clear brace over his teeth and rode a 1950s bicycle.

On Saturday nights, George copied out whole sections of the *Iliad* and the *Odyssey* in ancient Greek. After his first English class, George gave the teacher a folder containing a few of his translations. The teacher was very old. He opened the folder, looked perplexed for a moment, and then said, "Jesus of Nazareth."

During his freshman year, he stayed up for two days, listening to the Bach partitas over and over without headphones.

A week later George returned to his dorm to find his roommate's cupboard empty and his bed stripped to a mattress. A note on George's pillow said:

Dear George,
I've moved! But only a few doors down the hall if you ever
need a friend . . .
Joshua B

George wrapped CDs of Bach's French Suites into a little package with ribbon. Then he opened a bottle of gin and swigged from it several times before pouring some into a glass and mixing it with tonic water.

Then he took out a pad of paper and a pen.

He looked at his drink and then out the window—at the gently blowing tall trees that were all over campus. Then George carried the package down the hall and left it outside Joshua's new door with a note that read:

When Johann Sebastian Bach was nine years old, he copied out
an entire library of music. He sneaked out of his bedroom, went
downstairs, quietly turned the metal circle that lifted the latch
and worked quickly in a blaze of moonlight. The passions we
cannot control are the ones that define us.

G.

A few nights after making love to Rebecca, George relived the experience in a café close to his apartment. He tried to remember every detail, things she said, what they had for dinner. He wanted a photograph of her or a lock of hair, some physical token to remind him of the night—something he could actually hold in his hand as proof that he'd finally done it, and was in love.

SIX

The next day was Sunday. Rebecca woke up and took a shower. Then she tidied her studio. When everything was put away, she felt like going out and decided to visit the narrow lanes of the Monastiraki flea market. She picked out a pair of plain white pants, but nothing so tight as to have Monastiraki's thin-haired vendors barking at her to come over. She had outgrown the need to be admired by men she was not interested in.

The flea market attracted many different groups of people. The low working class who looked for things they could sell for a small profit. Bohemians (usually foreign) fascinated by the plethora of random objects and the cultural diaspora responsible for things like former Soviet Union military-issue binoculars (with a hammer and sickle hologram in the glass). Then there was the criminal element, who were omnipresent at most outdoor, public events in Athens, and who seemed interested only in looking about the crowd, as though picking out specific faces for their vicious fantasies.

For Rebecca, the most important member of the flea market community was the laturna man, a decrepit organ grinder with a music box on wheels from the 1850s. He would wheel his cart from corner to corner, stop, turn the organ wheel, and then sing. His voice was old and cracked, like the record embedded in his machine. To Rebecca, he was like some mythical figure from another time. And she found him beautiful without understanding anything that he said.

The heat on the Athens metro was dangerous. Old women fanned themselves with rolled-up newspapers. The seats were wooden and passengers faced one another across tables, as though seated for a meal that would never come.

She had eaten two croissants for breakfast, warmed on her patio in the sun. Then, barefoot, she drank ice-cold goat's milk from a bowl, watching cars swerve around a dead dog.

She climbed the steps from the metro station to ground level past two grimy teenagers injecting heroin. Monastiraki was packed—mostly tourists who'd spilled over from the Plaka. There were also scores of pickpockets trailing American and German tourists who had strayed from their tour groups.

The alleys of Monastiraki were dark and hot. Vendors hung merchandise from every possible corner of the street. Small alleys led to stairs that opened upon rooms of French tableware, porcelain dolls, family photographs, a silver headlamp quietly unscrewed from a Rolls Royce Silver Ghost parked at the base of the Acropolis in 1937. There were other things too, with a more sinister past. One vendor had a stack of Nazi soldiers' helmets with the letters *SS* painted on the side in gothic script, Nazi silverware, mugs of random bullets, knives, handcuffs, and old mouse traps rusted shut.

You could buy 1930s medical instruments, a collection of playing cards from hotels in the south of France, surgical masks, Venetian masks, and monogrammed butter knives.

Her eyes drifted over the mountains of junk that lay on blankets next to refugee women with scarves tied over their heads. Everyone was coated in sweat. And in some corners, stringy meat cooked on small gas burners.

Then a face in the crowd stood out to her. A man with black hair and dark eyes, unshaven. Rebecca strained to see with the vague feeling that she knew this man.

Breathless, she squatted to find a space in the crowd through which to view him better. A woman yelled at her in Russian, suspecting a thief. Rebecca stood and walked away briskly.

An hour later, perusing the many things for sale (but still in the fury of her experience), Rebecca spotted a rare book with a paper cover.

As she reached down instinctively to pluck it from a twisted ball of tattered clothes, another hand clasped the top of the spine. Without letting go, Rebecca looked up and saw the face of the man holding the book. It was the severe handsomeness her grandfather had once possessed. The dark eyes held her in place. He smiled, and would not let go.

She released the book and stood up. The man stared at her, holding the book.

"But I saw it first," Rebecca said impulsively.

"How do you know I haven't already paid for it?" the man said calmly.

Rebecca tried to make eye contact with the refugee woman selling the book, but she was busy shaking her fists at a small boy urinating on the wall behind her.

He opened the book and she watched. It was a first edition Colette with uncut paper. But the second half of the book was blank. He handed it to her.

"It's like they forgot to print the second half," she said.

The refugee woman wanted a few pennies for the book. The man gave her ten British pounds.

"Show-off," Rebecca said.

"Karma," he said, and then without officially agreeing to, they walked from Monastiraki to the Ancient Agora, inadvertently brushing hands as they threaded their way through the crowds and ancient lanes.

He stopped walking to introduce himself as Henry, and when Rebecca gave her name, he said it several times, as though it were a new taste in his mouth.

"These are the same streets Plato walked down," Henry said, after telling Rebecca a little about his work as an archaeologist specializing in human remains.

"Plato was after Socrates but before Aristotle?" she said.

"They all had great beards."

"Beards?" she asked, smiling.

"Like Santa Claus or Père Noel in French."

"What did he say?" Rebecca asked.

"Well, let me see, wasn't it 'Ho-ho-ho'?"

She laughed. "I mean what did Socrates write about?"

"I don't really know," Henry said.

"Yes, you do," she said.

"Okay, he didn't write, he just talked."

"Like us," she said.

At the gateway to the Ancient Agora, bony dogs lounged in a pile. Flies orbited their heads.

"This is the old marketplace," Henry said, "where Zeno came up with a few of his lines."

"I see," Rebecca said. She had no idea who Zeno was, but imagined a masked man with a sword in fishing waders. Then Henry stopped walking and recited something to a slumped dog under a bush.

"Every man has perfect freedom, provided he emancipates himself from mundane desires."

The dog sat up and began to pant.

Rebecca smiled. "He wants something to drink."

The Ancient Agora spread out before them as patches of half-collapsed marble.

Each mound was roped off. The paths were dusty and yellow. Patches of weeds had grown around the monuments obscuring each base. A few tourists milled slowly about, unsure of whether to go on or return to their hotels and lie down.

Lovers, too, dotted the shadier benches below the olive branches, more interested in each other than the ruins that lay around them.

Then Rebecca did something uncharacteristic.

When Henry took her hand and led her through the marketplace, she not only let him take it—but held on. He was certainly handsome, but for her it was more, as though in every movement, in every word and gesture she found herself thrilled—as though a spell had been cast and his mere presence filled her with an unimaginable happiness that was without reason or condition.

Henry explained the significance of each eruption of rubble. He talked a little more about his work, and the various bones he had personally uncovered.

They walked up and down the Panathenaic Way—Athens' ancient main street.

Henry described the statues as though they were part of his family.

Rebecca noted how the ruins looked chewed, as if by giant mouths. Henry said that most of the original structures had been torn apart by religious fanatics, war, or the most effective method of destruction, neglect.

They sat down in the only shady spot—at the Stoa of Attalos, a long covered porch of marble that led to a museum. Rebecca removed her sandals and lay her feet on the cool stone. On a podium next to them was one of the small fragments upon which the entire reconstruction had been modeled. A few original steps remained, worn into deep smiles by centuries of coming and going. People who passed behind them were visible only as shadows. Henry explained how the statues before them had been judged not good enough for major museums, but too interesting to sell privately.

Rebecca thought that this endowed them with a realistic sense of beauty. But she didn't say it. She let her eyes roll over the sumptuous torsi of Odysseus and then Achilles. But then she decided to say something. After all, she was a painter living in Athens, no longer a poor girl from a French village whose mother wanted nothing to do with her.

"I like these so much," she said, pointing out the figures before them.

"Why?" Henry seemed interested.

"Because they are imperfect."

"That makes them special?"

"It makes them more realistic."

Henry stared at them.

"I like what you're saying," he said. "It's something I would never have thought of."

Rebecca knew little of classical art. Her education had consisted of pragmatic middle-aged teachers reading loudly from books, gray gaping classrooms, windows that tilted to open. In the distance, windy fields in varying degrees of brown, a long walk to school, her tights always itching, her belly still hot from breakfast, a tractor moving slowly across the field towing birds like tiny kites.

Rebecca moved her feet because they were going to sleep.

Henry was talking, but in her mind, she saw only the hand of her old teacher writing something on the board.

It would soon be time to go home.

Her nose filled with the smell of her grandfather's stew.

The dull light of Tuesday afternoon.

The France of legend was a place unknown to Rebecca. It was a place from which the modern youth had been tacitly excluded. She had never been to central Paris—to the museums.

Despite wanting to be an artist, she was afraid she might see her mother and then scare her off completely, or worse, that she wouldn't recognize her. But she had seen the Eiffel Tower at New Year's Eve on television.

The Museum of the Ancient Agora was a long yellow corridor with tall glass cases and female security guards who took no pleasure in people coming in.

Henry led Rebecca to a case that at first looked empty.

Inside, was a shallow box that held mounds of dry earth from which fragments of bone were visible. Henry pointed to an abrupt line of jaw, a delicate femur, a few lingering teeth.

"It's the grave of a child," he said. "She was about three years old when she died. See those bracelets?"

Rebecca nodded.

"Well, she was buried with them on her wrists, and so they lie now in the position she had worn them when they laid her in the coffin."

"When did she die?"

"About three thousand years ago."

Rebecca looked at the child's remains for a long time. People walked around her.

"Why do I feel so sad?" she said to Henry. "She'd be dead anyway by now."

Henry nodded but didn't walk away until she was ready.

They shuffled slowly past cases of small stone figures, pots, bowls, a child's commode, and jewelry. They paused before a case of small lids with writing on each one.

"*Ostraka*," Henry said. "The names of people who the citizens wanted exiled."

"Why?"

"I don't know, maybe they were assholes."

Henry read the names of the assholes:

Onomastos

Perikles

Aristeides

Kallias

Kallixenos

Hipparchos

Themistokles

Boutalion

"If enough people wrote the same name, that person would be asked to leave the city for ten years," Henry said.

"I wonder what would happen to them," Rebecca mused.

"What happens to anyone in exile—they are finally free."

"That's a lovely thing to say," Rebecca said.

"Is it?"

"Yes, because it's us."

Henry laughed. "We're in exile?"

Rebecca nodded. "We're free from the duties of fate."

Henry smiled. "What a wonderful idea."

Then they passed a cabinet of things found at the bottom of a well. There were oil lamps—which Henry said were probably dropped in at night, after being balanced on the edge as the bucket was lowered and raised. There were fragments of bowls and a casserole dish, which someone who lived close to the well must have brought to fill. There was also a small vase in the shape of a child that would have been very valuable in its time. Rebecca told Henry that it was her favorite piece.

"Because," she explained, "it will always be a mystery why people toss out valuable things."

"They do, don't they?" Henry said quietly, pondering the idea. "Let's go somewhere and think about it."

Outside they found an empty marble bench. Henry opened the dusty leather briefcase he carried with him. Inside was a bottle of water, a slim book, and some interesting rocks he'd found.

He opened the bottle and offered it to her first. Instead, Rebecca impulsively pulled a notebook from his bag, opened it, and read a line.

"Why is there not nothing?"

"Isn't it the most interesting thing you've ever heard?" Henry said.

Rebecca grinned. "Yes—did you write it?"

"No," Henry said. "I copied it, but here's something," he said, passing her the bottle of water.

As she drank, several drops escaped her lips and rolled down her chest making tracks across her skin through the sweat and dust.

She saw Henry look, and their eyes met in a single moment of understanding.

In the marketplace around them, the sun was beginning to set and the narrow lanes of Monastiraki swelled with hungry people.

SEVEN

Henry's apartment was in a working-class neighborhood, beside the metro tracks. Although he had very little furniture, piles of books softened the space and gave it a sense of home. Henry and Rebecca sat on his balcony overlooking a fountain. Couples perched at its edge—leaning toward the water and dipping their hands. A few dark leaves had sunk to the bottom, held in place by the rushing water. Children lowered their small bodies carefully into the cool depths. Then an angry voice from a balcony and the children scattered like marbles rolling away.

On the rickety table before them lay two whole fish that Henry had rubbed with garlic and lemon before roasting.

A neighbor had left them in a box at Henry's front door, with instructions on how Henry should prepare and cook them. Henry also cut a brick of feta into thin slices, between which he slipped leaves of mint and basil.

"Dip them in oil like this," he said.

Then he opened more Greek wine by holding the bottle between his knees. He explained to Rebecca why he'd come to Athens.

Like her, he was from a small cottage, but in Wales, on a hillside.

"It was like camping every day," he confessed. "The house smelled of wet magazines and I shared my bed with a dozen animals."

"A dozen?"

"At least."

"Do you speak French?"

"In bits,"

"Like your work then," she said.

"Exactly—how did you know that?"

"When we were walking in the marketplace, you mentioned the bones."

"Oh."

And from the remains of the fish that lay on his plate, Henry explained how bones grow, how they change, and a few of the intricacies involved with his work.

Rebecca said that it was impossible for an artist to draw a person without seeing them alive, at least once.

Henry folded his arms appreciatively.

"Only Michelangelo could resurrect the dead," she went on. "I heard a story where a Roman statue was found about fifteen hundred years after it had been sculpted. It was intact except for a missing arm. Michelangelo was asked to sculpt a new one. Despite serious concern at the angle of the new arm in relation to the body, Michelangelo insisted that it was anatomically correct—that his arm was an exact replica of the missing arm. A few hundred years later, a farmer found a heavy piece of marble in his field outside the city of Rome, which turned out to be the original missing arm from the statue."

"And?" Henry exclaimed, ashing his cigarette.

"It was exactly the same shape and dimensions as the one Michelangelo had made."

"Amazing story."

"I'm not sure I'll ever make a living from painting," Rebecca admitted, "but if I work hard, I might get to a certain standard—maybe good enough to exhibit in Paris."

"That's exciting," Henry said, "and enviable."

"Enviable?"

"Yes," Henry explained, "most people don't have such a passion for something. When you do, it stands out."

Rebecca asked him if it felt personal, taking people's bones from the soil.

"No, but I suppose it is. I'm their last point of contact."

"It sounds as though you wish you could say 'hope,' their last point of 'hope.'"

Henry thought for a moment. "But I'm a scientist; I would never say that. There's a reason why people die, and it's often straightforward—nothing to get emotional about."

Then he looked over the balcony. A man was brushing his dog next to the fountain. The dog was standing very still with his tongue out.

"How about those human remains," Rebecca said.

Henry smiled at her.

"I wonder what will happen to mine," she laughed. "I wonder what will remain of my life—who will find my body."

Henry nodded.

"Will anyone remember the way I felt?" she said and then forked the last few pieces of flesh from under the spine of her fish.

Henry removed the plates.

"I'll be back in a minute."

Rebecca sat alone on the balcony as Henry disappeared into the bright kitchen. It was getting dark. More people had gathered at the fountain. Three old men had taken off their shoes. They lit cigarettes. The smoke drifted above them, unfolding its wispy arms until it reached Rebecca as the faint aroma of something on fire.

"Are you ever going back to Wales?" Rebecca shouted toward the kitchen.

"No," Henry bellowed. "Would you care for more wine?"

"*Oui, oui,* of course," she shouted. "I'm a French girl after all."

Henry returned with a fresh bottle and a packet of Greek cigarettes.

"Why did you come to Athens really?" she asked.

"I'm an archaeologist—so I need ancient places."

"But people die everywhere."

"But they have to have died a long time ago," Henry said, and found her hand under the table for the second time that day. "It's most interesting to me if they died before the invention of written language, because in the absence of records, the way someone is buried tells us so much about what was important to them when they were alive."

"Did you grow up close to Paris?" He poured a heavy glass of wine. Rebecca shook her head.

"I think someone once said that Paris is the most modern of ancient cities, while New York is the most ancient of modern cities," Henry said.

"Who said it?"

"I forget now—were you always a painter?"

She touched her chest. "In here, yes, but I worked for Air France for a few years."

"Air France?"

"As a flight attendant."

"Is that why your English is so good?"

She nodded. "I speak Italian too, and Dutch, but no Greek."

"God in heaven," Henry said with a lustful groan. "All men love flight attendants."

Rebecca raised her eyebrows with mild distaste.

"I love the little hats. Were you good at it?"

"I think so,"

"Did you ever have any difficult passengers?"

"Never," she laughed.

"That means they all were—tell me some more about it, I'm really interested, really interested!"

Rebecca brushed a few strands of flame-red hair from her face and took a drink before speaking.

"To see those people there like that, up there in the sky with me—some sleeping, some reading, but most staring up at the television, was very bizarre."

"Really?"

"I wanted to paint them, not serve little plates of warm pasta."

"Is it true that the pilots seduce the flight attendants?"

"No," she said, reaching for her glass, "I don't think that's true."

"Do you still have the uniform?"

"Yes."

"Really?"

"Do you want me to go and put it on for you?"

"Christ, are you serious?" he said. Then he got up and went into the hall. He returned with a clean ashtray and a blanket.

"In case you get chilly," he said.

They talked for another hour, staring at one another intently between sentences. When the last of the wine filled Rebecca's glass, Henry gathered everything up off the table and carried it inside. Rebecca followed him holding a cigarette.

Henry balanced the plates and bowls in the sink, then turned the faucet on. Rebecca sat down at the kitchen table and watched. The table was dark wood. There was a terra-cotta bowl of salt and a bowl of lemons. The lights were very bright.

"I think I'll do this tomorrow," he said, looking at the mess of dirty bowls and cutlery.

He went to the freezer and removed a small tray of baklava, which he cut into triangular pieces with a large knife. The plastic handle of the knife had been melted out of shape by the rim of a very hot pot.

Henry ladled thick cream over each piece and gave a plate to Rebecca with a fork.

"I don't want any," she said.

He held the plate in the air for a few moments, then set it down in front of himself.

"We'll share mine then."

They chewed the sweet, heavy baklava without talking. Rebecca looked at the cream.

"What's your surname?" she asked him.

"Bliss."

"You're joking," she said. "Bliss? Like happiness?"

His mouth was full, so he nodded.

"Henry Bliss," she laughed. "It does mean happiness, yes?"

"Pure, wanton happiness," Henry replied swallowing.

"Henry Bliss," she said. "It sounds nice, Henry Bliss, Henry Bliss, Henry Bliss, Henry Bliss."

Henry stopped chewing for a moment.

"What's your surname?"

"Baptiste."

"Jesus!"

And they both laughed without knowing why.

Then Rebecca said the light was very bright. Henry lit candles and turned it off. Their faces glowed in the darkness. Henry lit a cigarette and passed it to Rebecca.

"I can't believe I had dinner with a man I picked up at Monastiraki," she said.

"You didn't pick me up—I came with the book. Where is it, by the way?" He asked and then realized what had happened before she could speak.

"The foyer at the museum," she said. "Should we go back tomorrow?"

"I have to go away tomorrow."

"For how long?"

"Eight days."

"Should I miss you?" Rebecca said coyly.

Henry smiled. "Yes, please—it's only to Cambridge for a series of lectures on new carbon-dating technology that my boss thinks I should hear."

"Will you send me a postcard?"

"I will—and don't look so sad. Absence makes the heart grow fonder, doesn't it?"

"We'll see," Rebecca said.

Henry put down his glass and balanced his hand above the flame of a candle.

They both watched.

"*Agapi mou,*" he said. "My love."

Rebecca picked up her glass and swirled the contents, as though it were a tiny ocean at the mercy of her reticence.

"It's just an expression," he said. "I think I'm drunk."

"Sorry," she said, passing the cigarette back to him. "I just realized we were supposed to be sharing this. I suppose I should tell you that I sort of have a boyfriend."

Henry retreated from the flame of the candle.

"Damn," he said, then looked at her. "Is it serious?"

"Actually he's not really my boyfriend at all because I don't want to see him anymore." She reached for another cigarette. "Maybe I'm a bit drunk too."

With vague coolness, Henry said:

"Don't hurt him."

"What do you mean?"

"He probably loves you."

Rebecca sighed. "He does, I think."

"Well, don't hurt him."

"Why would you say that?"

"Because if I were your boyfriend, I would want it to be serious."

"He's not my boyfriend—I don't know why I said it. Anyway, what does serious mean?"

"Ask me in a year from now," Henry said, "and I might have an answer for you."

A cool wind pushed through the blinds.

Henry stood and leaned across the table to kiss her. The awkwardness of where he had chosen to embrace was quickly overcome when she stood and they both stepped into the hall, toward his bedroom, kissing and bumping into things. The floor felt cool against Rebecca's bare feet. His bedroom was dark. He handled her with gentleness, undressing her quickly but deliberately.

She let her dress drop and then stood out of it. Henry reached up her thighs with both arms as though quietly imploring. She squeezed his hands and guided them purposefully to the places on her body she wanted to feel him the most, any hesitation having long been dissolved by wine.

She opened her eyes when she felt the weight of his body shift. He was hard and his body was heavy. The feeling that began in the market that afternoon had grown in power. And from far away, something was dragging her to a place where she would momentarily lose herself. She dug her nails fiercely into his shoulders and bit him hard. He didn't flinch but slowed, suspending himself above her, strands of muscle in his shoulders like strings. She swirled in the currents of her life, where her sense of self was revealed as arbitrary, extraneous, and so easily washed away by the force of that singular intent.

She grabbed on to his black hair, exhaling savagely.

Afterward, they lay on their backs, holding hands. Two people divided by the illusion of experience. All was silent.

Like a single drop, she hung upon the edge of sleep.

He reached for her hand in the darkness and together they fell from this world and into another.

EIGHT

When Rebecca opened her eyes it was still dark. Henry was not in the bed, but standing against the shutters. Cool air was pouring in. She pulled back the sheet.

"That feels nice," she said.

He turned around. "You'd be shocked at how early it is."

Through the open shutters, Rebecca could see into a bright apartment across the street. A man stood shirtless over a pan of boiling water. Henry went into the kitchen and came back with two glasses of orange juice, which he set on the bedside table.

"Do you see him?" he said.

The man lowered several white towels into a nest of steam.

"What's he doing?" Rebecca said.

"Boiling towels."

"He looks miserable," she said.

"He has a right to look miserable."

Rebecca lifted her head from the pillow and opened her eyes very wide.

"That's the neighbor who left the fish outside my door."

"But why is he miserable?"

"Five years ago his wife and baby were hit by a taxi on the corner."

Rebecca gasped.

"The child died, and when the wife was out of hospital she left him and went back to her parents' village. The woman downstairs told me," Henry said.

"How did you meet him?"

"I haven't yet—but apparently all the neighbors know there's a foreigner living here."

"So he knows you're living here alone?"

"Yes, everyone does."

"Then why did he leave you two fish?"

"I don't know, maybe he thinks I look hungry."

"Or maybe he wanted to eat with you?"

"Do you really think so?"

"I think he looks lonely," Rebecca said.

"But there are always people on the street below his balcony—"

"That doesn't mean anything," Rebecca interrupted. "Loneliness is like being the only person left alive in the universe, except that everyone else is still here."

"That's beautiful," Henry said. "A really beautiful thing to say."

Then Henry told her about something sad from his childhood. Rebecca stared at the topless man. He stood at a tilt as though tethered to some terrible weight—some moment of his past that simultaneously defined who he was yet denied him life.

NINE

"Bye, Henry," Daddy said.

"You're not worried, are you, love?" Mammy said. "Because we're only next door if you need us."

Henry nodded.

"I know, Mam."

"If your brother wakes up, just run over and tell us, now, like a good boy."

"I know what to do, I can do it, Mam."

"And you're not afraid?" she said gently.

"He's fine, Harriet," Daddy said. "We'll be late."

The house was very quiet, but sometimes creaking, or a sharp tick from the kitchen, or the cat flap as Duncan came and went to do his business. The television was on. Henry sat down. There was a plate of rock cakes and a large glass of orange squash. It was still light out. Cars swished along in the wake of heavy rain.

When the cartoon ended, Henry wondered if they would come back. He stood in front of the television to see what would happen next.

There were pictures of Spider-Man on his underwear. He could see himself in the reflection of the television. The boy in the glass stood very still. They both waited to see what would come on.

Then Henry decided to check on his brother. It was his main job, after all. He was in charge when they were out.

Henry was five years older than his brother, but they looked alike. His brother always wanted everything—was always reaching his fingers into things, always touching—his face contorted with the difficulty of retrieval. Hanging saliva. The stench from his diapers—as heavy and hot as parcels of fish and chips. The violence of crying. His hair so wispy it might blow off. Henry remembered little black eyes when he came home from hospital. Mammy let Baby suck Henry's finger.

"That's how I eat gooseberries," Henry had said. Everyone laughed.

Baby didn't have any hair then. Now he was almost one. Henry liked to bounce him on the bed. His clothes were soft and blue. He was entered into them through a zip. There was a fish sewn into the cloth. It was smiling and blinked one eye.

Henry stood in his brother's room. The smell of disinfectant and baby powder filled him with despair. The blinds were down. The light was soft but bright enough to see.

His brother breathed quickly. His hands were very small, but wrinkled in all the correct places.

And then, outside a dog barked.

His brother's eyes opened quickly. He turned his head blinking. When he saw Henry, he smiled, but then began to cry.

"No use crying for Mam," Henry said. "She's next door."

Henry put his hand through the bars of his crib, but it didn't help.

Then Henry did a little dance and sang a song about bears he had learned at school.

"I'll teach it to you when you're older, like me," Henry said.

His brother's face was red with crying. His eyes bulged.

If only he would stop screaming. Mam and Dad would be mad that he woke up and blame Henry for going in.

Henry was about to run next door when he suddenly had the idea to give him a toy.

On his changing table, next to a pile of diapers, was a mobile that had once hung over Henry's crib. Henry's dad had said that maybe his brother might like it and he'd hang it tomorrow.

Henry grabbed the mobile and dangled it above the crib.

"This was mine once," Henry said. "So stop crying."

His brother stopped crying and reached up his hands.

"Would you like to play with it?"

The baby was laughing. His face returned to normal and the room was suddenly bright with the final moments of day. Henry dropped in the mobile.

Baby looked satisfied. His short, fat fingers explored little parts. He put one of the plastic animals into his mouth, then took it out and looked at it. He pulled on the strings, and tried to chew the wood.

"Go to sleep, little brother," Henry said. "Have nice dreams."

When Henry stepped out, he felt very proud. He would boast to Mam how he'd quieted his brother when a dog barked.

When his parents got home it was almost dark. There was nothing on television and so Henry had his toys everywhere. The house was now a place of shadows and Henry was too afraid to leave the glow of the television to reach the light switch.

"What a big boy," Mammy said.

"C'mon, young man," Dad said. "Time for bed."

Henry yawned.

"Did your brother wake up?"

"Yes," Henry said, "but went back to sleep after I went in and checked on him."

"You're such a good boy," his mam said. "I knew I could trust you to be the man of the house."

"Even though we were only at the neighbors," added his father.

As Henry zipped into his own pajamas, watched dutifully by his father, there was suddenly a piercing scream that seemed to go on for a long time. His father bolted.

Then shouting from his brother's room.

Henry watched through the crack in the door.

They had to use scissors to cut it off. Henry peed his pants but no one noticed.

Then the police came with an ambulance.

Neighbors appeared at the door in dressing gowns.

Henry was allowed to stay up and talk to the policeman.

TEN

For most of Henry's childhood, his brother's room was used for storage. They never talked about it as a family. Sometimes his mother cried in her bathroom. Sometimes Henry found his father in the garage staring at nothing.

As a teenager, he woke up gasping. Everybody knew his brother had died. In the supermarket, people would approach his mother.

"How are you coping?"

Even years later, the same question, the same grimace of sympathy. An arm placed gently upon her arm all helped to keep it fresh.

It was blamed on the toy; nobody knew anything beyond that.

By his final year at university, Henry realized that something wasn't right. The mechanism that allowed other students to form long friendships over rowdy nights at the student bar had broken in him, or had never worked.

The few relationships he'd had were quiet disasters. What began as genuine intent ended quickly with indifference.

And now Rebecca. It had begun like the others. Attraction, conversation, a night together. But there was something about her that was deeper and braver—something about her that compelled Henry beyond the details and feelings of the moment, as though they were both tethered to the same point in the future.

And so he told her some things, but not everything. Of course she blamed the toy, and Henry was safe to continue impersonating the man he should have been.

After a long silence, Henry awkwardly asked Rebecca about where she grew up. "In some French country house with shutters and garden hoses and beds of lavender and a vintage Citroën?"

"Not exactly," she said, still visibly shaken by his story.

"Where are you from in France exactly?" Henry asked.

"Guess."

"Well, not Paris, I know that. How about Champagne?"

"*Non.*"

"Bordeaux?"

"No, not Bordeaux."

"Dijon?"

"Is your geographical knowledge of France limited to what you can eat and drink?"

"Lascaux?"

"Good answer—being that I've made only sketches and not paintings yet, but no."

Rebecca reached for the orange juice on her bedside table, but then changed her mind and set it back down.

Henry went to the kitchen and returned with a glass of water.

"Thanks," she said.

She stretched out her body in the sheets.

They were both tired. As they lay down, Henry said, "I find proof of life, and you explain the significance of it."

"*Non*, Henry, I don't think that's it—I think you search for proof of your own life."

Henry thought for a moment. "And what do you do?" he said.

"I simply draw." She smiled. "For now."

"What's your boyfriend's name?" Henry said.

"He's not my boyfriend, I told you—he was just a friend, really."

"Greek?

"American. You'd like him," she said.

"Would I?" Henry puffed. "Why do you say that?"

"Because he listens to opera, drinks sherry in the afternoon with a small dish of dried apricots, and of course he knows all about archaeology. The ancient Greek language is his passion."

"Do people like that exist?"

"Here they do," Rebecca said.

Henry thought for a moment, and then said:

"Let's do that."

"Do what?"

"Let's make here our home—it's so far from our lives that we can be free."

She turned away and looked out into the darkness. Her pillow was soft and warm.

"But I just met you. I don't know you."

"I feel like you know me," Henry said.

Rebecca turned to face him. "If I think too much about what we're doing, I might get scared."

Henry touched her hair. Then he planted gentle kisses on the back of her neck, and she soon fell asleep.

In the morning, Henry dressed and went outside. It was cool. He untangled the strap on his helmet and looked up at his own balcony. Then he mounted his rusty Vespa and rode north, until pulling free of the city.

He slowly climbed the mountain road that led to the scorching, sun-drenched hole he was digging, with what Rebecca would later describe as an expensive toothbrush. By early afternoon, he would leave the site with his briefcase of notes and get on a plane bound for London. A Cambridge University minibus would ferry him to his dormitory for the week.

Rebecca stayed in his apartment until noon. She washed in his hot yellow bathroom, then cleaned the dishes from supper. After dressing, she bought oranges from an Albanian in the street, propping open the front door with an empty wine bottle. She put the oranges in a small bowl and left them on the kitchen table next to the lemons with her address. Before closing all the shutters for the day, Rebecca noticed the topless man who had been boiling towels in the building opposite. He was sitting at the kitchen table with a cigarette and pulling at his hair.

ELEVEN

George spent most of the afternoon in bed, a bilingual volume of poetry by Kazantzakis split over his body like a small church. It was open on a page that read:

Beauty is merciless. You do not look at it, it looks at you and does not forgive.

It was about a week since he had seen Rebecca. His apartment smelled of spilled wine. Wilting vines of dill lay on the kitchen counter in thick bunches, while empty wine and liquor bottles occupied most corners and areas where George didn't need to walk. He repeated the line of poetry a few times until he knew it by heart.

He was meeting someone at noon, and so got up, dressed, and made his way to a popular café on the corner of his street. George's lunch companion was early, and stood to greet him. They did not shake hands, but were pleased to see one another.

"How are you, Costas?" George said. "Did you order?"

He shook his head.

"Thanks for meeting me. Here are cigarettes and the bottle of ouzo, before I forget."

The man's look of dull shame brightened for a moment. He tucked the cigarettes into one of the many pockets of his heavy coat, but held up the bottle of ouzo and made a great pretence of reading the label. This was an attempt, George suspected, to hide that fact that he was actually illiterate.

"Looks like a nice one, interesting history," the man said.

"It's excellent, just like your English."

Costas nodded appreciatively. He was a dark-haired man of about fifty, but due to his circumstances he looked considerably older.

"So what have you been up to since our encounter?"

"Honestly?" said George.

Costas nodded.

"I've gone and fallen in love with someone."

"A woman?"

George nodded.

"Greek?"

"French."

"Oh," Costas said. "Very nice."

"But," George said, "I haven't heard from her in a week."

"Have you telephoned?" Costas suggested.

"She doesn't have a telephone, but I've been round a few times and she doesn't appear to be home, or if she is, she doesn't open the door when I ring."

"Maybe she's busy," Costas said. "But then all women are mysterious, no?"

Costas scratched his chin, then reached for one of George's cigarettes. "May I?"

George nodded. "Of course."

Finally the waiter approached along with the owner—a stout man with a heavy gold chain.

The owner stood at their table, arms akimbo, and glared angrily at Costas.

"Sorry, we're closing," he said.

"Closing?" George said incredulously, "But you've just opened."

Costas laughed heartily.

"Both of you get away from here," the owner said.

"But why?" George said. "We're only here for lunch."

"Well, this is a neighborhood café, not a charity kitchen."

George stood his ground. "I've always paid my bill, and tipped you generously."

"This is true," the owner said. "So why you know this man if you're so respectable," he said, pointing to Costas—who was already packing up and getting ready to leave.

"I'm very disappointed," George said, standing up, "that you've lost the nature of what hospitality is. You guys invented it."

The owner's lips trembled slightly, but he said nothing.

As they walked away George turned around and waved. It was a peculiar habit of his that often confused people. The waiter, who had said nothing, waved back, and the owner gave him a few harsh words.

"Sorry about that," George said. Costas smiled magnanimously and asked George for another one of his cigarettes. They smoked at the edge of a fountain and watched people pass.

"Strange world we live in, isn't it?" George said.

Costas nodded. "Very strange."

"Look," George said, turning to face his friend, "I promised to buy you lunch, so how about we just get some souvlaki sandwiches and take them back to my place."

"I don't know," Costas said, "I really should be going soon."

"I know," George said. "There's nothing like being waited on. We could also pick up some wine to drink with our meal—I know you like a drink as much as I do."

"Okay," Costas said. "That sounds nice. Then maybe you could tell me more about the French girl you're in love with."

George purchased two sandwiches and a bottle of wine from a kiosk, then led Costas up to his apartment, which overlooked Kolonaki Square.

"I don't much come to this area," Costas said.

"Why not?"

"Because the police don't like people like me here with all these beautiful foreigners spending money."

"But it's your country," George said, "and you have a right to go where you please."

"You're a nice boy," Costas said. "I wish you were Greek."

When they were inside, George helped Costas take his knapsack off. It was most awkward to maneuver on account of two thick blankets strapped to the bottom with rope.

George asked Costas to sit down and then served him some wine.

"Just a cheap house red," George said, "but it's wet."

"It's wet, yes," Costas repeated after a long gulp. He held up his glass for a refill.

During lunch, George told him all about Rebecca—the late dinners, the long romantic walks, her ambition to be a great artist, the awkward lingering on her steps. Costas listened politely, and nodded where was appropriate.

After lunch, they drank Armagnac and George thanked Costas again for his generosity the previous week. Costas shrugged. Then he wrote down the address of a derelict house in Athens, where he'd made a bit of a home for himself with a few others.

"If you get lost, come to this address and ask for me."

TWELVE

To celebrate his night of passion with Rebecca, George had decided on an all-day drinking session. After leaving Rebecca's apartment that morning, he spent the afternoon flitting from café to restaurant, nibbling on sandwiches and small pies, reading, and drinking as much as he could without drawing attention to himself.

By the early hours of the morning, however, the only bar open was an Internet café. It served until 5:00 a.m. and generally catered to backpackers from a nearby hostel.

George paid to sit at a computer, where he sat drinking and feeling sleepy in the bright glow of the monitor. If people were watching him, he was certainly not aware of it.

When the Internet café closed, he decided to sleep in a park. Morning was almost upon the city, and despite the inevitable but harmless advances of men who lurked in the bushes, he was comfortable and safe.

He crossed a bridge over the railway lines toward a mass of trees and empty paths. He skirted the edge of the park railing—hoping he would come upon an opening. Then he suddenly realized that he was surrounded by a group of men. Something poked into his stomach and George looked down to see a sort of pipe, which he later realized was a gun. The men went through his pockets quickly. He could feel their hands upon him like mad animals. Despite the violence of what was happening, however, George was quite relaxed. It was an event beyond his control, and so all he had to do was surrender to it and wait for it to be over. Afterward, they muscled him to the floor and ran away. George lay there, unharmed but in shock.

A homeless man under some cardboard boxes witnessed the incident and took pity on George, who, like himself, he judged to be nothing more than a harmless drunk. Costas helped George to his feet, brushed him off, and offered him a place to sit down with some wine and something to smoke.

After a few swigs of liquor and the remains of a cigar that Costas kept for emergencies, George fell asleep on the cardboard. Costas covered him up with one of his blankets and covered himself with another.

The next morning, George thanked Costas for his generosity and begged him to be his guest for lunch in a week after he'd sorted himself out. Costas accepted, and George told him the address of a café on his block that served excellent fish and even more excellent wine. Costas nodded politely and said he would see George then. George also promised a pack of cigarettes and a bottle of ouzo as a return gift for the wine and cigar stub he'd smoked at Costas's expense.

THIRTEEN

As Costas packed up to leave, George had an idea.

"Listen," he said. "If the police don't like the look of you, then let's change the look of you."

George disappeared into his bedroom and returned with a suit and a pair of loafers.

The suit was a little baggy, but the shoes fit with three pairs of socks.

"It's very nice," Costas said, stroking the fabric. "It's been twenty years since I wore a suit."

"Splendid," George said. "Fits you very well, and actually looks good with your T-shirt underneath, like you're from California."

"I'll take these," George said, pointing to Costas's old clothes, which lay on the floor in a dark heap. The smell of sweat and urine was quite strong, and for a second, George was reluctant to pick them up.

"No, no," Costas said reaching, "I'll take them—you can never have too many clothes."

George saw Costas to the front door, and they shook hands. There was a dignity in fine clothes that George felt was vital to a person's sense of self.

Many of George's heroes—archaeologists and linguists from the 1930s—wrote in their books as much about their tailors as they did about their expeditions. They climbed blazing hot sand dunes in linen suits from Savile Row. They explored Himalayan caves in tweed with full brogues and sock garters—and but for some grave injury or temporary paralysis, they were never unshaven.

The suit George gave Costas was one of several tailored for him in Paris. His button-down shirts had been sewn on Jermyn Street in London, and his shoes were from Alfred Sargent. In George's opinion, bow ties had never gone out of style, and his shaving accoutrements were from Geo. F. Trumper, as were a few of his more eccentric possessions—such as a narrow silver device meant for making Champagne less fizzy.

FOURTEEN

George's father left Saudi Arabia and returned to his home in the United States when George was in his final year at Exmouth, about three years before he went to Athens. He wrote to George and said he wanted to be his father again.

He said he also wanted to give George money—to make his life more comfortable, to do fatherly things and make sure he was a well-set-up young man for the future.

For the past three years, he visited George when he felt like it, about twice a year. Five months ago, his father had come to Athens.

After a long dinner with several bottles of wine, George had walked him back to his hotel through Syntagma Square—past the Parliament Building and up that long stretch of boulevard to the Athens Hilton. He then helped him upstairs, and waited in the sitting room part of the suite as his father knocked about in the bathroom. After ten minutes, George went to see what he was doing and found him asleep on the floor in his clothes.

George unknotted his tie, loosened his shirt collar, unhinged his belt, took off his shoes, and pulled a blanket over him.

On the dresser was a large envelope with George's name on it. Inside, a wad of bills in U.S. dollars and, as always, a gift certificate for Hermès—his father's idea of tailoring.

Before leaving, George folded his father's clothes and tidied up. He also set some empty vodka bottles outside the door for the maid. He straightened up the golf magazines on the desk. He drew the curtains against the city and sat on the bed. For a few minutes he watched his father sleep. Then he got up and left, closing the door quietly behind himself.

George stopped to chat with the desk clerk on his way out, and asked that they check on his father in a few hours, as he hasn't been feeling well. Then George took a taxi home and put himself to bed.

Homer's *Odyssey* was George's favorite poem of all time. He had copied it out and translated it into English. Part of the story is about how a boy's father goes missing.

FIFTEEN

George woke up in the early hours of the morning. It was still dark. The liquor store would not be open for several hours. He read a little of the poetry from the book on his bedside table.

> There is only one woman in the world. One woman, with many faces.

Then he got up and ate some cold potatoes with yogurt, lemon juice, and chives.

He had written Rebecca's name in ancient Greek and taped it on his refrigerator. He had even tried to compose a few lines of poetry for her, which he kept in his pillowcase with an emergency packet of cigarettes and the birthday cards from his father, which went back as far as his seventeenth birthday.

George unwrapped a bar of chocolate. He hoped the sugar would make him feel better. The world was too hard to live in when he was sober, because everything felt precious. Like some devout follower of an obscure religion, he was moved to tears frequently by what he perceived as divine moments— like rain on the window or the smell of apples, or a man reading a book with his daughter in the park; a flock of birds, the flash and clatter of a passing train, and the silent beauty of faces.

Booze washed all that nonsense away. It shallowed his perception. As a drunk, he was free to explore the earth without having to digest every moment as if it were his last.

Outside the window above his bed, a dull blue sky meant dawn was near.

Somewhere across the city, among the thousands of thumping hearts, was the one he wanted.

After thinking about it for a minute, George decided it had been much too long and that he should walk several miles across Athens to her apartment where he would smoke, swig from the bottle of ouzo he would buy when the shops opened, and then soak up the imagined impression of her slumbering body from beneath her balcony.

Perhaps he would even ring her buzzer and then run away (if he wasn't too drunk to find it). He imagined leaping into a bush as she rushed down to see who was there.

George was in the habit of leaving his apartment with everything on, including lights, the radio, and once even the shower—which he'd drunkenly forgotten to get into in the first place. Without turning around, he found his keys and took from a drawer the gift certificate his father had left him—an orange envelope with a horse and cart engraved upon it. He thought it might be a nice impromptu gift, or serve in place of an excuse should his presence be discovered.

The elevator tapped quickly in its descent, and George remembered the sound of housemasters' shoes echoing through tall arched corridors of the dormitory.

A year before he graduated from Exmouth, his only real pleasure, aside from translating ancient texts and music, was drinking single malt against an obelisk set in the manicured grounds of the school. He liked to sit there, drink, and hum Bach. The obelisk was known as the Exmouth phallus. Once, drunkenly, George wrapped his body around its base and screamed:

"Thrust me deep inside, O great Exmouth cock, where no mortals dare spread fragile wings."

If it hadn't been parents day, nobody would have heard and George wouldn't have got into any trouble.

Some of the colder mornings brought great joy. Before dawn, after a night of heavy frost, George wandered the white dreaming garden through clouds of breath and the forever nothing of stars. Like a silk puppet, he glided through the grounds, the only living witness to that day's birth.

George had entered boarding school when he was seven, soon after his family split up.

The flight from Lexington to Boston was uneventful. He was served a bag of animal crackers and the beverage of his choice (Fanta). Someone from the school named Terrence drove to the airport to pick him up.

By the time George reached Rebecca's apartment building around seven in the morning, his memories of Exmouth lay scattered behind him. He had bought some liquor on the way and was now too drunk to focus on anything above the second floor. He simply stared at her building and tried to make sense of the blurred colors.

When George eventually found the courage to cross the street, he realized he had been staring up at the second floor of the wrong building, and so he gave up and fell asleep in a park nearby.

He slept unceremoniously until early afternoon.

When he woke up, he walked carefully through the bright sunshine to the closest metro station. He felt ragged and nearing sobriety. His lungs ached for the heaviness of smoke. Like the veteran of his own private war, he painfully and crookedly ascended to the platform.

A train pulled in.

He watched people spill from the doors, waiting for an opening so he could board. Suddenly, Rebecca was in front of him, with a bouquet of white flowers.

"Rebecca!"

She seemed surprised. Her eyes were a beautiful shape.

George tried to stand straight. "Sorry if I frightened you," he stammered.

"What are you doing here, George?"

"Oh, well, I had to collect some official documents from the library up the road." He motioned one way and then looked in the other direction and motioned that way too.

"Have you ever been there?" he asked, touching the heads of her flowers.

"Where?" she said.

"You live here?" George asked.

"You know I do."

"Just coming home?"

"Yes—why do you have leaves stuck to your pants?"

"These leaves?" George said and looked down at his soiled suit trousers, laughing. "I took a nap in the grounds of the academy—it really needs a good rake, to be honest."

"I thought you said it was a library?"

"It's both, in a way, I suppose—hasn't it been ages since we saw each other!"

"Looks like you need to sober up."

"Rebecca," he said breathlessly. There was so much he wanted to say, but was unable to think past the syllables of her name that filled him like some delicate music.

She looked down the platform, in the direction of her apartment.

"I'll sober up very soon," he said. "I have something for you too."

He reached into his pocket and handed her the orange envelope.

"It looks important," she said. "Is it a letter?"

"Sort of, open it later."

She faltered, but George insisted and she put the envelope in the pocket of her dress. Then she looked again in the direction of the steps.

"I have to go, George," she smiled.

George raised his fingers to his face.

"Is my nose bleeding?"

"I don't think so," Rebecca said, standing on her tip toes.

"I've been having some trouble with it."

It was a lie he made up which he instantly regretted.

For a moment George thought she might ask him over for a nap or a cup of tea. She may even have a little wine and some hard Greek biscuits to chew on.

Sensing her departure, he said:

"I'm pretty sober now, as it happens." But then realized he was carrying a can of freshly opened beer he'd just purchased at the train station kiosk.

His shoes were also covered in dark stains, which he suspected was urine.

Rebecca had on her light blue ballet flats. She sighed heavily. Her arm with the flowers fell.

"George," she said. "Can we sit down here and chat for a minute?"

She guided him over to a bench seat at the top of the stairs, and they both sat down.

"This is nice, isn't it?" George said.

Rebecca surveyed him carefully before she spoke. "Can we just be friends from now on?"

George said nothing. Then he laughed. "Friends?"

"Like we were when we first met, having coffee or dinner from time to time."

George said nothing.

"I think it's for the best," she said.

"Why?"

"I love your company, but I've just been thinking and this is where I am right now in my life."

"Is it my drinking?" he said, dropping his eyes to the can.

"That's part of it."

"What's the other part?"

"I can't be your girlfriend."

"Ever? Or just anymore?"

Rebecca frowned.

"Ever," she said.

And then George began to sob.

People looked.

"George," Rebecca said quietly.

But he continued sobbing. It was quite loud. A woman passing said something to her in Greek.

"George," she said again. "Please stop crying. It's not that bad."

"I can't," he said. His face was very red. Two of his shirt buttons had come undone and displayed a few unflattering inches of stomach.

"Just tell me why you're so upset."

George rubbed his eyes and took a swig from his beer. When he seemed to have himself under control, a fresh wave of sobs came. If a train hadn't pulled in, they would have been surrounded by curious locals.

"Just tell me why you're crying, George."

She touched his hand but he pulled away.

"Because I'm slightly upset."

"Why?"

George didn't answer, but fumbled for his cigarettes. Rebecca lit one for him quickly. More than anything, she wanted the scene to end.

He took another swig from his beer.

"I just thought . . ." he said, wiping his eyes, and raising the can to his lips again.

"Oh, George," Rebecca said desperately. "Can you stop drinking for five minutes?"

George set the can on the platform. By the sound it made, they could both tell it was empty.

"Are you crying because you're drunk?"

George began sobbing again, and very loudly. A train pulled in, but hardly anyone got off.

"We should talk about this when you're sober," Rebecca said. Then for the first and only time in her life, Rebecca caught a rare glimpse of George's temper.

In a low growl, he said:

"How dare you, how dare you judge me, Rebecca—you just gave up that right, so just you stop talking before you insult both of us."

Rebecca wasn't sure what he meant, and suspected he wasn't either, but she saw it as her cue to exit and stood up.

"Good-bye, George," she said. "I wanted to talk to you about this rationally, but you're too . . . upset."

George let his head fall into his hands. Then without getting up, he kicked the beer can toward the tracks. It rolled in noisily. Someone shouted something from down the platform, and Rebecca walked away. When she was almost to the end staircase, she turned around. George was standing up. "Rebecca! Rebecca! Rebecca!" he shouted.

She went home and cried. Her first attempt to connect in Athens, and she had failed on all counts. It must run in my family, she thought—an inability to maintain any kind of emotional connection. And then she remembered Henry, and longed for him, despite the shame that hung over her.

SIXTEEN

The next morning Rebecca woke to someone knocking forcefully on her front door. She slipped into a floral print dress and padded across the cold floor.

"Hello?" she said.

"It's Henry!"

She flung open the door and threw her arms around him.

"I missed you so much," she said, but then fell silent.

They were soon in bed. She could feel his muscles tightening over her, and she opened her thighs to take in as much as possible. Afterward, they lay on their backs.

Henry said he was taking her up to his dig.

"Is that your idea of romantic?"

"Actually, yes."

"Well, I have nothing to wear."

Henry looked around her room. "How about a pair of trousers, a cotton blouse, a pair of sensible shoes, and a silk scarf?"

"There's no such thing as sensible shoes."

"What do you mean?"

"Shoes are either beautiful or sensible, and I have only beautiful."

Henry laughed.

"It's Air France's fault."

The events of the previous night's confrontation were starting to lessen. The feeling would soon break into fragments and cease to affect her.

They kissed again. She reached down and put him inside. They kissed without moving their bodies.

Later on as she was getting ready, Henry said:

"I love the way you tie up your hair."

She turned to look at him from the mirror.

"Well, you're lucky, because that's my favorite way to wear it."

"I can see your neck."

"Do you like my neck?"

"It's my second favorite part of your body."

"What's your favorite part?"

"The rest."

She rushed over and kissed him several times on the lips. Then she went back to the mirror. Henry sat on the edge of the bath.

"When did you fall in love for the first time, Henry?"

He thought for a moment.

"I was eleven. I used to take a bus to school. The bus was blue with writing across the side in cream letters. It used to stop in front of a ballet school and pick children up. From my seat on the left side, I could see over a tall fence into a bright studio where girls about my age were warming up in front of a mirror. I remember the beauty of their arms, the slow arches, the ghost-like sweeping away. Sometimes they would all move together, in a sort of elegant dip. There was one girl in particular with light brown hair, not as tall as the others. And I was in love with her." Henry got up and stood behind her.

"Did you ever meet her?"

"No, but she looked at me once, and then it was the end of school term and in the autumn my parents moved and I went to a different school in another town."

"You still think about her."

"She wore her hair like you."

"Like this?" Rebecca said, taking Henry's hand and holding it against the back of her head . "It's how I wore it for Air France—but pulled very neat."

"I would have fallen for you in the sky," he said and then left her to get ready.

After drinking some coffee, they raced down the stairs holding hands and laughing. His hand felt very strong, and as they neared the last few steps, Henry stopped and pulled her to him.

He hadn't shaved that morning and the profile of his warm, slightly perspiring cheek renewed her desire for him.

They mounted his old Vespa and dropped off the curb into a light stream of traffic.

It was already hot. After about an hour, they crossed a bridge that coughed them on to a dusty road that seemed endless but was in fact climbing to a high, hot peak that Henry said had not seen consistent human life for thousands of years. There was a white tent in the distance, and several tables of large stones, and an old car that seemed to have been abandoned. They parked beside one of the tables. A tent flap went up like an eye opening, and a figure stood looking at them, shielding his eyes from the sun.

"Good morning," the man said. "And who is this?"

"Rebecca," Henry said.

"Not her, you," the man said.

Henry laughed.

"I haven't seen you in a week, Henry. Where have you been?"

Before Henry could speak, the man patted him on the back.

"Good to have you home, Henry. Now, who might this be?"

"Hello," Rebecca said, extending her hand. "Rebecca Baptiste."

"Baptiste, eh?" the man said, and then turned toward the tent.

"Come on in and have some water—I'm Professor Peterson, by the way."

Henry took Rebecca's helmet and followed her under the flap.

They sat in canvas chairs. It was very cool and smelled faintly of vinegar. Several tables inside the tent were covered with tools and stones. There was also a sink connected to a large bucket, and a plastic washing-up bowl with some white sticky substance in it.

"What news, Professor?" Henry said.

"What news? Well, take these first—" The professor handed them each a glass of cold water. Then he lit his pipe and looked at Rebecca from the corner of his eye. He held the match into the stomach of his pipe—it flickered as he puffed, and then the tobacco caught and sizzled with each shallow intake of breath.

"Giuseppe has gone back home for a week at least, his poor old mum is not well again."

"Again?" Henry said. He turned to Rebecca. "When Giuseppe's mother misses him, she becomes so ill that he goes to her immediately."

"How are we going to get the script on that discus analyzed?" Henry said.

"We'll have to wait."

"Is that what you wanted to talk to me about?"

"Yes," Professor Peterson said. "If you do go down to the university, don't mention that Giuseppe is not here."

"I won't."

"They're looking for any excuse to get rid of us."

"Are they?"

The professor removed the pipe from his lips. "Well, I always think so."

After a little more conversation, they found themselves outside again in the heat. The professor gazed past Rebecca and Henry at Athens in the distance. An uneven film of smoke hung over the city like tufts of wool. They were many miles from Athens, but the heat, the energy, and the sense of human plight could be felt—even from such an isolated cliff.

"If you want to be useful, my dear—" the professor said to Rebecca, "and I'm old enough to make such requests without the least awkwardness—feel free to sketch a few of the things on the table for the British school newsletter. I can pay you either in rocks or in compliments, or by sorting Henry out when he behaves intolerably."

"Finally, a man who understands women," Rebecca said. "I'll take the rocks."

"Henry tells me you are a gifted artist."

"But he's never seen my work."

"Yes, I have," Henry called up from his pit. "I glimpsed a few sketches on the living room floor this morning."

"But that was this morning," she said.

"I was right though, wasn't I?"

Rebecca followed the professor to a table covered by a sheet of plastic that was anchored by bricks. Then he pulled out a box of old British dental tools and explained what they were doing with them and where things went after being found, and which ones she might like to sketch.

A few sketches later, Rebecca dozed in the hammock beside the tent. She had fanned herself with a faded copy of *The Economist* until falling asleep.

Professor Peterson stepped to the edge of Henry's pit.

"You're awfully quiet today, Henry—all this marriage business with Rebecca no doubt."

"Marriage?"

"Steady on, Henry—anyway, where has that leg gone?"

"It ran away."

"Very good."

"It was picked up yesterday, so it should be at the lab."

"Righto."

Henry gazed up and smiled at his old friend. The sun was too bright to make out the expression on the old man's face.

"You're doing a fine job, as usual, my boy," he said.

Then Rebecca appeared. Her face glistened with perspiration.

"Was I asleep for long?"

"Not long," Henry said. "An hour, tops."

"Henry found a femur last week," the professor said.

"I think it belonged to a woman," added Henry.

"How can you tell?" Rebecca said.

"I get a sense of the shape, somehow."

"How does it feel holding the leg of someone who once lived?"

Henry thought for a moment, cleaning the blade of a small shovel on his apron.

"I wonder about their lives—not the main events, but small things, like drinking a glass of water, or folding clothes, or walking home."

The professor rolled his eyes. "Well, I'm going back to work."

Rebecca wobbled down the ladder into Henry's pit.

"Sometimes I find the bones of children," he said. "These bones are very different than the bones of their ancient parents—I mean they feel different. Even though the children would still be dead if they had lived long lives, it just amazes me somehow."

Rebecca picked up a rock.

"Is this anything?"

Henry leaned in and surveyed it.

"Do you think our lives stand for nothing and we are all destined to die and be forgotten?" she said.

"In some ways," Henry said. "I suppose you could say that we're already dead—already lost—in some ways."

"Well if that's true, Henry, then I'm going to lie down in your pit so that you can find me."

On the way back down the mountain, the world blew through their hair.

The skin on Henry's arms was a dark, deep brown, and warm to touch.

When they entered Athens, the air was still and heavy.

Henry raced through the city center, swerving around trucks destined for points far away. Restaurants were opening for dinner.

Rebecca held on under Henry's linen jacket. The rushing coolness made her feel light, and for a few moments fearless. She would tell him soon about her childhood, for she could feel the love growing between them as a rare and unspoken trust that allowed her to reveal herself. If it continued, she felt sure that if it ever came time to fall, she would spread her arms and fly.

SEVENTEEN

As they neared his apartment in central Athens, Rebecca squeezed Henry to stop. He pulled to the side of the road, but didn't turn off the motor.

"What's wrong?"

"Nothing," she shouted. "Can we stop here for a minute?"

"Okay," he said with slight reluctance. Rebecca climbed off and Henry pulled the scooter up on to the sidewalk. Rebecca took off her helmet and scarf. Her hair was wet.

"I need to go to a shop near here."

"Aren't the shops closing?"

Rebecca pointed to a row of buildings on the other side of the fountain.

"I think it's just over there somewhere," she said. "With all the foreign boutiques."

It was still hot and the air was dusty.

The normally packed shopping precinct had thinned to single people hurrying home with small packages of meat or fish.

"Let's go in here and get you something," she said as they reached a heavy brown door. "I found this in my dress." She held up a small orange envelope. "I want us to use it and get rid of it."

"I'm all dusty," Henry said.

Rebecca held the door.

"I really don't want anything," Henry insisted, "but we can look for you."

"No, I can't buy myself anything with this—let's just use it for you."

The shop had several display cabinets of scarves and a long table set out for a full dinner with plates, cutlery, and napkins.

In the middle of the shop were two saddles and a selection of equestrian accessories.

"This place is amazing," Henry said, picking up a riding crop.

"It's French," Rebecca said, "like me."

The saleswoman glided toward them. She was in her late fifties and had short hair. She smiled at Rebecca and said in a deep voice, "Hello, mademoiselle."

Rebecca smiled. "I'm here to find something beautiful for this strange man."

"I really don't need anything," Henry said to the woman.

"We're not about need in here," the saleswoman laughed, "we're about want, and everybody wants something beautiful— if only to remind them of someone beautiful."

Henry shrugged. "That's the best sales pitch I've ever heard."

"How about a man's shirt?" Rebecca said.

The saleswoman led Henry and Rebecca to a wall of dress shirts.

"Pure mother-of-pearl buttons, and barrel cuffs," she said, taking one down.

"Interesting," Henry said, taking it from her. "It's so simple."

"If you understand that," the saleswoman said, "then you understand the most important element of style—which would explain why this young lady has taken a keen interest in you."

"I'm not keen," Rebecca said. "But I'm certainly interested."

The saleswoman laughed and walked back to answer a ringing phone.

Henry chose a white, cotton poplin shirt with an Italian collar. The saleswoman shut the lid of the orange box and tied brown ribbon around it.

"Very pretty," Henry said.

"And practical," Rebecca added.

"Like the two of you," the saleswoman said, handing them the box. "Put it to good use, please."

EIGHTEEN

Henry decided to pick dinner up from the restaurant on the corner. He suggested eating on the balcony again.

Once in the street, he stopped and looked up at his own apartment. Rebecca was inside.

A couple of lights were on.

He wondered if he could ever confess how his brother had really died. It wasn't his fault. Everyone had said so. And when he woke up screaming, Dad always came in and held him.

Rebecca was upstairs. He wanted to love her, and almost could—but something restrained him. He'd felt it all his life, like arms holding him back from the happiness that would destroy him.

Soon, Henry thought, we'll be eating on that balcony. And even though they would spend the night in each other's arms, he would yearn for her.

Walking slowly back from the café, he recognized the moment he felt something other than lust. It was in the museum, when she lingered over the remains of the child. He could see that it upset her, and it was when he felt closest to her—when he knew she was capable of understanding him. She had anticipated the event that rooted him to loneliness. She could feel the winter that defined him.

NINETEEN

After Rebecca left the station, George sat back down and lit a cigarette. Then he sobbed a little more. The scent of her perfume lingered, deepening his sense of loss.

A train pulled in. George stood up and stepped forward.

People rushed from the carriages and pushed past him. He felt the urge to fall over and be trampled, but instead moved to the side of the platform and sat down again.

He listened to the sound of footsteps fading.

A man stopped walking to look for something in his pocket.

Another train in the distance. No one on the platform in front of him. An easy lunge. But deep down, he knew it was the impulsiveness of being drunk. For like the Russian petruska dolls that fit one another in varying degrees, the real, sober George lay still, at the core of his life—the true self from which all the other likenesses had been fashioned.

·   ·   ·

When it got dark, and he felt cold, he decided to walk to an area north of the city center, a dangerous place of broken-down houses and drug addicts. The sort of place where only the boundaries are patrolled by city police.

It took George about two hours to get there. Once he had entered the narrow labyrinth of streets, he stopped walking and lay down on the ground. The small bottle of vodka he had bought was empty, and he could barely walk anymore.

There were people in the shadows. They seemed to move very slowly, until he was completely surrounded. He withdrew his wallet and threw it at them. Shadows moved quickly to pick it up, while others pulled and dragged George over to a wall.

The shadow holding him said something in Greek. Someone in the background laughed. And then he felt a crushing blow above his eye. He looked into the darkness, dumbly aware of a distant silvery thread that flashed with every blow. Something smashed against the top of his head and then a force to his back. And then, as he lost consciousness, a familiar voice.

When George awoke, he was on a mattress in a very dark room. Someone was sitting beside him. When he turned his head, a glass of water appeared, and he took it shakily.

"It's me, George," Costas said.

"What happened?"

"You got beaten up on your way to my house."

"Beaten up?"

"Yes, quite badly."

"How did I know where you lived?" George said.

"Because I gave you my address."

"But I don't have it."

"Don't worry about it, I had to give you some stitches."

"Stitches!" George said. "Did I go to hospital?"

"No, no, I used to be a doctor in another life," Costas said.

"You were a doctor?"

"That's why they didn't kill you, because without me they would have no one to help when they overdose or get stabbed over squabbles. So I have a little pull here, but not much—if they were sane they wouldn't be here, remember."

"Where am I?"

"In the house I share with a few harmless junkies."

George opened his eyes. "Why aren't you wearing the suit I gave you?"

"Because I sold it," Costas said. "To buy alcohol. You of all people should understand that. But I was touched, George, by your generosity."

George lay back down. They talked for a bit longer, and then he went to sleep. He wondered what Rebecca was doing and remembered their night together. Her slow breath and silent eyes. Morning not quite sketched against the window. The happiness of breakfast and the unfolding of a day.

All things, George suspected, that he would never have again.

In the morning he saw that he was in a room with about twelve other people, but Costas was not one of them. He quietly stepped between the sleeping bodies, each on their mattress. Then he climbed through the ground-floor window that functioned as a front door, ripping the lining of his jacket in the process. On the way home, he inspected his injuries in the reflection of car windows. He fingered the stitches on his cheek that Costas said would dissolve and wouldn't need taking out. One of his eyes was badly swollen. With each step, he tried to re-trace his final conversation with Rebecca on the platform, still utterly perplexed as to why she was committed to never being his girlfriend. He thought about her all the way home to his chic but empty apartment in Kolonaki Square.

Then he put himself to bed and hoped never to wake up for a very long time.

TWENTY

Over the next several days, Rebecca made sketches she thought were getting close to what she wanted. Her pencil scratched the canvas paper softly while her mind wandered over moments shared with Henry on his balcony.

After each drawing, Rebecca took a cold shower to wash away sweat that had formed on her body. Then she started to feel lonely.

She sat on her balcony thinking about her mother.

In the evening when the heat broke, Rebecca smoked cigarettes and imagined her mother getting home from the office. The clack of glamorous shoes on a tile floor. Something cooking. Voices from the television. Her boyfriend not home yet. He rides a scooter with fairing. She takes her shoes off and stands beside the microwave in her tights. An expensive cheap pocketbook with loose coins and gum inside. Rebecca wondered if they even looked alike.

The last Christmas card she received from her mother was

six years ago. She had brought it with her to Athens. There was a letter missing from her name, but it sounded like "Rebecca" if you said it aloud. Her sister had received one too, but recognized the handwriting on the envelope and threw it away without opening it.

The next day, Rebecca was on her final sketch of the laturna man from the marketplace when something strange happened. Instead of drawing his shabby overcoat and weathered face, her pencil began to move with its own intelligence. Like a newborn animal learning to take a few steps outside its cage, she let her hand carefully and slowly impress upon the canvas paper its own vision. She lost herself, and after several minutes she realized she was no longer drawing the organ grinder, but the topless man who lived opposite Henry's apartment. From what she could remember, her sketch was the keen likeness of someone from a distance—but it lacked the intimacy she prided herself on with other subjects.

As the pink flesh of dusk swallowed Athens, Rebecca cooked several small fish in a frying pan, and then ate them with hummus she'd made from grinding chickpeas in a bowl with a squeeze of lemon, salt, oil, and tahini. There was half a bottle of wine left in the refrigerator, and so Rebecca (wearing nothing but Henry's white shirt) took the cold bottle into her studio and drank it down like water, looking at her sketches.

She thought how perfect it would be if Henry were to show up at that moment with more wine and cigarettes. Then she took off all her clothes and went to bed.

The next morning, Rebecca drank milk on her balcony and sketched from memory the topless man standing over his steaming pots. When she stopped to make coffee, she decided that her exhibition would consist of a series based on modern Greek tragedy.

The topless man would be her first subject.

She quickly dressed, packed her pencils into a box that she strapped to an easel—then slipped several sheets of paper between the straps. It was a sweltering noon, but she hoisted the gear onto her back and set out across the city.

On the metro, her mind cast back to one of her first memories, and one of the only moments with her mother.

They were at home. Her mother had come down from Paris for a few days.

One night, unable to sleep, Rebecca crept out of her room and saw a light on downstairs. She was six or seven years old. Her mother was on the couch smoking. When Rebecca peeped her head around the door, her mother smiled.

"Come," she said.

Rebecca remembered walking slowly toward her, anticipating at any moment, that her mother might just as easily dismiss her back upstairs.

She was leafing through a book of paintings.

They read the book together. It was very quiet. Rebecca hoped her sister wouldn't wake up.

"Look at this one," her mother said. "Aren't the colors pretty?"

Rebecca nodded. Her mother turned the page.

"I used to paint, Rebecca."

"I can paint too!"

She dragged slowly on her cigarette.

"This one is nice," Rebecca said.

"That was one of my mother's favorites," her mother said. "She died long before you were born. I can barely remember her myself."

Rebecca nodded. "But you're not going to die?"

Her mother stubbed out her cigarette.

"You never know."

Their eyes went back to the book of paintings.

"I love this one," her mother said. "I really, really love it."

Rebecca stared at the painting. A girl in a pretty pink dress lying in a meadow. A farmhouse in the distance.

"Is she trying to run away or trying to go home?" Rebecca asked.

"Both," her mother said softly. "She's trying to do both."

She drew on the cigarette, tapped her ash directly onto the picture, and closed the book.

Sometimes children, not long exiled from that silent world of softness and gesture, can feel in their tiny hearts the nuances of what adults say; and though powerless to act, they sense fully those feelings that creep like figures behind the veil of language.

And though Rebecca would never admit, even to her sister, the feeling that passed over her at that moment, she knew with certainty that something was terribly wrong. And though in the coming years she would yearn for her mother, in truth, it was not *this* woman she yearned for, but the idea of her— without the terror she was too young to recognize as madness.

. . .

It was easy getting into the topless man's building, as the door had been propped open. People were making their way home for siesta. Small children peddled their bicycles barefoot on the street outside.

Rebecca ascended the stairs that led to his front door.

The echo of children's voices lessened.

Then, by the time she reached his floor, she could no longer hear the children, nor the low hum of distant traffic, nor other voices—just her own breathing and the tapping of her easel as she conquered each step.

The hallway was heavy with steam. There were two names scrawled on his door in blue pen. Rebecca listened. She could hear him inside walking around.

She knocked.

The walking stopped. But nothing happened.

She wondered if he would answer at all, then a voice.

"*Neh?*"

"Hello," she said. "Hello, monsieur."

The door opened.

He was topless, and hot steam poured into the hallway.

"*Neh?*" he said, but with more gentleness.

Rebecca smiled broadly and motioned with her hand that she wanted to come in. For a moment he didn't move. Then he turned slowly so that she might enter his apartment, but she froze and felt suddenly faint.

TWENTY-ONE

Henry was a child archaeologist.

At nine years old he dug up a piece of flint that resembled an axe head. His father took him to the University of Swansea. They asked for the archaeology department and were directed to a tall concrete block with untidy rows of bicycles outside.

A long-haired student asked if they were lost. Henry produced his flint, as though it were proof of something. The student stared at it.

"Do you have an appointment?" he said.

"No," said Henry's father. "We thought we'd just pop in."

"Well, I suggest you look for Dr. Peterson's office," the student said, tossing his mane. "He's good with this sort of thing."

Professor Peterson was much younger then, but to nine-year-old Henry he seemed a very old man. He scrutinized the artifact with a magnifying glass. Then he looked at Henry with his magnified eye.

"I can deduce that it's extremely old," he said. "May I ask how old you are, young man?"

"Nine," Henry said. "Actually, nine and a half."

Professor Peterson set the magnifying glass down on a piece of felt and looked at the artifact again. "I'm afraid it's a great deal older than you."

"I knew that," Henry said excitedly. "Is it as old as dinosaurs?"

"Older," Professor Peterson stated without flinching. "Your artifact would have been used to hunt them."

"To hunt them?"

"Oh yes," said Professor Peterson. "Not only for food, but for their pelts."

"Their pelts?"

"The ancients wasted nothing."

"What should I do with it?"

"There's really only one place for it."

"Where, Professor?"

"In your bedroom under a glass bowl for protection."

Professor Peterson handed the flint back to Henry.

His father stood up to leave.

"Actually," said Henry, "I want you to have it." He held out his rock to the professor with two small hands.

Professor Peterson blushed.

"You should keep it, Henry."

"But don't you need it for research?"

"But, Henry—you found it—it belongs to you."

"But if it's so precious, doesn't it belong to everyone?"

Professor Peterson took the flint and set it on his desk.

"Please sit down," he said to Henry's father.

"Years from now, I want you to look me up, and when this young man is older, I'd like to help with his education—if he's still interested in all this."

"I definitely will be," Henry interrupted.

"That's nice of you, Professor," said Henry's father.

"Nice has nothing to do with it," Professor Peterson snapped. "I need men like your Henry. People with faith."

Henry's father looked away. His wife was at home in the bedroom they use for storage, sitting on the carpet. She would be out when they got back—walking in the fields beyond the house.

He would fry eggs and make toast. Henry would watch. They would eat together in front of the television, watching *Blue Peter*.

Professor Peterson took the flint and set it next to an ashtray of old stamps. Then he took a key from his waistcoat pocket and opened a glass cabinet behind his desk. It was full of strangely shaped things. He carefully removed a fossilized dinosaur egg and turned around.

"Here," he said, handing it to Henry. "I was given this when I was your age by my father. It belongs to you now."

For the next twelve Christmases, a box of the year's archaeological books and journals would arrive by post to the small semidetached house in Wales where Henry spent his childhood.

After about three years, however—Henry realized that all he'd found in the garden that afternoon was a flint in the shape of an axe head.

He wrote this in a letter to Professor Peterson, who was in the Middle East at the time. A month later, Henry received a postcard from somewhere very far away with writing he didn't recognize.

Mosquée Ste. Sophie.   Constantinople.   آيا صوفيه جامعى

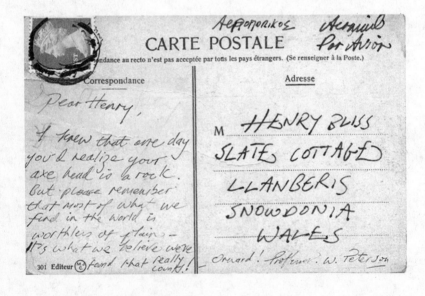

ΑΕΡΟΠΟΡΙΚΟΣ   Aerienne
Par Avion

CARTE POSTALE

...ndance au recto n'est pas acceptée par toüs les pays étrangers. (Se renseigner à la Poste.)

Correspondance   Adresse

Dear Henry,

I knew that one day
you'd realize your
axe head is a rock.
But please remember
that most of what we
find in the world is
worthless of plain —
It's what we believe were
found that really
counts!

M HENRY BLISS
SLATE COTTAGE
LLANBERIS
SNOWDONIA
WALES

Onward! Professor. W. Peterson

301 Editeur

TWENTY-TWO

On a mountain high above Athens, two figures leaned over a kitchen table in the blazing sun.

"This is peculiar," Professor Peterson said, handing a magnifying glass to Henry. "I have a funny feeling it might be Lydian."

"That doesn't seem likely."

The professor was referring to a discus the size of a dinner plate.

Henry spent the afternoon not thinking about his work. His old British dental tools scratched the ground but revealed only more questions about Rebecca. About eleven o'clock, Henry washed his hands over the sink, pumping the foot pedal to draw water. The professor appeared from the tent.

"Let's take that discus down to the college now," he said. "With Giuseppe away, it's our only chance."

"I was going to have lunch," Henry said.

"Good, good, we'll eat together at Zygos's Taverna."

Professor Peterson's car occupied the extremely rare privilege of being the most battered automobile that had ever clunked and overheated its way along the Athenian roadways.

It was a dirt-brown Renault 16 the professor said he had bought when he still had hair. He had driven it over 1.3 million miles, most of which were accrued on long desert roads in the Middle East. According to the professor, the mileage clock had broken in 1983 and then started going backward in 1989. The professor said that when it got to zero, he would give it back to Renault with a ribbon tied around the bumper.

The dashboard was a mass of twisted wires (one of which was live) and the instruments were too dusty to read. Pinned to the sagging upholstery roof were photographs of the car at famous digs in Europe and the Middle East. According to the professor, the car had led a far more interesting life than any one person he had ever met. It was once stuck in the sand in Egypt and had to be pulled out by camels. It took two bullets running the Iraqi border into eastern Turkey with a half-ton statue strapped to the roof that Professor Peterson had stolen from thieves who had stolen it from pirates who had stolen it from an international arms dealer. In the end it turned out to be a fake.

In snowy Poland at Biskupin, the old Renault had rolled down a small embankment, almost crushing a Polish archaeologist, who was saved only by her enthusiasm for archaeology—the depth of her excavation pit. It was stolen in Nigeria, only to be abandoned that afternoon when the thieves realized the entire backseat had been taken over by a fourteen-inch Hercules Baboon spider.

The professor sat in the car with his foot on the brake pedal while Henry removed the bricks from under the wheels that prevented it from rolling off the cliff.

The car was missing several windows and the sunroof had rusted open in 1986 during an African rainy season.

The professor had converted the trunk of the car into a soft nest of blankets and hammocks—not as a place to sleep, but as a safe haven for whichever artifact he was transporting at the time. The professor boasted of the various artifacts he'd had in the backseat the way a teenager brags about sexual conquests.

They careened down the side of the mountain without talking. Then they trundled through the iron bridge, at which point the professor began to talk and talk. Henry could hear nothing except the engine, and a strange banging that came from underneath whenever Professor Peterson tapped the brake pedal.

At the first traffic light on the edge of the city, Henry was finally able to hear what the professor was saying.

"And did you know I once had an infestation of killer bees in this car?"

Henry replied that he did not know, but suspected a joke. The light turned green.

At the next red light, the professor was suddenly audible again.

" . . . with several newborns. Newborns!"

When the light changed, the professor pulled across six lanes of traffic to the fury of other drivers, and then turned abruptly down a side street. He was a dangerous driver—which in Athens meant he was safe. Despite being almost eighty years old, he had adopted the Greek custom of ignoring every important red light and only pulling out to overtake a slower car when he spotted a vehicle racing toward them in the opposite direction.

As the professor swung the Renault down an even narrower side street, a figure stepped into the road from behind a parked car. The Renault's fender clipped him hard and from the corner of his eye Henry saw a body sprawl onto the sidewalk.

The professor skidded to a stop. Henry threw open his door and sprinted back to the motionless body of the man on the ground. He was wearing a crumpled tan suit that was torn under one arm. Henry knelt down and began a routine he'd practiced in his first-aid classes. The man was alive and breathing—but seemed barely conscious. He also appeared to have a black eye and stitches in his face.

"My god, look at him," the professor said. "What have I done? My god, my god."

"I won't know how badly he's hurt until he comes around and I can talk to him—or we take him to hospital ourselves."

"My god," the professor said. "This is unbelievable."

"I know—his face has taken a bit of a knock."

But then the man on the ground opened his eyes. He took a long breath and let his gaze fall sullenly upon the two men standing above him.

"Something's happened to me, hasn't it?" he said.

Professor Peterson and Henry recoiled at the stench of anise, fennel, and raisins—the ingredients of ouzo.

The professor nudged Henry and mouthed the words, "He's blind drunk."

"Yes," the professor said. "Something has happened to you."

"You speak English?" Henry said to the man.

"I clipped you with the car," the professor interrupted. "You stepped out into the road, you understand," the professor leaned down. "I'm very, very sorry, old chap."

The man tried to sit up.

"No, no, it's all my fault," the man admitted. "Wine."

"You're drunk?" Henry said.

The man seemed not to hear.

"Are you in pain?" Henry asked.

"Not any more than usual, I suppose," the man admitted with a strange smile.

Henry and Professor Peterson helped him to his feet. He introduced himself as George. His pants were also ripped and there were bloodstains around the tear.

"Sorry we almost killed you, George, but tell me," Henry said, "what are all those bruises on your face and the stitches?"

"Oh, these darlings?" George said casually. "A common misunderstanding."

"Have you been to hospital?" the professor asked.

George shook his head. "There's little point—the human body is capable of sustaining much worse."

"Well, George—I'm Professor Peterson, an archaeologist digging here in Athens, and I have rooms at the university, you understand. Let's go there now. Henry here—who has a certificate in first aid—can patch you up properly and make sure you don't need any X-rays."

"If you really think I need looking after," George said. "I'll go with you."

Henry helped George climb into the long backseat of the Renault.

"It's filthy back here," George muttered.

"Would you mind driving, Henry?" the professor said.

"Why is it so dirty back here?" George said again.

"Ever hear of a Nigerian Hercules Baboon spider?" the professor exclaimed.

"Definitely not," George said.

Henry watched him in the mirror—not with coolness or relief, but with a compassion that extended beyond the moment, as though behind the bruised eyes and the quivering mouth he could sense the presence of a small boy the world had forgotten about.

TWENTY-THREE

Professor Peterson's office was the most dangerous place on campus. Books piled ten feet high leaned dangerously in various directions. On the tallest tower of books, a note had been hung halfway up:

> Please walk VERY slowly or I may fall on you without any warning, whatsoever.

There were three oak desks with long banker's lamps that the professor liked to keep lit, even in his absence. On his main desk were hundreds of Post-it notes, each scribbled with some important detail or addendum to his thoughts. There were also hundreds of pins stuck in a giant map that had been written on with a fountain pen. The ashtrays were full of pipe ash and the room had that deep aroma of knowledge: old paper, dust, coffee, and tobacco.

"This is my dream home," George said, trailing Henry through the stacks toward a battered chaise.

"It's like a museum, isn't it, George?"

"A museum that should be in a museum," George said.

"Don't mind the stuffing," Henry said, when they reached the chaise. "This couch once belonged to a princess of Poland whom the professor said he was in love with."

"So how did he end up with her chaise?"

"Who knows," Henry said. "I can't imagine Professor Peterson with a woman unless she's been mummified."

"Nice you spend so much time together," George said.

"Well, we work together."

"That's even better. What was he like growing up?"

"Growing up?"

"Did your mother come along too?"

"My mother?"

"To the archaeological sites, I mean," George said ardently.

"No," Henry said, quite confused. "My mother never came to work with me."

"So it was just you and your father."

Henry laughed. "Professor Peterson is not my father, George."

"He's not?"

"Well, in a way—he's like my second father."

"It shows," George said, looking around the room. "Don't suppose you have anything to drink here?"

Henry eyed him with mild scorn. "Well, perhaps after I've patched you up. The professor has some single malt somewhere."

George sat on the battered chaise.

"If you want me to look at your knees you'd better take your trousers off."

George quietly undressed.

"I'll unbutton my shirt too," George said. "I have a feeling my back is grazed."

"Okay."

"Is my nose bleeding?"

"It doesn't look like it."

George stripped down to his pinstriped boxer shorts, but kept on his black oxford shoes, black socks, and sock garters. Henry opened a rusty tin box with a red cross on it and removed pads, gauzes, swabs, and disinfectant. Then he gently felt the area on George's leg where the wound was.

"There's actually quite a bit of swelling," Henry said. "But I don't think we need to have an X-ray—unless you're really in a terrible mess and hiding it from us."

"A terrible mess?"

Henry peered up at him.

"Are you in a terrible amount of pain, George?"

George hesitated.

"Not really," he said.

"Then I'll just clean and bandage."

"How do you know all this?" George asked.

"Two terms at medical college spent looking at bodies."

"So you've had more than a first-aid course."

"Yes I have—the professor likes his jokes though."

As he wrapped the bandage around George's knee, the sensation of Henry's hand brushing his leg slowed George's breathing. There was such tenderness in Henry's hands that George felt quite giddy and had no memory of falling asleep.

When George opened his eyes, Henry was staring at him from a chair he had placed next to the chaise.

"What were you dreaming about?" Henry asked.

"I didn't even know I was asleep," George said, struggling to sit up.

Henry switched on a few floor lamps, and then cooked some Greek coffee on the professor's rusty stove. When the coffee was ready, Henry looked for the professor's single malt and then poured some into their coffee cups.

"You're not here with the American School of Archaeology?" Henry asked quietly.

"No," George said. "I graduated two years early from university and wanted to get a head start on my PhD."

"Where are you from in America?" Henry said.

"Morris County, Kentucky," George said. "Originally. Very pretty if you like woods and meadows."

And then Henry asked George to tell him more. George spoke in a soft voice. Henry closed his eyes to imagine trees swaying, clear rivers, and then summer—an unbearable heat, green wilderness packed with the tightness of a fist.

"Sounds like paradise," Henry said.

"It's close to it," George said. "But I spent most of my childhood at boarding school in the Northeast."

"They have boarding schools in the States?" Henry asked.

"Oh yes," George said. "With uniforms and everything."

Henry pointed toward George's ankles. "I like your sock garters. I have a pair too, somewhere."

George asked for more scotch.

Henry brought the bottle back to the chaise. He took a swig and then passed it to George, who took a long drink.

"So what do you do here, George?"

"Apart from drink and get my heart broken?"

"And get run over," Henry added.

"I'm exploring the vast field of ancient languages."

"Interesting," Henry muttered, suddenly preoccupied. "Can I show you something?" He rushed over to the professor's desk and found a paper copy of the script written on the professor's discus.

He handed it to George. "Can you make any sense of this?"

George scrutinized it for a minute. "Honestly?"

"Yes, honestly."

"No," George said.

Henry looked disappointed.

"Because it looks like Lydian," George said. "And that's very hard to translate."

As the afternoon light deepened into gold, the two men leafed silently through centuries-old dictionaries in a bid to translate the text before the professor returned.

Henry switched on the radio, and the turning of pages was accompanied by the crackle of Haydn's *La Fedeltà Premiata*. They moved only to smoke and drink coffee.

The translation would have taken much less time had George and Henry not been constantly sidetracked by interesting but unrelated chapters, which they felt compelled to share with one another.

The sentences and paragraphs that Henry found interesting George copied into his orange notebook.

George liked to read his digressions aloud without looking up from the page.

Henry listened. The sound of George's voice made him feel as though he were drifting above his life.

When he opened his eyes, the recitation had ceased.

"It's like we're long lost brothers," George said.

When the professor burst in an hour later, he found George and Henry asleep on the chaise. George was sitting upright, while Henry lay partially upon George, using his shoulder as a pillow.

George was the first to wake up. The professor stared down at him superciliously. He was holding George's translation that Henry had pinned to the door.

"I hope, George," Professor Peterson said, lighting his pipe, "that you don't have any plans tomorrow."

"Tomorrow?"

Then Henry woke up.

"Thought you might like to see the dig where you'll be working from now on," the professor went on, puffing out smoke.

The tobacco sizzled.

"Where I'll be working?" George said.

"Excellent," Professor Peterson said. "It's all settled then. Welcome to the family."

TWENTY-FOUR

Rebecca and the topless man stood facing one another in the hall. It was very hot. The skin on his chest and shoulders glistened. Rebecca set down her backpack and easel.

"Do you speak English?" she said. "French?"

She hoped he might motion her inside again.

"*Liga*," he said, finally. "Speak little English. What do you want?"

Rebecca explained that she was a friend of the foreigner for whom he had left the fish. She said that she was an artist and wanted to draw him.

From the short time she had lived in Athens, she had learned that there is little point in trying to deceive a Greek. It was an art they had perfected even before their victory at Troy.

Rebecca explained how she'd seen him from the window. He didn't seem angry or saddened by her request but just stood very still gazing at her. He had walked down the backs of his sandals. The radio was on in his apartment and played some ancient opera.

"You real artist," he said in a way that wasn't clear whether he meant it as a statement or a question. But then he moved aside for her to enter and she did.

His apartment was empty but for a few straw chairs, an old television with thick dust on the glass, and an industrial broom. The radio sat on top of the television. Clean folded towels were stacked on a table in one corner, and on a chair were slung several dirty towels. From the kitchen she could hear bubbling. Rebecca wondered whether she should ask why he boils towels when he suddenly explained how the towels were from a nearby hospice, and that after someone died, the towels needed to be boiled clean.

He asked her to sit down by pointing at a chair. Then he went into the kitchen. The faucet squeaked. He returned with a glass of water.

"*Nero,*" he said.

He tilted his head to one side as she drained the glass. Then he took the glass back to the kitchen. The walls of his room were yellow with cigarette smoke. The only single piece of decoration was a painting hung beside the window—a reproduction of Munch's *The Storm*. A white, veiled figure running from dusk into wilderness. This man's life, Rebecca felt—is a slow plummet.

Pain drawn out by thought.

He returned with a second glass of water. She took a gulp and put it down. He watched. Then he asked where she was from and about her childhood. She said: "My mother abandoned us." He shrugged. "Tell me a nice moment," he said. "Remember something nice for me and I'll let you paint me."

And so she let herself fall back through the past, until her memory with seeming randomness pulled a postcard from her life, and she told the story of an old piano she and her sister found washed up on a beach. They were bright little girls then, vacationing with their grandfather in rainy Deauville. The next day the piano had gone, carried back out to sea on the tide. She was especially upset. Later that night her grandfather found some paper and told her to draw it, to bring it back with her memory.

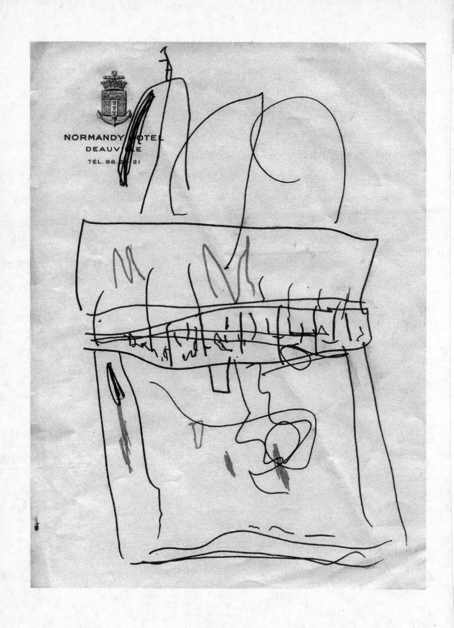

Rebecca's drawing of a piano that washed up. Age 6.

The topless man motioned with his hands upon an imaginary keyboard and then lit a cigarette. Then he offered the pack to Rebecca, and they smoked together.

As Rebecca set up the easel and unpacked her pencils, she noticed her fingers were trembling.

He remained naked from the waist up, and his flesh hung lazily from muscles that still bore the frame of muscular youth, like something beautiful in the early stages of decay. His face was poorly shaved. His cheekbones were high, almost regal.

After an hour of silence, he asked if he could smoke again. Rebecca put down her pencil and they both lit cigarettes.

"I unlucky," he said.

"What do you mean?"

"Tragic things happen."

"I understand," she said. Her tragedy had been slow, whereas his needed only a few seconds.

"It was my fate," he said.

"I'm sorry for you," Rebecca said.

"Yes," he said. "Like Oedipus—it was my fate."

He lit another cigarette.

"You cannot change fate," he added.

Rebecca nodded.

"It's set, you understand? Like the weather."

Rebecca nodded again and raised her eyebrows as if she had just understood. He seemed pleased and went into the kitchen, where he began feeding towels into hungry pans of boiling water. He returned after a few minutes and sat back down.

"I'm ready," he said.

Rebecca told herself that she did not believe in fate. She believed that she alone was responsible for everything that happened to her. If there was such a thing as fate, she thought, her mother would be blameless. It would have been her fate to abandon her daughters.

But it was not her fate.

It was her decision.

Fate is for the broken, the selfish, the simple, the lost, and the forever lonely—a distant light that comes no closer, nor ever completely disappears.

The topless man was a good subject, except for the occasional twitch the way a person does when falling asleep. After two more hours, he held an invisible cigarette up to his lips.

"Smoke?"

"Yes," she said. "Smoke, I'm almost finished."

Rebecca dabbed the sweat from her face with a linen scarf. He did not sweat, though his skin maintained a constant level of moisture that contrasted with the hard black of his hair.

The man held his cigarette by the neck as though it were an insect he had caught. When the paper and tobacco had burned away, he didn't stub it out, but just lay it flat in the saucer he was using as an ashtray.

After a few final strokes, Rebecca motioned for him to come around to her side of the picture.

"No," he said, shaking his finger.

"But don't you want to see how I've drawn you?"

"No," he said. "You see any mirrors in here?"

Rebecca looked around, embarrassed by her sudden vanity.

She removed the paper and sprayed it with a substance that would ensure it didn't smudge. Then she packed away the easel. The man fetched her a fresh glass of water.

"You come back if you want to draw me again."

"I will," she said.

"Okay," he said.

He made her promise that she would come back.

As she was leaving, he put his hand upon her shoulder. Then he took it off.

"Wait," he said. He ran back into the apartment. Rebecca was holding the front door. She heard the slamming of cupboard doors and he was suddenly back.

"Take these," he said, thrusting a few pieces of paper into her hand.

Rebecca looked down at three children's drawings. In each one the sun dominated the sky. The people on earth were drawn as little sticks with stubby lines for limbs. Flowers as tall as people with drooping heads. Cars bouncing along in the background with stick drivers.

"I too like to make art."

Rebecca looked at them, trying to think of something to say.

He mistook her silence as awe.

"You're kind," he said. "When you come back, I make more for you."

It was late when Rebecca stepped onto the cool street. The drawing was under her arm. Her first serious work.

TWENTY-FIVE

She lingered momentarily below Henry's balcony, hoping that perhaps he might see her. But it was cool and walking for a while would feel good after being inside for so long.

Then a voice called out.

"Rebecca!"

"Hello," she said, looking up.

"What are you doing?"

"Why don't you come down and get me," she said.

"Okay, let me put some clothes on."

"Don't come down, Henry, I'm coming up."

Then suddenly a voice from another balcony.

"Make your minds up! My children are trying to sleep. And let him come and get you," the voice commanded. "You shouldn't be chasing men at your age."

A pair of shutters slammed.

She entered his building and waited for the elevator. When it arrived Henry was in it wearing pajamas.

"I told you I was coming up," she said.

"But the voice——"

When they reached his floor, the door was open. From the bathroom, Rebecca could hear rushing water. She set down her easel and her drawing on the couch. Henry explained how he was trying to get a few spots of blood out of his clothes.

"Did one of your specimens come back to life?"

Henry laughed and she followed him into the bathroom, where a shirt was slung over the side of the bathtub. He kneeled down and continued scrubbing. Rebecca watched.

Henry turned off the faucet and explained what had happened.

Rebecca listened and then fetched salt and lemons.

She touched the back of Henry's head. His hair was soft. She fingered the bumps of muscle between his neck and shoulder. She wondered if she would ever truly know him, if their togetherness would shape her life, or if, like the summer, he would fade into the beauty and sadness of all summers.

There was no way to know the future. At times she felt she might open to him, but then something he said, or a subtle change in mood—and she would close again, very suddenly.

In the end, they hung his sopping clothes on the balcony. Faint dark spots remained where the blood had soaked in.

Henry was very moved by her story of the topless man. He made her a sandwich with cold strips of lamb which he smothered with *tzatziki*.

"It felt as though he'd been waiting for me—as though he'd been waiting for someone to draw him."

Henry nodded.

"But then just as I was leaving," she went on, "I understood why he had allowed me to come in."

Rebecca showed Henry the three childlike drawings presented to her.

"Jesus," Henry said. "What are these?"

"He's an artist too," she said.

Henry gave the drawings back to Rebecca.

"He told me that he believed in the idea of fate," she said.

Henry sneered. "I'm sure he does, but the truth is probably that his wife just wasn't looking where she was going. The idea of fate is for cowards."

"I'm not sure I think that anymore," Rebecca said. "Do you know the truth of what happened to that man? Do you know what it's like to find someone you love dead in front of you?"

Henry's eyes dimmed.

"Sorry."

"It's okay," Henry said. "It was such a long time ago anyway."

"You don't have to say that."

"What do you mean?" Henry said fiercely.

"I mean that it's who you are."

Henry snatched his wineglass and smashed it against the floor. For a moment, he just stood there. Then he stepped over the broken glass and went into his bedroom.

Rebecca found the broom and cleaned up the glass. She thought about what happened. Ten minutes passed. Then she saw Henry standing in the doorway.

She continued sweeping.

"Did I scare you?"

She nodded.

"Are you going to tell your mother I turned out to be crazy?"

"No," Rebecca said plainly, "because my mother abandoned Natalie and me when we were seven."

"Natalie?"

"My sister, didn't I tell you that—"

"She abandoned you? Your father had to bring you up?"

"We never knew our father. My mother wouldn't tell us, so no French house with shutters, no garden hose, no wine cellar, no vintage Citroën. We lived with our grandfather, and we took care of each other. And now she's gone off with some bastard in the south of France, and I'm here cleaning up your broken glass."

Henry just looked.

"You're not the only one with tragedy," she said and then started to cry. Henry held her and then walked her gently into his bedroom, where they lay down in the darkness.

A few hours later, Rebecca's life was spread before him like models of each event.

Henry would never know exactly how she felt when she remembered those moments of her life, but his desire to know was the beginning of a seriousness he had never known before with a woman.

After, he made chamomile tea. It was very late. The flowers softened in boiling water. They sipped it slowly with honey.

Then they kissed. Her necklace caught between their lips. Moonlight spilled across the bed, purifying them with its pale fire.

They fell asleep without making love, but were closer than ever.

The shutters were open, and a stiff breeze had claimed Athens, filling bedrooms, rearranging the tops of desks, touching everything and nothing, as if searching for something it no longer recognized.

Then Rebecca woke up. She wondered how much time had passed. She turned to Henry's sleeping face. It opened and closed with the shadow of her watching.

Rebecca wondered if her mother had once lain in bed with her father under such a spell of happiness. She imagined swimming with Henry in the steaming waters of the Aegean. She would take him to Aegina. His hands on her waist, guiding her through the water. Then his cool brown flesh after swimming—his beaded skin not quite dry.

She imagined taking him home to France.

A flock of bending trees.

Orchards.

The telephone about to ring.

Her grandfather cutting an onion with the slowness of age.

The bag of bags behind the door.

Sitting in the garden together—maybe her sister would come.

All the different cheeses. Plums from a tree in the garden.

Then driving back to Paris on the A11. Speaking English in the car.

Walking in the courtyards of the Louvre Museum. It was a place she had always dreamed of going, but she had never found the courage to enter central Paris in case she saw her mother.

The crunch of stones beneath her feet.

The excitement of doing nothing.

New sandals.

Cool marble steps.

A few clouds unfurling against the porcelain blue of dusk.

A bath together in the hotel on Rue du Bac.

The sense of something larger, something grand and overpowering, like some great historical event unfolding silently around them.

What happens to one person is felt by everyone. The time to hide has come and gone. She must give everything to survive.

But then she fell.

Like a statue falling off a ledge into its own reflection, Rebecca plunged headlong into sleep.

TWENTY-SIX

Morning felt like a different life.

The curtains had stilled to a slow blaze.

Her thoughts somehow washed away by the currents of sleep.

She woke to a room on fire with pools of morning. Henry lay on his stomach with his palms against the sheet.

And then his eyes opened.

He looked at her without smiling.

"You're here," he said.

"Me?"

"I've been waiting."

Rebecca put her hand on his forehead. "Are you dreaming?"

Henry sat up quickly.

"Were you dreaming?" she said.

"I don't know," he said.

"Was it bad?"

"I don't know. I've forgotten it."

"Would you tell me if it was bad?"

"Yes, I think so."

"Funny how we feel emotion when we're asleep," Rebecca said, turning away. "I wonder if we can when we're dead too."

It was still quite early, and so they didn't have to rush.

They mounted the Vespa around nine o'clock, and then joined the stream of traffic that would carry them past the towers of apartment blocks and factories, under the peeling bridges, past smashed cars rusting, past inaccessible fruit trees high up in the jutting rocks, and then out into the open heat of sand and scorched trees.

Rebecca rested her head on Henry's back. She could feel the vibration of the motor in his body. She felt very tired. Dreaming must have kept her up.

She was wearing the same clothes as when she painted the topless man. She imagined him in his kitchen boiling towels. The hospice van picking up the clean and dropping off the dirty. That would be the next drawing. The steaming pot. She wondered how she might sketch the steam. She thought of Edward Hopper struggling with the angle of his brush as he curved the glass in *Nighthawks*. Steam from the drinks machine. It was raining the day he painted it. He was drinking coffee for sure. His wife, Jo, asleep in the next room with one leg outside the covers. His brush kept time to her breathing.

When they arrived at the dig, the Renault was not there. Henry parked. They pulled off their helmets and carried them up to the tent.

Inside it was cool and dark. The artifacts lay in their bins as if in a deep sleep.

Henry pumped Rebecca a glass of water from the plastic barrel. Then he pumped himself one.

"I'm sorry about last night," he said.

"A lot came out."

Henry set down his glass gently and admitted that he felt very close to her, closer than he had ever felt to anyone.

"Make love to me," Rebecca said. Henry picked her up and lay her down on the long bench.

When they heard the Renault clunking its way up toward the tent, he didn't stop.

"Henry, I hear something,"

"Don't worry, they have to find the bricks for the wheels."

Outside the tent, in a world that was somehow disconnected to their lovemaking, Rebecca heard one car door shut, and then two distant voices.

One was the professor's, while the other lighter, younger, less certain.

Afterward, as they dressed quickly, Rebecca strained to hear the voices outside. Henry kissed her slowly on the lips.

"Thank you for telling me about your childhood last night," he said. "Now come and meet the genius we almost killed."

TWENTY-SEVEN

Rebecca opened the tent flap, but was blinded by the sun. George stopped walking when he saw her. Dust rose around his feet.

"Rebecca?"

Blinking wildly, she walked toward George, but stopped a few feet away.

"What happened to you?"

Then Henry came out.

"George!" he said. "This is my girlfriend."

The professor shook his head. "I may be old, but this is all very confusing—George seems to know Rebecca—which means that we all know each other already."

Henry gasped. "How do you know each other?"

George simply stared.

"Well—" Rebecca interrupted. "We've been friends for a while—pretty much since I moved to Athens."

"And why have you never told me about him?" Henry said in mock reproach.

"I did," Rebecca said. "The American."

"Jesus," Henry said with a laugh. "You were talking about George?"

George stared at the faces around him, not completely understanding what anything meant.

Time passed, in which George was dimly aware that through some strange coincidence the two main characters in his new life, the two people that he cared for the most, would soon be forced to wash him away for the sake of clarity. He felt the deep bite of loneliness. He thought of the cemetery in New Hampshire, and he longed for the cold simplicity of it. Fractured sunlight through the orchard. The eternal sea beyond, churning the names of the dead.

George followed the professor into the tent smiling weakly, but Henry reached out and took his arm.

"I had no idea she already had a boyfriend," George said. "She didn't tell me."

Henry just looked at him. "We can talk later."

"Okay," George said.

"I don't want our friendship to suffer," Henry admitted.

The small fist of anger in George's throat loosened.

"I'm just sad, is all," George said. "I really—"

"I know," Henry said. "But let's try and work it out."

For the rest of the morning, the professor made continual remarks about what a coincidence it was that George and Rebecca knew each other.

Then over lunch he went on about the various coincidences he'd encountered in his life, and how he'd experienced several especially complex ones in the Sinai Desert in 1974—which to this day, he had no explanation for but which continued to plague him.

George laughed out of courtesy.

Rebecca spent part of the morning with Henry in his pit, watching him scrape away the dirt with patient hope. Then she went to visit George in the tent.

"Hello," she said.

"Hello," George said without looking up from his dictionary.

"Are you okay?"

"Not really," George said. "But it's clear why you like him." Then he looked up at Rebecca. "I'd break up with me for him too."

"Oh, George, I never broke up with you."

"I know," George sighed. "Even though we slept together, we were never together."

Rebecca wanted to touch his hand, but was too afraid of what he might say next.

"And I'm not ready to give up drinking," he said.

She stood over him for a few moments and then went back outside.

George worked on various shards and plates for the rest of the day. Every so often he would consult his books, holding open the pages with washed stones. The professor brought hot cups of tea and digestive biscuits every half hour, and then read the translations over George's shoulder.

Over tea, Professor Peterson complimented George on the

sensitivity of his work. And then, at exactly 3:00 p.m., the professor gave them all a little wine and they stopped working. George gulped his wine mercilessly. The professor poured him another and said, "Steady on, George."

Rebecca and Henry watched.

Outside the tent, the sky was getting dark.

"I haven't seen clouds like that in a long time," Professor Peterson remarked, looking out through a raised tent flap. "There's going to be one blighter of a storm."

"Will it be soggy in the pit tomorrow if it rains?" Rebecca asked.

"Probably not," Professor Peterson replied. "The sun dries everything up rather quickly. Still, it's not ideal for various reasons I won't go into—but which in actual fact are the very reasons I'm ordering the three of you to go island hopping."

"Island hopping?" Henry asked.

"But what about the trays?" George asked. "There's still so much to do."

"Those artifacts have been here for approximately twenty-seven hundred years, George. I don't think another day will make any difference to them—though the fact that it does make a difference to you makes a difference to me, if that makes sense."

"Are you really giving us the day off?" Henry asked.

"Yes. I'm even going to pay you—all of you."

"Even me?" Rebecca said. The professor nodded.

"What's the catch?" Henry said.

"No catch," replied the professor with a wink. "But I have to leave Athens for a day, so get to know each other even better and then come back ready to find the rest of that Lydian woman's bones."

By the time they finished talking, clouds had swallowed up the tent.

Athens was no longer a nest of lights in the distance, but a place that had to be conjured by memory.

As they were tying up the tent flaps, a few drops fell with soft, heavy thuds against the fabric.

"To the Renault!" shouted Professor Peterson. "We're evacuating."

"I'll ride my scooter if you take these two," Henry suggested.

"Leave it here, and I'll pick you up the day after tomorrow—you'll get killed in this weather."

They all squeezed into the Renault 16, and then opened the two umbrellas Professor Peterson kept in the backseat to ward off anything falling through the sunroof, whether it be rain or snow or volcanic ash.

The engine spluttered and then died. Professor Peterson turned the key again, and with several small explosions, he put the car in gear.

"We'll coast down the hill and hope it starts properly as we roll onto the motorway."

Driving back to Athens was easy. Most cars had pulled to the sides of the road. The windshield was so steamed up, however, that the professor had to requisition one of George's socks to wipe the condensation.

As they neared Henry's apartment, the professor asked George where he wanted to be dropped.

"Drop him off with us," Henry said.

"But I really should catch up on my reading," George protested. "I should go home."

Rebecca's mouth flickered.

"We're all in this together now," Henry said, looking at Rebecca. "I suppose you could call it fate or something."

George looked out into a drowning world. In the reflection of the glass he could see the outline of a man, a few lines, a specter suspended by light and dark, by falling rain. A life that was yet to be decided, despite everything that had already happened, every moment is yet to be decided and connected to the one before it by illusions.

TWENTY-EIGHT

As the professor pulled up to the curb, the rain was falling fast in hard drops.

"See you boys day after tomorrow at six sharp," he shouted.

"Six?" Henry protested.

"Of course. We have to make up for lost time. As for you, my dear," he said, extending his hand to Rebecca, "it was a genuine pleasure."

Rebecca kissed him on the cheek. They all rushed from the car into Henry's building. The professor chugged away in such a low gear that a taxi behind him swerved and almost hit a telephone booth where a man and his dog were sheltering.

Once inside, they toweled their hair dry at the kitchen table while Henry made Greek coffee. Rebecca switched on the radio. The only station Henry received with the least crackle played classical music.

"It's one of the French Suites," George said as music filled the apartment.

"What?" Henry asked.

"It's Bach's French Suites."

"Turn it up then," Henry said.

They listened with towels on their heads.

"Very beautiful," Rebecca said. "It makes your hot, humid apartment seem like a grand palace in Vienna."

"What do you think, George?" Henry said, giving Rebecca a cigarette. "Is she full of it or what?"

George shrugged. "I think I might go home."

Rebecca nodded.

"No," Henry said. "Please don't go home."

George looked at the floor and moved his feet around. "You two have each other—and it's clear why, so what do you need me around for? You don't owe me anything."

He stood, but Henry blocked his path. "No," he said. "I want both of you here."

George picked up his bag.

"I'm fucking serious," Henry shouted, standing in front of George. "I really, really want you to stay. I know it's selfish, George, but please let's just try and work this out—don't discard me because of a weird coincidence."

"It's hard," George said. "I just didn't expect it to turn out like this."

Then Rebecca spoke. "You haven't lost anything, George. Think about it—you have my friendship and now you have Henry's."

"I don't know—I feel like I've lost something."

"You have," Henry said. "You've lost the excuse to be alone."

"Then why do I feel more alone?"

Henry shook his head. "But you have us."

George finally sat back down.

"Just imagine how happy we can all be if somehow this ends up being okay," Henry pleaded.

George nodded, but seemed unconvinced.

"You said I was like your long-lost brother," Henry said. "Was that just bullshit?"

"No," George said.

Henry put his hands on George's shoulders.

"So let me take care of you—let's share a hundred afternoons looking through old books," Henry said. Then he turned to Rebecca. "I want to take care of both of you."

George looked down at his hands.

They all sat listening to the rain.

"Why don't you start taking care of us by taking George and me out for dinner?" Rebecca said finally.

Water dripped from the balconies and gushed in small rivers to iron grates. Any oranges that had lain in gutters now bobbed against the drains. The only way to tell if the rain had stopped was to watch passing cars for the swish of wipers.

George's shirt was still too wet to wear, and so Henry went to his room to find another one. A few minutes later, he came back holding a white cotton shirt with French cuffs.

"This was a gift from someone special, and I just got it back from the dry cleaners. I think you should wear it."

"Okay," George said, inspecting it. "And it's my favorite brand."

"Then it should fit you perfectly."

George squeezed into the shirt.

Rebecca watched.

After drinking two bottles of Greek wine, they descended in the slow elevator. Henry argued they should all stay at his apartment on account of the weather and how it would be better if they were going to catch an early boat to one of the islands.

"Are we really going?" George asked.

"Of course we are," Henry laughed. "We're young and free, and all this is fine."

"Strange that we are all together like this," Rebecca said. "Like we're the only three people left in the world."

George stopped at a kiosk to buy a large can of beer. The others waited. Then Rebecca walked ahead slowly.

George offered the can to Henry.

They walked in silence through the narrow, wet streets. Men in sandals nodded to them from doorways of shops with little inventory.

As they crossed a main avenue, the rain began again—first in slow, heavy drops, then small, fast pellets.

And then it stopped suddenly, and the sun fell through distant clouds. Henry turned to say something. It was very bright and their shadows overlapped.

Around them, at unthinkable speeds, planets tilted their bodies of fire and ice.

TWENTY-NINE

Henry pointed to a neon sign up ahead.

"Let's eat there," he said.

Then it started to rain again and they ran up the street to the restaurant.

Inside, it was small and noticeably dirty, with plastic tablecloths, slow ceiling fans, and slabs of meat on trays in stainless steel cabinets. The dirt in the restaurant was the sort that accumulates slowly over time—the sort that hides itself from the owners through gradualness.

They sat in a corner next to a couple. The woman wore a cream cotton blouse that was tight around her breasts. Her husband wore a black T-shirt that said JOHNNY BOY, AMERICAN LEGEND, with a sequined skull embroidered underneath.

When the waiter switched on the main lights, the sequins on the man's T-shirt caught the light and the skull came alive with a grin.

The couple was brought a tray of spanakopita. The smell

SIMON VAN BOOY

of spinach and warm cheese filled the restaurant. The waiter balanced a cigarette on his bottom lip, and when he faltered slightly, so did the cigarette, which made it seem as though he were not a waiter at all but an acrobat performing a trick that involved smoking and serving spinach and cheese pie.

Despite Henry's habit of eating at the restaurant once a week, the locals and the staff regarded them with coolness.

The waiter's hand trembled as he wrote down their order. At Henry's suggestion, the waiter promised an assortment of what he could vouch for personally. When he left, the owner of the restaurant—a tall, muscular woman with thin lips—came up to the table and asked them if they liked Greek music.

George asked her in Greek to bring three glasses of raki. The woman stared at him. A smile curled at the edges of her mouth.

"You make a good effort with Greek," she said. "And so I have something better than raki for you—something you've never had, any of you."

She disappeared into the kitchen and then a few moments later, the lights sank and slow painful bouzouki music came through the speakers. A few of the locals laughed.

"Is she doing this for us?" Rebecca asked.

"I'm afraid so," George said.

Then she came out with three glasses of red liquor.

"Mournoraki, my friends."

"They each took a glass."

"*Yamas,*" George said and then drained the glass of its thick red liquid.

Henry took a sip and spat it out.

People laughed.

"What the hell is this?"

"Probably something from her village," George said, and then called out to the woman in Greek. She answered back in English.

"From Crete," she said.

"I like it," Rebecca said. "It's like blood."

And then some food arrived.

"This will warm us up," Henry said.

"Look at me—I'm still soaked," said Rebecca.

Two Greek men turned from the counter and looked at her.

Then a large tray of steaming lamb, which the waiter carried above his head.

"Let's get up at five and take the underground to Piraeus," Henry suggested, spooning food onto Rebecca's and George's plates.

"That's a bit early," Rebecca said. "I'm going to the toilet."

George stood as she left the table.

"What a gentleman," Henry said.

"Just a habit," George said shyly.

Henry stared at him for a few moments.

"I'm going to take care of you, George," he said.

"Thanks," George said.

"How about we find you a beautiful Greek girl who loves that red stuff?"

When Rebecca returned from the bathroom they ate mostly in silence and listened to the music. Then Henry paid for dinner and they put their coats on. The rain had stopped. The streets were hot and clean.

Instead of going straight back to Henry's apartment, the three of them wandered the streets of the Plaka, which were choked with tourists buying alabaster busts and leather sandals. The lanes were muddy. Water dripped from tarpaulins onto anyone inspecting the wares.

Then suddenly a man stepped in front of them.

"Very nice Greek place here!" he said, pointing toward a shabby building.

"What kind of music?" George asked.

"Greek music," the man said rudely.

"Rembetika?"

"Yes," the man said.

"I don't believe you," George said.

"What is your name?" the man said gruffly.

"George Cavendish."

"Well, Mr. George, I am a traditional Greek dancer with good steps," he said. "The songs tonight in this place are rembetika songs."

"You mean hasapiko," George insisted.

"No, no, no," said the man sternly. "Traditional songs, rembetika."

Immediately after entering through a curtain, they went up some narrow stairs past a woman sitting behind an enormous cash register. The restaurant was very dark, except for an empty stage lit with upward-facing lights.

There were about thirty tables, but only two or three were occupied.

"This is the first time I've ever been to a tourist trap," Henry said quietly.

"Not me," said George. "I've been overcharged and robbed since the day I arrived in this country."

The stage was covered with rose petals. Rebecca picked some up on her way to the table and put them in Henry's and George's pockets.

"It's going to get much worse," George said, smiling. "But they'll get us drunk—because if they don't we'd never pay the bill."

"What's rembetika?" Rebecca asked.

"It's one of the most beautiful forms of all music," George explained. "It's alchemy."

"Is that what we're going to hear?" Henry asked as they sat down.

"I doubt it," George said. "Most proper places are closed this time of year, and they are usually in areas where there's no tourist trade—like empty markets or neighborhoods where there are lots of factories."

"How do you know all this?" Henry asked.

"Because I've spent months just wandering the streets alone," George admitted. "I've met some real characters."

Henry, Rebecca, and George lost count of how many glasses of homemade liquor they drank—for after every long sip, a hairy arm would reach across the table with a bottle, and the glass would be replenished before it was empty.

When the bouzouki player finally left the stage, he did so by stepping down into the audience and kissing and hugging everyone he could, expertly cradling his bouzouki to one side. Henry, George, and Rebecca all took turns hugging him.

The next singer who came out was a transvestite. He took the microphone off its stand and flicked his blond hair back, winking at an old man in the front row. George told Henry and Rebecca that they should go, as there were five more live acts and it was late. They agreed and, after stuffing themselves with flaky baklava, found themselves outside the restaurant, standing aimlessly in the street with lit cigarettes. It was half past two in the morning.

"I'm drunk," Rebecca said. "You don't mind, do you?"

Henry put his arm around her. "Only if you don't mind that I am."

"Cretan firewater," George said loudly. "They make it in the hills. Last time I drank it I got run over."

"That's probably why you survived," Henry said, buckling with laughter.

Rebecca held George's and Henry's arms for balance, but couldn't help from swaying.

"I think we should find a taxi," she said.

And then, as such things happen in states of insobriety, a taxi seemed to suddenly appear at their feet, and then they all seemed to be in it, speeding somewhere they couldn't quite remember how to get to.

In the taxi, Henry didn't stop talking. And then he tapped the taxi driver on the shoulder.

"This is my brother back here," Henry said with slurred affection. "He says he's my brother."

The taxi driver nodded.

Then Rebecca told Henry how she had met George, how she had seen him and thought he looked interesting. George admitted he couldn't believe it when she spoke to him.

They alighted at the corner of Henry's street. George put an arm across Henry's shoulder and the two men strolled together.

"I'm so very drunk," Henry said. "So very drunk."

"It's hard not to be," George said, "when you drink that much."

"You don't mind what I said in the taxi, do you?" Henry said. "I know you're an American, but who gives a damn—the age difference is right at least."

"Thanks," George said, fumbling for his cigarettes. "I like it all."

Outside Henry's building, Rebecca stopped walking and looked up at the moon.

"It's almost full," she said.

"Almost—my beautiful, wonderful air hostess," Henry said. "You should know the moon better than any of us because you spent years flying through the heavens like a shooting star."

"Let's go inside," she said, "before I collapse."

"Did she?" George said.

"Did she what?" Henry said.

"I don't know," George said. "Did she?" And they both laughed.

They all sat in the kitchen for some time. George drank the rest of the wine and talked with Henry about human remains.

"Henry talks a lot about interesting things, but not much about himself," Rebecca said to George. "Isn't that true?"

"My life isn't that interesting," Henry slurred. "I'm sorry I'm not perfect."

"I don't believe him," George said.

"That he's not interesting?" Rebecca said.

"No—that he's sorry," George said, and then roared with laughter. "What are we talking about again?"

By 4:00 a.m., Rebecca said she couldn't keep her eyes open. She kissed both men on the cheek and went into Henry's bedroom, closing the door behind her.

Henry got up and poured himself a glass of water, then poured one for George.

"C'mon, Georgie boy—let me make up your bed."

Henry went into the hall cupboard and got some sheets and a pillow, then made up his bed with the slowness of a drunk. George stood by the window and looked outside. It was raining again and there was no other sound but the falling of drops.

Then, in the distance a taxi splashed up the street, changing to a lower gear and then disappearing too quickly to be remembered.

"What do you think of that?" Henry said, looking down at the makeshift bed he'd made for his friend.

"You should work in a hotel," George said.

"Well, it certainly feels like I do—which reminds me that I need to lend you my spare pair of swim shorts in the morning."

"Good night, brother," George said quietly.

Henry leaned awkwardly into his friend and embraced him. For a few moments they stood very still.

"Good night, good night," he softly said.

Rebecca was already asleep.

Her clothes lay on the chair, arranged in the order in which she had taken them off. Henry removed his clothes and lay them on top of hers.

As he sank into the sheets, two hands reached around his back.

As he closed his eyes, Rebecca's body moved under the sheets. He lay on his back, conscious of her but in the shadow of another dream.

THIRTY

They arrived at the port of Piraeus much later than planned. The port was empty as most of the tourist boats had already departed for the islands.

A few deckhands skulked about smoking. A dog followed them with its tail up. The air was salty. An old man in a cigarette kiosk was asleep. His radio was loud, but no one seemed to notice.

They stood for a few minutes and looked around.

"I have a feeling we've missed the boat," Henry said with a smirk.

Rebecca lifted her foot to adjust the strap on her sandal.

"What are we going to do?" she said.

"I'm going to find the ticket office," Henry said. "Maybe there's another boat,"

George nodded. "Good idea."

After he walked away, Rebecca said she was hungry.

"We could all go for lunch," George said.

"No, I really need something now," she said holding her stomach.

"Are you okay?"

"I can't drink anymore, George, I really can't."

"I'll help you stop."

They both laughed at that. Rebecca pointed to a small market with wicker baskets of fruit.

"Let's go over there and buy something."

Next to the wicker baskets was a mechanical ride-on horse, stripped of color by the wind that whirled through the square off the sea.

They bought a bag of fruit and three small bottles of water.

As George opened a bottle for Rebecca, he saw Henry running toward them waving.

"C'mon!" he shouted, motioning with his hand. "The captain is holding the boat for us."

The dog noticed people running and barked. There were only a dozen or so passengers onboard. They sat on plastic orange chairs and ate peaches.

Then George excused himself and went to find the toilet. After locking the door and closing the window, he pulled a small hip flask of vodka from his pocket and drained it. As he climbed back on deck, the water was getting choppy. When the boat ploughed through a wake, spray flew up the hull and slopped onto the deck.

Rebecca put her arm around Henry and kissed him slowly on the cheek.

"I feel a bit guilty," she said.

Henry turned to her.

"Why?"

She smiled.

"Why do you think?"

George stood at the railing and looked out to sea. As they neared land, he felt a hand touch his.

"What are you doing over here by yourself?" It was Rebecca.

"Thinking."

Rebecca turned to Henry.

"He's over here thinking," she shouted.

"He thinks too much," Henry shouted back. Then the boat began to slow.

"I think you're the artist," she said.

"Me?" George said sadly.

"You're probably some great genius and don't even know."

George laughed. They were suddenly the only three people on deck.

"When the nature of all things rational," George said, looking over Rebecca's shoulder, "equipped each rational being with his powers, one of the faculties we received from his hand was this: that just as he himself transmutes every obstacle or opposition, fits it into its place in destiny's pattern, and assimilates it into himself, so a rational being has power to turn each hindrance into material for himself and use it to set forward his own endeavors."

"What do you mean, great speaker?" said Rebecca.

"He means there are no mistakes," Henry said. "Take a bow, George."

George bowed and they entered the small port of an unknown land.

THIRTY-ONE

As the boat kissed some old truck tires nailed against the dock, Henry explained how Aegina had been a superpower in ancient times because of the island's geographical position, but when the Aeginetans allied with Sparta, the Greeks finally had an excuse to destroy them.

"There were also coins," he added. "Apparently the first coins in Europe were minted on Aegina—they had little turtles on them—so if you find one, please give it to me."

At the dock, fishermen sat on upside-down buckets and sewed nets. Old women stood behind them and talked to their children on mobile phones.

"What else?" George asked.

Rebecca grinned. "Thirsty pistachio trees lower the water table a few feet per year."

Henry looked at her incredulously. "How do you know that?"

"Nuts grow on trees?" George said.

"From a documentary that's on all Mediterranean Air France flights," she replied.

They stepped off the boat into a bustling market that lined the two main streets of Aegina. The square was packed. Small women in black with carts pushed past them.

"Let's buy food here and take it to the beach," Rebecca said.

"Perfect," George said. "I'll get fruit."

"We've got fruit—why don't you get fish?" Rebecca said.

"Fish would be good," said Henry. "I'll get one of those little grill things—otherwise we're eating sushi for lunch."

"I'll see about renting mopeds," George said, pointing to a line of dilapidated motorcycles with a rental sign propped up against them.

From the long line of motorcycles, there were only two mopeds that actually worked. Rebecca insisted on having her own, so George and Henry rode together—a little lower to the road than the owner of the rental company would have liked, but he was amused that Rebecca wanted her own and told them not to drive too fast. Henry and George took turns driving, changing over at spots they thought might possess archaeological significance.

After passing a few coves too rocky for swimming, Rebecca found what looked like a hidden beach, though the map showed no beach whatsoever, just a strip of tall cliffs. The road that led to it was not really a road, but a footpath through yellow scorched rock. They rode very slowly across the rough ground, their engines ticking. When they reached an uneven cliff path,

George announced that he'd rather walk than risk being driven to his death by a British archaeologist. Rebecca agreed it was a good idea, and they hiked for half an hour down a steep slope toward a strip of beach they could now see tucked underneath the overhanging cliffs. They could also see several openings to caves, which George said he'd explore after lunch.

"Will the bikes be okay up there?" Henry said, stopping to look back.

"Why, did you leave a deposit?" Rebecca joked.

"Yes, I did, actually—quite a lot as it happens."

"They'll be okay then," she laughed, waving everyone forward.

"I hope so," Henry said, "for your sakes."

The sand on the cliff was very fine and coated their feet and ankles. When they reached a ledge after twenty minutes of careful descending, the beach came into full view. The sand was so white that from a distance it resembled snow.

When they finally reached it, George dropped his bag of food and towels and stripped down to the bathing suit he was wearing underneath his cotton slacks—one he'd borrowed from Henry. Then he ran into the sea and swam quickly into deeper water.

As Henry entered the clear waves, he felt the urge to submerge his entire body. He waded deeper, then held his nostrils and fell backward. In the second it took for the water to swallow him up thoughts unraveled in him, long-held thoughts, thoughts of which he was conscious but could not articulate, an unceasing sentence of thought like thread from a falling spool.

He ascended after a few seconds from the sandy bottom, breaking the surface with tremendous power—as though divinely anointed for what was soon to come.

After swimming for a little while, the aroma of grilling octopus and sardines on the disposable barbeque lured Henry and George back to shore. Sand coated their legs. They squeezed lemon halves into the milky white contours of octopus.

After lunch Rebecca entered the sea slowly.

Henry sat up and looked out to sea. "Maybe happiness is just finding the right people at the right time."

"But how do you find them?" George said.

"Just run them over."

George was then suddenly interested.

"But say you do find the right people—how do you love without smothering them?"

Henry looked uncertain.

"How do you not suffocate them with all the love you've built up in their absence?" George said.

Henry thought for a moment. "You don't," he said. "And that's the whole point—it works in a way it just wouldn't with other people."

After sleeping for a while, they woke up and saw that Rebecca was still in the sea. They strolled to the water, still chatting, and then swam to the rock upon which she was resting. George swam out a little farther and splashed around.

"I've been loving you from a distance," Henry said.

Her mouth broke into a smile, but her eyes didn't change—as though attached to thoughts beyond the moment. "I was thinking," she said.

Henry touched her cheek. "About what?"

Then George appeared. "I'll tell you soon," she said.

"I thought we could swim around there," George said.

They found they had swum into a cave that widened into a larger space. The sand was dark and compact. Without carrying the sun on their backs, the cave felt almost cold. Their voices were louder and more distinct. The ceiling of the cave was ridged like the inside of a mouth.

The cave echoed with the breath of each wave, and through spaces in the rock sunlight fell in columns of yellow.

They talked for an hour and then swam into the darker, deeper hollows of the cave, which were teeming with so much life that things brushed up against their legs. For a while they lay on their backs on the cool wet sand. Then the tide swept in and washed over them. They swam against the current and out toward the beach—to their jumble of possessions in the glow of early evening. They packed up without saying much.

When they reached the top of the cliff, George and Henry found the scooters and wheeled them quietly toward the road. Just as they were about to mount them, Rebecca stopped.

"I want one more look at the place where I was so happy," she said.

They turned around and walked back to the edge of the cliff.

Rebecca found George's hand. "I'm so glad we're working it out," she said.

The sun was beginning to fall behind distant rocks. It was very quiet and they stood for some time before anyone spoke.

"My whole life," Henry said, "I've felt as though I were missing something, that the happiness assigned to me existed always at a distance, somewhere, in some place that was somehow beyond me—and when I moved, it too moved, always away but never so far as not to haunt me with the feeling of what it might be like to be happy."

"But with you," he said, turning to George and Rebecca, "I feel as though I am leading the charge toward death. Happiness and I have swapped places, and now it's pursuing me for its very existence."

"No matter what happens from this moment on," Henry announced. "Here, in this place, I will always have my defining moment of victory against sadness."

"I wonder if we'll ever come back here," Rebecca said.

"I think we will," George said.

Waves broke against the cliffs.

Rebecca fell into a deep, dreamless sleep on the boat back to Athens.

George and Henry chatted about the coming day, hypnotized by the lights that grew nearer and brighter as their boat skimmed home in the quiet dusk.

THIRTY-TWO

Henry's apartment was warm and dark. It was not late, but they were all very tired and had nothing to say. Rebecca fell asleep again on the metro from Piraeus. George agreed to stay over if he could borrow some clothes. The professor was expected early the next morning.

Henry brewed some tea, but Rebecca and George were already asleep by the time it was ready. The smell of peppermint filled the kitchen. Henry drank a cup and thought about their day together. He checked on George and then went into his bedroom, where he shed his clothes silently and slipped into bed with Rebecca.

A scooter went past.

Light from the hall fell upon their bed like a spine.

Henry turned to kiss Rebecca and saw that she was awake.

She looked at him and stroked his face with her hand.

"I love you," she said.

"I love you too."

Then he asked what she had been thinking about when he swam out to meet her.

She hesitated for a moment. "Can I tell you tomorrow?"

Henry smiled. "Is it something about George?"

"No, it's about you and me."

Henry blinked quickly.

"But not tonight, Henry, maybe tomorrow when we're alone."

"I think we should talk tonight," Henry said. "Otherwise I'll worry about it tomorrow."

Rebecca touched his arm. "Can we please wait?"

"George is dead asleep—I checked."

Rebecca closed her eyes. Henry turned abruptly to face the shutters.

"Are you mad at me?" she said.

"A little," Henry said. "If there's something you need to say—say it."

"I'm afraid to."

Henry turned to face her. "I've spent my whole childhood with people too afraid to speak—so if there's something you need to say, say it, Rebecca."

Rebecca sat up.

"So?" Henry said.

"George is really asleep?"

"He's dead asleep."

Rebecca covered her face with her hands. "It's serious."

"Whatever it is—I'm yours," he said. "I love you now."

"I'm afraid that if I tell you, you'll leave me and I'll turn out just like my mother and sister."

"What does that mean?"

"It means I'm pregnant."

Henry's face dropped.

"At least, I think I am."

"How?"

"I missed my period and then took a test," she said. "And the test was positive."

"Jesus. Jesus," Henry said.

Rebecca reached for him, but he pulled away into some private world.

"Henry," she said softly, but he seemed not to hear her. "Henry," she said again.

"It's awful," he said, "so awful, you'll hate me."

Rebecca threw back the covers and went over to the window, where she stood, a shadowy outline against the starlight.

"There's something I have to tell you that's awful," he said.

"Tell me then," she replied coldly.

His instinct at that moment was to hold her, but Henry found himself suddenly pinned by the sight of his baby brother, not asleep but dead. His parents screaming. They pulled at his body with scissors.

The only baby Henry had ever held was no longer living.

Rebecca watched him cry. When she finally came near, he escaped into the bathroom and vomited. Then he sat quietly on the tiles.

By the time he went back into the bedroom, determined to admit everything, Rebecca was asleep and it was nearing dawn.

Henry got into bed and held her so tightly that she opened her eyes and smiled.

THIRTY-THREE

The professor kept his word and pulled up to the apartment at six o'clock sharp. The car was very loud. Henry heard it coming down the street while it was still far away and quickly dressed. He had spent most of the morning awake, staring at the window, watching the ghostly arc of passing headlights lessen against the glow of dawn.

George was fully dressed when Henry emerged from his bedroom.

Henry combed his hair in the mirror then went to find his briefcase of notes.

Rebecca was still sleeping. Only half her body was covered by the sheet.

Henry imagined a life growing inside her.

He knew things like this could be taken care of in a few hours—like a tiny candle blown out with a puff. He wondered if it was what she wanted.

A moment before leaving the apartment, he hoped Rebecca

would wake up so he could reassure her they would work it out together. But she was motionless and Henry let her sleep. George held the door. His face was slightly burned.

"Is Rebecca not coming?"

"She's still sleeping."

Nobody talked on the drive up, so Professor Peterson turned on the radio. The sky was very bright. George rolled down his window.

If they had the child, where would they live? Would she give birth in France? And what if the child were born dead? What if the child came out in a tangle?

It would all take place within a single year.

Unsolvable questions swirled in Henry's mind.

A mile or so from the dig, the professor started whistling. Then he skidded to a stop in the dust.

"Which one of you boys is going to find the bricks?"

George volunteered. Once the bricks were under the wheels. Henry got out and walked over to his Vespa. There was condensation on the inside of the dials. He tapped the glass.

A dog had barked once, and his brother's eyes opened for the last time.

For most of the morning, Henry worked quietly in his excavation pit, scratching the ground with little enthusiasm.

He knew that he would see her later. That a decision had to be made somehow, and that they would both stick to it.

And then, not long before lunch, another side of Henry began to emerge—a part of him that was just a little further ahead in his life than where he was now. And in his mind, he saw himself in a tweed jacket in Regent's Park, pushing a stroller along some beautiful Sunday path, the child giggling with joy. He imagined packing up the car for summers in Wales. Skipping through meadows of tall grass, and the light, bubbling laughter of a child trying to keep up. Learning to swim in the cool water of Bala Lake. The wobble of first steps. He sensed closeness too. Rebecca in some heavy pocketless coat, with snow falling. A weekend in Paris. The happiness of afternoons.

He would give up his search for the dead and live for the living.

Love is like life but longer.

END OF BOOK ONE

In my end is my beginning.

—T. S. Eliot

The final moments of her life Rebecca lay crushed under tons of rubble.

The fruit she had been eating was still in her mouth.

Her eyes would not open.

She could sense the darkness that encapsulated her.

She could not feel her arms.

Then her life, like a cloud, split open, and she lay motionless in a rain of moments.

The green telephone at her grandfather's house next to the plant.

She could feel the cool plastic of the handle and the sensation of cupping it under her ear. She could hear a voice at the other end of the line that she recognized as her own.

The weight of her mother's shoes as she carried them around the house, wondering when she would come home.

The idea that she'd grow up and have to wear such things.

Running through the forest of owls with her sister.

Their white faces.

A twin.

The strangeness of a living mirror.

And then the rain of her life stopped, and she was in darkness, her heart pushing against her ribs.

Muted noise as though she were underwater.

Then the rain of moments began again until she was drenched by single esoteric details:

Morning light behind the curtain.

The smell of classrooms.

A glass of milk.

The hope for her mother and the imagined pressure of her arms against her.

Passengers' faces.

Quietly beating hearts.

Wings held steady by moonlight.

Market stalls.

Orange trees.

Sandals.

Laying her head upon Henry's cool back in the morning.

It was as important as being born.

George and the street children.

Clogs.

Sweets.

Her grandfather again, but a character in his own dream—walking barefoot by the lake calling out to someone far away.

A bungalow in France.

A daughter.

Granddaughters.

His elbows as he drove them in the rain to the shops.

And then two very small hands growing inside her belly.

A small head.

Thumb body, surging.

Life knitting something in her womb.

Then Rebecca realized she could not feel her body and was unable to shout.

There was no sound. Nothing stirred but the silent movies projected on the inside of her skull.

She was not so much aware that she was dying as she was that she was still alive.

Had she more time, she might have nurtured a hope of being rescued by George and Henry. Instead, memory leaked out around her.

Mother.

This memory was not painful to her now. Her life was an open window and she a butterfly.

If not for her intermittent returns to darkness—the body's insistence on life—she could have been on vacation, swimming in the sea, each stroke of her arms a complete philosophy.

Henry.

The morning he came back from Cambridge.

And then she smelled her grandfather's coat, hanging behind the kitchen door with a bag of bags and a broom.

On the back of Henry's Vespa.

She wondered if she had lived her entire life from under the collapsed building. That life is imagined by a self we can never fully know.

The softness of hands. A child's hands. A small house somewhere. Gloves on a cold day.

And then with the expediency of the dying, she fell in love with the darkness and the eight seconds she had left in it—each second like a mouthful of food to someone starving.

At that moment, a French girl living in Paris called Natalie fainted in the supermarket.

People rushed over.

In order to possess what you do not possess
You must go by the way of dispossession.

—T. S. Eliot

BOOK TWO

NIGHT CAME WITH
MANY STARS

THIRTY-FOUR

You couldn't wait for the day to end. She would be delighted with your change of heart. There would be practical things to sort out, like hospitals and names, a house to live in with a garden.

But just before lunchtime it came. George was at the entrance to the tent, holding up a pitcher of water. George fell over. The water spilled.

And then it came and just battered everything.

You tried to cover your ears, but you were soon on the ground too. No one could see because of the dust. You had no conscious thoughts. If you had died, your last feeling would have been pure terror.

It seemed like hours; thought lay in a mess at your feet. Below the mountain, buildings were crumbling. People's lives were ending within a few seconds.

And when it stopped, the silence on the mountainside was deafening. You remember sprinting to the top—toward the tent—through the dust. George was standing again, but very still. His face seemed grotesque, as though it were hung upon his skull the wrong way. Then you felt each other as if to physically confirm what your eyes saw. You remember being at the edge, looking for Athens in the distance.

"Stop! Stop! Stand where you are!" screamed the professor. "Don't move, the ledge may be unstable—there's been an earthquake and there may be another any second."

But from where you were standing you could see enough.

Athens had disappeared under a cloud of dust.

The professor was shouting.

"I have to secure the artifacts. I have to secure the artifacts."

He turned to you and George.

"Go and get Rebecca—bring her up here where it's safe."

The Renault had rolled backward into the rock face. The entire back end was smashed in.

The professor said to abandon the car if you got to something you couldn't drive around. He also told you to steal whatever you needed in order to survive. Then he handed you a small gun.

"For emergencies," he said, shoving it into your hands. "Use it if you must."

Then he disappeared.

"Try and start the engine," George said. "I'll push it off the rock."

It started after a few attempts. George jumped into the passenger seat.

"The whole back end is smashed in," he said. "Totally smashed in."

Approaching Athens, you saw that the stream of cars leaving the city had become a stationary line of vehicles on both sides of the road. There were at least thirty helicopters in the sky. You drove most of the way along the steep grass embankment, stopping only to steer around steaming cars packed with panic-stricken Athenians.

For a two-mile stretch you drove along a sidewalk, blasting the horn. People scattered like insects. Entire houses had slid onto the road and there were small fires everywhere. You passed two men having a fist fight.

When you arrived at your apartment, it was intact, with only a few cracks up the walls. You both rushed around calling Rebecca's name. Then you glanced at something on the kitchen table.

Dear Henry,

I am going home for a bit to think about all this. If you can, come over when you get back. I want you to know you can tell me anything about your life. I could never hate you for anything you've done. We should also talk about what we're going to do. I want it to be our decision. I care about your happiness, so please be honest, Henry.
I love you.
See you for dinner.
R

P.S. Maybe don't tell George yet.

It took a further four hours to reach Rebecca's apartment. You stopped twice. Once to change a flat tire, and the other to help lift a section of roof off a family who were having lunch. The mother had managed to crawl out—but the others were trapped. When there were enough people to lift the roof, it was clear the children were dead. They were still in their seats like dolls.

It was hard to find Rebecca's road. Everything looked different. The air smelled of sewage and burning plastic.

Young men were directing traffic and trying to keep lanes open for troops now coming in by the truckload. Army helicopters patrolled the city in menacing formations.

You and George ditched the car a few blocks from Rebecca's house and ran the rest of the way. You hugged and shouted when—from a distance—her building looked perfectly intact. You even looked for her among the faces on the street. As you ran toward the entrance, a young boy called out to you and pointed up. Somehow you had missed seeing it. The walls of the building were standing, but the building had collapsed in on itself.

You just stood there.

Then you looked into the crowd for anyone who didn't seem to be doing anything. You grabbed a teenage boy and asked him something.

"Answer me!" you screamed, but then he pushed you off and ran away.

"We have to go in," you said to George. "She might be trapped."

The only way to get in was through a broken window in the first-floor lobby. The entrance was blocked with rubble—but strangely, the glass in the front doors wasn't even cracked. George pulled his shirt over his mouth because the dust had not settled. You could smell electricity and steered George around a live cable dangling from beneath the staircase. The elevator shaft was open and filled with bricks, pieces of marble, and books. There was a hammer on the floor and George picked it up.

You found what remained of the staircase and, before ascending, looked at one another, knowing that the building could collapse at any time. A cold, logical voice kept telling you that she probably hadn't survived and that you should get out, but the impulse to save drove you blindly on.

It's difficult to explain what it was like inside because everything was smashed and topsy-turvy. You were able to climb to Rebecca's floor because the nature of the collapse formed a sort of natural ladder. In the places that were too high, George piled up rubble or found some furniture to stand on that would take you both to the next level.

When you reached what you thought was Rebecca's floor, it was uneven, but largely horizontal. You realized there was going to be no quick way of getting to her room because of several collapsed beams. Your fingers were already pierced and bloody. The dust higher up was not as thick, otherwise it would have been impossible to breathe.

You took turns smashing the beams with George's hammer. You remember George saying he thought you were in her hallway. You were both sweating. George had taken his shirt off. His skin was covered in dust, and there were dark circles of blood, from where he'd torn his skin open. The path you made for yourselves from the hall was tiny. It was so dark you could hardly see what you were doing. There were pieces of broken marble everywhere. George hammered through a length of ceiling tiles, kicked through some drywall, and you found yourselves in her bedroom, which seemed to have escaped damage, except for the dust everywhere. Although you could smell gas, George kept lighting pieces of paper and bits of rag in order to see.

A wall had fallen out, or been ripped out with her balcony. You remember looking out into Athens from a fourth-floor apartment now only two stories up. The air was very cool and there was something calm about being so open to the night. It felt good to breathe. You could hear the roar of traffic, endless police sirens, and the occasional scream.

A bowl of oranges lay on the side table white with dust. Then you realized you were in Rebecca's bedroom. A few inches from the bowl, a slab of ceiling lay where Rebecca's bed should have been. Then you noticed a hand on the ground. It must have been severed by the impact. When you began screaming, George didn't know what to do. Then you felt his weight on your back.

You shook free and started smashing a block of rubble with the hammer.

"Stop it," George commanded in a low growl. "You're going to kill us both, stop it, stop it." He lunged for your swinging arm, but you stopped before he could grab on.

"We have to get out of here," he said.

"Not without her," you pleaded. "I'm not leaving without her."

"She's dead," George kept saying, and you then realized exactly what he meant—that Rebecca was no longer alive, that you would never have any contact with her again, that any child growing in her womb would never live, never be delivered, never run around the garden of your imaginary house.

Her life would wear the mask of paradise.

"We can't leave her here," you said desperately.

"We have to get out," George said.

"Listen to me, George—we can't leave her here. She'll be trapped in here for days, maybe weeks. We can't leave her body here like this."

"And if we dig her out, what then? Where are we going to take her?"

"We'll take her to my apartment."

"Henry, no, absolutely not."

You picked up the hammer, but George got hold of your arm. His strength was enormous. "Put it down," he said. "We'll take her to Aegina."

You imagined the secret beach glistening in moonlight, perfect and serene. And you knew without any doubt that George was doing this for you—not for Rebecca, nor for himself, but for you, only you.

It was the greatest act of friendship you would ever witness.

When it seemed impossible to move the block of marble, you found some knives from the kitchen and began slicing your way through the mattress. If you could cut open a path in the fabric, you could somehow wriggle her out.

You mapped the position of her body and worked quietly. You lost your breath when blood poured through the foam and springs and onto your arm. George said you must have nicked her body. And then the blood stopped and you both kept cutting.

When you finally got to her, it was a relief to find that her body was in one piece. But it was very stiff, like a store mannequin, and it didn't look anything like the Rebecca you knew. Her eyes were open and her face was a hard, pale wax. No trace of the woman you loved, just a body, just a shell from which all life had escaped.

You went to the other side of the room and sobbed.

George watched.

Then he came over and tried to console you.

"I killed him," you said.

George looked at you with no expression.

"I killed him," you said again. "I gave him a toy and it strangled him and he died."

"Who?" George said.

"My baby brother."

George looked horrified. "You never told me."

"Because you would have hated me."

"No, I wouldn't."

"But it was my fault."

He let you sob for a while and then started wrapping Rebecca's body in artist's canvas.

"Help me with this," he said.

You hadn't actually thought how you were going to get her out. But there was only one way—so you tied the canvas at each end with clothes you found lying around. Then you checked to make sure there was no one standing in the rubble below. There was some movement, but George said it was a dog.

The canvas landed with a thud. The dog began to rip at it

with its teeth and then barked and barked. You felt a burst of panic, so you pulled the pistol from your trousers and cocked it. The dog must have sensed the impending gunshot, because it ran away before you could steady your arm.

It took an hour to crawl back through the building and into the cool morning. George went to find the car and some water. The sky was beginning to lighten.

Your throat was so dry, you could hardly breathe without coughing. You waited with the body. A man who said he was a cop came over and asked if you had been trapped in the building. Then he asked if it was a body wrapped up on the ground. You told him it was. He nodded and told you to wait with it until someone came to take it away. You just stared at him. You think he was lying about being a cop. And you think he knew that, which is why he disappeared before George got back.

There were quite a few people out, mostly going somewhere carrying things. Nobody was wandering in a daze anymore. A new day had begun and brought purpose. The majority of Athenians had been evacuated, but parts of the city still burned.

George said the car was gone, so you carried Rebecca's body through the streets, setting it down every few hundred yards to rest. George's shoulder was bleeding badly. Then a truck full of soldiers pulled over and asked if you wanted help.

"Piraeus," George said.

"Not hospital?" the blond driver said in English.

"No, Piraeus, please take us to Piraeus," George said.

The driver said something to someone in the passenger seat and then said okay.

"That's where her people are," George said to the driver, who then understood immediately that you had a body wrapped in the canvas. He honked and several soldiers climbed down and helped load Rebecca into the back. Some of the soldiers were speaking Turkish.

The soldiers were about your age. They looked at the body and then at you. As you neared the port, one of them took the crucifix and black beads from around his neck and offered them to you.

"I don't believe in God," you said blankly.

"He'll catch you in his net," the soldier said and slipped the crucifix and beads into the canvas with Rebecca's body.

You explained to the soldiers that you were going to Piraeus in order to get her to Aegina. You told them you were taking her to the place where she had been happiest.

They seemed to understand.

The truck stopped only once to pry a female corpse from a car crushed by a wall. It happened moments before you arrived. The man who implored the truck to stop was her husband. He had been buying something at one of the few kiosks that was open. He saw it collapse. The soldiers lay the body of his wife on the street. Bits of glass had stuck in her face and they glinted in the morning sun.

By the time you reached Piraeus, the canvas was starting to smell. The soldier who offered the crucifix helped lower the body to the street, and then several soldiers found a boatman who was standing on the deck of his small ship watching everything quietly. George stayed with the body.

You begged the boatman in broken Greek to take you to Aegina. He shook his head that he wouldn't. The soldiers eyed him with quiet intensity. He looked past you at the body and the army truck in the square. "Sorry," he said in English.

Then one of the soldiers pulled out his revolver but without raising it above his waist. The boat captain shrugged calmly and went into his cabin. A minute later the engine started and the soldiers helped carry the canvas on deck.

The engine was very loud and the boat shuddered as black smoke surged from the rear engines.

Within ten minutes, you were way offshore. There were no other boats and the sea was quiet. The soldiers watched from the harbor wall. When they had lessened to a smudge of green in the distance you heard the snapping of rifle fire.

The captain stayed in his cabin, emerging only once to hand George a bottle of some Greek liquor. George gave you the bottle first and then gulped half the contents.

On reaching the port at Aegina you both realized you had been asleep.

It was evening.

There were hundreds of people at the harbor, as if waiting for your boat. You didn't know what they were doing and were afraid for some reason that they would attack you. After docking, you realized they were praying for people on the mainland.

People rushed over as the captain attached the lines, but were immediately disappointed when they saw only three men. They shouted at you for news. George yelled at them in Greek.

You don't know what he said, but they repeated it to one another and then went back to praying.

A couple of teenage boys helped you carry the body of Rebecca from the deck and onto the harbor. They must not have known what it was because when her hair fell out through a tear in the canvas one of them dropped the end he was carrying and ran off.

You and George carried the body away from the harbor to a bench in the square. Men were shouting at the fisherman who had brought you.

You don't know what time it was, but the boat must have taken several hours.

George went to find water and came back with a car. You didn't ask where he got it.

Rebecca's body wouldn't fit lying down in the back seat, so you had to sit her up. After drinking as much as you could from a bucket George had filled at a fountain, you drove through the town and then thumped up the mountain in third gear. Halfway there, you almost collided with a moped that came hurtling toward you at an intense speed.

When you reached the cliff, George didn't hesitate in steering off the road onto the scrubland.

He drove slowly until the land was too uneven for the axles.

When you got out of the car it was dusk and everything was quiet. A cool wind was blowing in off the sea.

Rebecca's body seemed to lighten as you neared the edge of the cliff.

You swung it a few times for momentum and then let go at the same time.

When you got back to the car, George just stood there in a daze. He asked if you would drive. You couldn't find the headlights and so drove down the mountain in darkness.

It took all night to get from Aegina into the city again. By the time you had penetrated Athens at dawn, confusion had turned to uncertainty. Soldiers stood on every corner with machine guns, smoking cigarettes and reassuring the elderly. George's apartment was shaken, but remained standing. Most of his neighbors had left the city for country homes. You both slept for a few hours in his bed. Then you woke up and decided to go back to your apartment. George wanted to come, but you left while he was in the bathroom.

THIRTY-FIVE

You no longer wanted to live.

Standing on your balcony, you felt your heart had already stopped, and each soft thud in the dark, each faint push between your thumb and neck, was only the ghost of your heart and its memory of something beautiful.

You imagined the ensuing moments if you jumped off:

The square beneath would be remembered as the place where a foreigner died. Local children would grow up wondering who you were.

Shouting. A single scream. A body has fallen from the sky. A tapping of shoes. People running toward you. Faces flash at windows. Doors swing open. Old women hold children back.

By the time you found Rebecca it was too late. You will feel useless for the rest of your life. Your hands will always remember what they couldn't do.

An old man turns you over.

He kneels and puts his head to your chest.

You see your hands spread open, palms down. The rhetoric of descent.

Your hands were tiny once. Easily cupped on cold mornings by your mother and father. Swinging between them: one, two, three, jump!

You see the scuffed tips of your Clarks, a lighter blue. Your pockets glued together by sweets. The sound of your name meant something to eat or something to see.

And you rose, you rose—anchored by your parents' hands, the sun above you smashed and dazzling.

Once all hands seemed bigger than yours.

Hands everywhere.

Now there are hands on you again. Hands you will never know, but that will remember you in the way they touch the living.

Your hands are motionless on the cobbles below your balcony.

Those same hands once held against a father's bristly cheek on Saturday morning—one Saturday long ago.

A single day fallen from the deck of days past.

"Wake up, Dad," you say. "We're going fishing."

The curtains so white.

The deep brown glass of his morning eyes.

"My little Henry," he mumbles.

The sadness in his eyes is not only for his other son. You blame yourselves, but never each other.

It is cold. The hard blue of dawn.

You remember him tapping the ground with a branch.

Then worms everywhere.

You hold some in your hands, laughing.

It's drizzling, but you're warm from breakfast. You hold out a worm to your father in wonder. The worms think the tapping is rain. They can't help it. They can't help but rise to the light. It's an instinct beyond their control. Something draws their ascent into another world.

You feel the wet grass for more.

Your father kneels and places his hands upon yours. He holds them fast against the earth.

"Don't ever forget this moment," he says.

It takes a while for the car to warm up. The engine revving by itself. The morning air thick with diesel.

Crows stare from trees.

A light, uneven rain.

The gearstick is tall and vibrates when not held.

Worms in a silver bucket on the backseat.

They lie on top of one another and move with the silence of snow.

The body is a disguise.

You lifted Rebecca in your arms, but felt the weight of a stranger.

You wondered if she took the memory of who she was. Is it possible for love to go on if not attached to memory?

Is it possible that, after death, she feels your absence without remembering who you are? You imagine her memories folded up and packed into a suitcase that's forgotten on the platform.

People stand around your body. A Greek boy watches from his window.

Finally he understands why his baby brother resists sleep.

Like all children, the boy becomes a part of what he sees. And that night the boy sneaks into his brother's room and holds his tiny hand. He has found someone in the darkness and will never let go.

The old man you imagined turning you over just stands around.

He is shaking.

His hat has fallen off and sits upright on the ground. If you were alive, you would pick it up for him.

You are like her now but will never know.

The dead do not breathe.

They cannot see or hear or move or speak.

They feel nothing.

THIRTY-SIX

On the streets there is still rubble from the earthquake. The broken glass has been swept up, but hundreds of tents still fill the parks of Athens. People are too afraid to go home in case it happens again. In your living room there is a large crack that runs the length of the wall—neatly dividing your life before and your life after.

George is somewhere in the city. He keeps coming over. Sometimes you let him in. He sits down and you drink hot tea at the table without saying anything. Sometimes you walk around the block. You talk about what happened. And he knows the truth about your brother, but not the pregnancy.

You need him desperately, but don't want to see him.

You make chamomile tea before bed. It's evening. Streetlights come on by themselves.

You close the door to the balcony. The noise outside pushes softly against the windows but barely enters.

You boil water.

The strip of kitchen light was always too bright. Cooking feels like some clinical procedure when you don't wish to live. Utensils glint menacingly. A faint buzzing from the lights. The table has drawers too small to keep anything in.

The kitchen floor is unswept. Gossamer sleeves of fallen garlic lie undisturbed where the linoleum meets the cupboard. Rebecca once sat at the table drinking tea with both hands. You shared baklava from the same dish. You remember that first night. The thick cream. Taking your cigarette. The long walk home. A missing book. Unceasing heat. Her body stretching out under you like a map of your life to come.

You wait for her to burst in at any moment.

You've learned since her death that everything you are afraid of will never happen. It's the events you cannot conceive of that happen.

But at night you forget everything.

Then you wake up and begin again.

You raise your hands against the glowing stove. The friendliness of steam. The water bubbles with quick pops. You suspend your hands above for comfort.

In your imagination, you see other fires from long ago. Deep glowing coals. The sound of rushing air. The house of your childhood in Wales.

Your mother polishing shoes for school in the morning. The gentle, quick-scratching of the shoe brush above the television. The chirp of plates being dried and stacked in the kitchen by your silent father.

You remember things—but the details are not of your choosing.

It's cloudy. Washing on the line nods weakly, unsure. Everything is too large for your hands—even night seems longer, darker, unmanageable.

You surface from the depths of memory to eat lunch, to have a bath, to walk around some ancient ruin that can never be rebuilt. The future lies on the other side of what's past. We go back to move forward.

But going back is like returning to a house where everyone moved out long ago; for the only life that dwells within memory is the shallow breath of your misplaced desire.

Athens is still warm, but the evenings are very cold. You feel the cold in the core of your body. Hot baths work for only an hour or so. You take them in the afternoon when the light is pretty.

People hurry home through dusk without stopping.

Lights go on in kitchens by early afternoon, and doorways of hanging beads, where bodies once lingered, are now simply doors, with square frosted windows and handles worn with turning.

Televisions have been carried in from balconies—extension cords folded away. And the stray dogs that lay in the shade of orange trees at the roadside are no longer part of the evening landscape. Without anyone noticing, they have carried their old bodies elsewhere.

You have a radio, a couch, a bed, a small desk, and a washing machine in the bathroom that doesn't work—all of which were in the apartment when Rebecca was alive.

Your desk has a black marble top. It was the first thing you moved when you entered the apartment. You set it beside a window. The desk is so polished that it reflects everything. Birds swim through the table as you work.

Summer has ended and the square below your balcony is empty.

Once full of footsteps, people talking, and people sitting down alone to watch the others—the gaping square is an open mouth with nothing to say.

It's where you want to kill yourself.

It's where you plan to, but never will.

Occasionally a dog wanders up to the fountain, looks around for a moment, and then turns away without barking.

Newspapers blow across the cobbles like small sails.

Everything you do is a secret because nobody sees or knows.

You remember being a child again.

Shouting: "Look, look, look at me! Look. Look at me."

In bed you listen for the noises that once comforted you, but hear only a stream of inaudible names from a distant tide of traffic.

You like to sit on your balcony and look at cars as they line up at lights. They are all different colors. Sometimes a driver is smoking, or talking to his wife, or simply staring out at nothing.

Sometimes you carry out a bowl of coffee in both hands and sit very quietly. Sitting there makes you feel good. Your lips see themselves approaching in the reflection of the coffee. You find steam beautiful.

You remember the steam from your father's coffee. The cup rests on a small table with folding legs in the middle of the fishing boat.

A light mist unfurling across the pond like a spell. The hollow clap of the boat bobbing. The unscrewing of a thermos. The smell of pond water.

Sometimes you see birds from your balcony. They pass without flapping their wings.

You imagine what it would be like to simply drift through the air with no effort.

You go to bed.

The days are broken by light.

Most nights you lie in one position. By contrast, your sleeping mind cannot dwell on one thing for too long. Your sleeping mind, like a ghost, drifts from place to place, from person to person.

In the morning, you wake to see what has washed up on the tide of dreams.

You stay in bed.

The morning is very white.

Someone in the square is talking on a cell phone. Sometimes people wait there for things.

You feel the world going on without you. And soon you become starkly aware that in the great history of life, you mean absolutely nothing.

THIRTY-SEVEN

In the weeks that followed, you spent long spells at the kitchen table in your underpants and socks thinking. Rebecca and your child lay at the bottom of the sea, a world within a world, existence without existing.

Professor Peterson came to check on you. He wanted you back at work, but you had no interest. George kept coming by, too. He wondered if her family knew, and if you should somehow find the sister. But you pushed them away.

You went out once a week to the market, but didn't linger there as you once did. Rebecca liked to pick out oranges with the leaves still on and then arrange them in a terra-cotta bowl beside the bed.

"What about all the little insects in the leaves?" you said, the first time she set the heavy bowl on the bedside table.

She peered admiringly at the bowl of fruit. "What about them?"

About six weeks after the earthquake, you opened your eyes in the middle of the night and realized something was very wrong with you.

It was still dark.

You managed to sit up. It was difficult to breathe and your hands were shaking. You reached for your notebook but couldn't write anything.

Then you realized that you couldn't move your legs.

You looked around the room, at the pattern of weak street-light chalked upon the wall and the outline of your things in the darkness.

Your life was nothing more than a quick sketch and you a character not fully brought to life by the artist.

Then you must have fallen asleep because the next time you opened your eyes, you had fallen out of bed. You were sweating, but at the same time felt very cold. You remember being able to see a few stars from where you lay.

You were very thin, almost skeletal—but you were too tired to drag yourself out to the balcony.

When you were half outside, you think that you passed out again.

When you awoke, there was a strange taste in your mouth, a lead taste. Your shirtfront was also wet.

Then a cool wind blew against your face. It felt lovely and you opened your mouth to swallow.

There was light traffic on the street. You imagined smoking men at the edges of their balconies in undershirts, enjoying the cool evening. And farther down the boulevard, a knot of tired prostitutes dwindling at the curb, dazzled by the glare of a few passing cars.

You began trembling violently and felt suddenly that your lips were very sore and wet. When you found the energy to raise a hand to your face, you withdrew it quickly to find blood. You realized that your shirtfront was not soaked with sweat but covered in blood. Your lips were shredded and you didn't know why. Your nose was numb, and you felt the tickle of blood inside.

You had fallen without falling.

You were discovered unconscious on your balcony by the boy from downstairs. The broken washing machine in your bathroom was not broken after all. The water valve in the basement was simply turned off. When workmen checking the foundation turned a lever to see what it was, the washing machine in your bathroom gushed to life.

When the ceiling buckled in the apartment below your bathroom, Mr. Papafilippou and his son raced upstairs. He banged on your door. When he heard no answer, father and son pounded on it together. Two large hairy fists, and two small ones.

Mrs. Papafilippou watched from the bottom of the stairs in an apron with her hand over her mouth. When the first few drops fell onto the Papafilippou living room rug, Mrs. Papafilippou shouted at her husband to break the door down.

As Mr. Papafilippou rushed into your bathroom and searched frantically for the shut-off valves, his son calmly explored the apartment. Stepping into the bedroom, he saw a motionless foot on the balcony. Curious, he approached it, wondering who it belonged to. He touched it, but nothing happened.

Mr. Papafilippou and his son carried you to their Fiat van and took you to hospital.

As they sped through central Athens, the boy reached back and put his hand on your forehead. You vaguely remember this, because you wondered who they were. His father nodded and said in Greek: "Good thinking, son."

Then you came back to life and remember being lifted from the van.

The desk clerk at the hospital wasn't really a desk clerk—he was an Alzheimer's patient who had simply chosen what he thought was a comfortable seat in a safe place. The real clerk was outside arguing with her boyfriend on a cell phone.

"We found him on his balcony," Mr. Papafillipou said breathlessly as he carried your body through the foyer.

"How kind of you to bring me flowers on such a pretty day," the fake receptionist said, getting up to kiss Mr. Papafillipou on the cheek.

Mr. Papafillipou drew back. "We didn't bring flowers."

His son looked on the ground. "No, we must have dropped them."

When the pretend desk clerk asked about the spinach pie, Mr. Papafillipou just carried you into a ward and put you into the first empty bed he saw.

The other patients sat up and wanted to know what was going on.

It took George three days to find out where you were.

Then he visited you every day.

At first you both just sat in silence, as if waiting for news to arrive. Then he brought a book and read it aloud. When he finished that book, he brought another, and then another. It went on for weeks and weeks. The last book he read to you was *The Wind in the Willows*.

You were also on heavy drugs. One day George showed up with a small suitcase. He wore a suit and was freshly shaven.

"You smell good, George."

He sat on the bed.

"I'm thinking of leaving Athens," he said.

"When?"

"This afternoon."

"Today?"

"Yes."

"Why?"

"I've accepted a job with an American university in Sicily."

"I see."

"Will you be okay, Henry?"

"Yes. Are you still not drinking?"

George nodded.

"How long now?"

"Forty-nine days tomorrow."

"I'm proud of you, George."

"I'm proud of you too," he said.

"You've been a real friend to me," you said.

George looked away. You could tell he wanted to cry. The echo of his footsteps was steady and pure.

·   ·   ·

A week later, you were told you had to leave hospital.

The doctor insisted.

"You're better, Henry—go home."

"I'm not better," you said. "And I don't think I should leave."

The doctor was quite young. He generally joked around with you, but this time he folded his arms.

"I can't leave," you insisted. "I like it here."

"It's not a hotel."

"I'm still not well."

The doctor kneeled at your bedside. "I know what happened to your girlfriend was tough, and that you are depressed, and all those other things which led to you coming here—I know all this, Henry—but now you're making progress—the broken nose from falling out of bed, the malnutrition, the virus, we've cured you of everything—all you need now is a shave and a haircut, and maybe something to look forward to."

"I'm not ready."

"You're still a young man," the doctor said standing up. "I know you don't feel like it, but maybe one day you'll realize you've got more ahead of you than behind you."

An old man in the next bed with an oxygen mask over his face turned slowly to face you both—then he carefully removed the mask to say something.

"I wish I was you," he said, smiling.

"No, you don't."

"I do," he insisted.

"Put that mask back on," the doctor ordered. "You're supposed to be resting."

THIRTY-EIGHT

You left the hospital in a taxi still wearing pajamas and a hospital gown. The driver smoked and said in Greek:

"You sure you're better?"

Your apartment had been taken over by someone else. You didn't even have to go in—the curtains had changed and the balcony was overrun with tall, thin plants.

You imagined your few things in a box in the basement. Your Vespa would be locked up at the university or stolen. The professor had visited you in the hospital too. He was planning on closing up the excavation and heading back to North Africa—you forgot where exactly because the doctor had you on some new kind of drug that week.

You took one final look at your apartment from the back of the taxi and then asked the driver to take you to the airport.

You had drachmas in your pocket from wages the professor had brought in a brown envelope.

You entered the terminal in George's pajamas. They were

light blue cotton with white piping. He also brought you a pair of black Church's slippers, which you were wearing. He'd sewn his new address in Sicily into the fabric of the left slipper. The dressing gown was the property of the hospital, but you'd grown quite fond of it and so decided to take it with you.

You half expected the airline staff to look at your plastic wristband and call the police. But they just glanced at your passport and counted the money you gave them.

You boarded the aircraft.

Deep down you knew it was time to leave Athens—even though you had nowhere to go and the people on the plane just stared at you.

THIRTY-NINE

Asleep on the short flight to London. A flight attendant woke
you after landing. She was pretty, but there was something
sinister in how she barked at you to get up. You imagined Rebecca in her uniform. Her eyes, the way she stared at you. You
wish now you'd confessed everything about your brother.
She would have understood. She would have helped you let
him go.

You found out that you were actually in a place called
Luton—which was close to London, but not in London.

"Why are we in Luton?" you asked another passenger who
had also slept through the landing and was now collecting his
belongings.

"I ask myself that every day," he said.

You continued sleeping at the airport. It was much colder
than Greece.

In the early hours of the morning a Jamaican cleaner
woke you up and asked if you were okay. He wanted to know

where you got your pajamas. He gave you some ginger beer from a plastic bottle. The ginger beer was very sweet and stung your throat. The man insisted that the burn of the ginger keeps away colds and spirits. Then he went back to work, swishing past you from time to time with a mop and a chuckle.

When the airport began to fill, you went outside and asked a taxi driver to take you to the nearest branch of your bank. You also asked the driver if he had a bag. He looked around on the floor under the passenger seat and shook his lunchbox from a plastic shopping bag that read TESCO SUPERMARKET.

"Here you go, mate," he said. Then with his eyes still in the mirror, he said: "What are you doin' wearing bloody pajamas in this weather? You all right?"

You told him it was a long story.

Inside the bank, you asked to withdraw your life savings— the money from unspent student loans, plus the inheritance from your grandmother, which was meant for you to buy a flat when you got married.

The teller asked you to take a seat somewhere more private. Then a tall Sikh came out and introduced himself as the manager. He asked if you were feeling okay. You told him you were, but that you just wanted your money.

"But our policy is to—"

"Just give me my goddamn money," you snapped.

The manager nodded reluctantly and said, "I can tell that these are strange and original circumstances."

·   ·   ·

Only about a quarter of the bills would fit in the Tesco bag. The teller and the manager watched with a mixture of curiosity and horror.

"Please, please, Mr. Bliss," the manager implored you. "At least take the rest in travelers checks—if only for safety."

You returned to Luton Airport in the same taxi with approximately £48,000 in a shopping bag, and £160,000 in American Express travelers checks.

When you got back into the taxi with a bag of money, the driver was amazed. "Did you just rob that bloody bank?"

On the way back to the airport, you noticed an air freshener hanging from the rearview mirror. It was shaped like a child and said BABY ON BOARD.

You asked the driver to stop the taxi. He wouldn't. You screamed and he did. You got out with your shopping bag. He was reluctant to just leave you. It was windy and gray. The grass at the side of the road was very green. Birds flew against the wind. In some places the grass was soggy and you felt the cold soak into your slippers. At the side of the road were many things: a pink teddy bear, a pair of workman's goggles, empty cigarette packets, broken bottles, pieces of bumper and shards of headlight from a late night of flashing lights.

And there you were—walking in your pajamas at the side of the road. Children looked out and wondered who you were, where you were going. People you will never meet, and who knew nothing about your life, carried you for a few miles as a silent flush of compassion.

The cold didn't bother you, but it was hard sometimes to cross roundabouts because nobody wanted to slow down.

You were the Oedipus of legend, the doomed soul, left to wander blindly in the wilderness.

In the distance burned the lights of the airport.

You stopped midway and bought coffee from a van selling hot dogs. The lights of the planes were beautiful in the gray light.

You followed the path of planes coming into land. It was very cold by the time you arrived, and you felt like you might fall down. The world behind you had fallen into darkness.

You sat still for a few hours, and then ate minced-beef pie and mashed potatoes in a café. A bit later you found a British Airways sales desk and asked to buy a ticket.

It was getting late. Only a few flights left. The woman leaned forward and smiled.

"Where is your destination, sir?"

"When's the next flight?" you mumbled.

"To where, sir?"

"Anywhere?"

"In Europe?"

"Yes."

"Well, there's a flight to Dublin leaving, but they're closing the gate. There's a very early flight to Milan if that's helpful—"

"It doesn't matter," you said. "Everywhere's the same to me now."

FORTY

When you arrived in Milan, the airport was packed with handsome businessmen smoking and touching their hair. There was a place to buy fresh orange juice, and so you bought some and then drank it quickly on the spot.

You decided to see the city, and after visiting the Bureau de Change, you took a taxi into the center of town. You walked around with a shopping bag full of money. Your pajamas were getting dirty, and you wondered if you should buy some real clothes.

It was very busy.

People talked loudly on phones as they walked. Vespas threaded their way through traffic. Taxi drivers talked in groups with sweaters tied around their shoulders. It was almost like Athens, but beautiful and organized.

When you were hungry, you found a bustling restaurant close to a courthouse. The counters were long rivers of brushed steel.

The ceiling fans were slow and clean. Each blade was slightly angled. The tables, the chairs, and the floor were all cut from the same dull steel—or perhaps after decades of use, the shine had worn off.

Everyone chewed in silence and looked at one another.

You pointed to a plate of something in a glass case on the counter. The young waiter nodded.

"Signor," the waiter said, pointing to an empty seat.

A few minutes later your meal arrived. You noticed several other people at nearby tables eating the same thing. And then you noticed that all the meals in the glass case were exactly the same.

There were no children in the restaurant, and you wondered why.

The restaurant was part of a tobacconist's shop, and after lunch, you picked up your shopping bag and wandered over to it. Everything in the shop was streamlined. Even the white hair of the tobacconist was brushed back and glistened under the shop light.

Although you had stopped smoking in hospital, you bought a few packets of cigarettes because the boxes were beautiful. You received your change in a chrome ashtray, not in your hand.

As you went to leave a man blocked your path.

The man stood between you and the door.

"Signor," he said.

You looked at him and gripped your shopping bag.

The man held up some lottery tickets and a small pencil.

When you finished marking one line, the man pointed to the next. When you finished all the lines, the man held the card at a distance from his eyes.

"Foreigners are sometimes good luck," he said.

You walked around for an hour and then went into a shop that sold crucifixes, hoping to use the bathroom. There were hundreds of crosses in the shop, in all different colors, but with Jesus wearing the same expression in most of them.

The manager said, "If you want to use the bathroom, buy a crucifix."

"But I have nowhere to hang it," you said.

The owner shrugged.

"I'd really like to use the toilet, without purchasing an action figure nailed to a piece of wood."

"Please leave the shop," the man said. Other staff drifted over.

"I can pay you," you said.

"Just buy something with Jesus on it," the owner said. "The toilet is over there behind those shelves."

"Actually, I think I'll go."

You left the shop and peed against some recycling bins nearby. In the alley beyond the bins, sitting atop a black garbage bag, was a typewriter. You went over and pushed a few keys. Then you put it under your arm and walked away.

You ambled back toward the center of town, studying the design on a packet of the cigarettes you'd bought.

Then you noticed a gang of teenagers watching from a park across the street. You had seen them before outside the lunch place. You looked down at your money. How could they know? But then you thought that maybe it had something to do with the typewriter. You considered putting it down and walking away.

You strolled a few blocks to see if the teenagers would follow. They didn't seem to be behind you, but when you thought you'd lost them, they suddenly appeared ahead of you—a tight group of boys in whitewashed jeans, like a scene from *West Side Story*.

Instead of waiting for them to come upon you, you turned and sprinted down a narrow street. At the end was an opening that led on to a very wide and beautiful street—a street far too handsome to get robbed on.

You looked back and saw two of the boys enter the alley running, and so ducked quickly into the nearest shop. The bell rang violently.

The shop was empty, but smelled delicious—as if someone had been smashing grapefruits. Mannequins in metallic dresses glowed under the lights.

A woman approached you. A mole on her lip made her mouth look exotic.

"I need clothes." You opened the shopping bag by letting go of one of the handles. "And do you take pounds because I've run out of your currency?"

The woman peered into the bag.

"I think we probably could," she said.

Then she asked if you'd like to put down your typewriter and try a few things on.

Three hours later—after a local tailor was called in to make adjustments—you left the shop in a double-breasted navy suit and a sky blue polo shirt.

The tailor had told you off for carrying money around in a plastic bag and helped you pick out a black alligator briefcase that smelled faintly of mints.

At a nearby barbershop, you received a haircut and a shave. Hanging on the walls were pictures of dead movie stars. The barber was very old and kept going into the back every few minutes to tap something with a spoon.

After another hour walking around on the streets of Milan, you stopped to rest on a street called Via Palomba. There were display cabinets for bottles of men's perfume, and you thought of George.

You realized then you were starting to feel hopeless and tired, and so decided to go back to the airport. Your briefcase was heavy because it also had the typewriter in it.

It took over an hour to get to the airport in a taxi. It was uncomfortable because the driver wouldn't open the window and you were too depressed to ask.

You caught the next flight by running to the gate.

Alitalia Flight 522 to LaGuardia Airport in New York City landed on time.

It was a bright morning with many birds.

You walked from the terminal to the hotel in Queens across the freeway. A few people honked.

You lasted a week at the hotel, living off free breakfast bagels and watching cars from your window inch their way along the Grand Central Parkway. There were a few rainstorms but they didn't last very long.

Nothing out of the ordinary happened at the hotel except for a day spent naked when you sent your suit and polo shirt out for cleaning. You cranked the heat and took long baths with the television up loud.

On your last day in Queens, you realized it had been three

weeks since you had spoken to George, and so you wrote something on the Italian typewriter with the intention of sending it to the address in Sicily that George had sewn into your left slipper.

HOWARD JOHNSON

Lodge

Hello George,

Well I'm out of hospital, and found this typewri-
-ter in the street in Milan after it was thrown
away--though I am discovering that it has a ~~fwew~~
few problems.

I don't know what I'm doing really. It's only
been six months since the earthquake and I'm
still a mess. I wanted to stay in hospital
but they wouldn't let me.

I'm now in a place called Queens, New York,
but don't write to me here.

          H.

p.s I miss ner to tne point tnat life has no meaning

You left Queens on a Tuesday and by early Wednesday morning you were at Keflavik Airport in Iceland.

The airport reminded you of an art gallery, with several interesting sculptures of people running, and very tall windows of uninterrupted glass.

Three German men drank beer with their breakfasts. You sat down and ordered a glass of beer too. You stayed in the airport for thirteen hours—most of which you spent drunk.

Then you took Flight 1455 to London.

And then a long flight to Tokyo.

And then Brisbane.

And then Auckland.

You took your meals on the flights, and got most of your sleep in the air too.

The Continental flight crew was by far the most caring, and if you were able to get on a Continental flight you didn't care where it was going.

On a Royal Air Casablanca flight, a small boy wandered into the cockpit while the passengers were boarding and the pilots were busy chatting with girls in the business class seats. Within a few minutes, the boy pilot had started an engine and almost raised the landing gear.

Sometimes your flight would be packed and you wondered who *should* be sitting in your seat—and where they would *not* be going because of you.

Sometimes at the airport, you sat with the lost luggage until a destination announced on the loudspeaker piqued your interest.

.   .   .

In order to choose a hotel for the night, you simply stood outside the terminal and got on the first bus that stopped without asking the destination—even if the bus had been chartered to pick up returning U.S. Navy staff for submarine command in Connecticut.

UNITED STATES NAVY

Hello George,

You wouldn't believe where I've ended up--
th ough I'm sure the stationary gives it away.
It was all a misunderstanding, but they were good
enough to let me spend the night as they like to
keep the gates closed "after hours."

Apparently, the bus driver mistook my
navy suit for navy blues.

I'm staying in Captain Hart's room (it says so
on the door), though he's not here. I hp hope
he doesn't mind me using his stationary.

This place makes me miss the professor; I hope
he's note tooworried. If you're in contact
with him, please tell him I think of him often.
I think of you too.

    OVER & OUT

     henry

WESTERN UNION

A. N. WILLIAMS
PRESIDENT

1204

The filing time shown in the date line on telegrams and day letters is STANDARD TIME at point of origin.   Time of receipt is STANDARD TIME at point of destination

Dear George,

Greetings from Greenland.

It's not really green though, just cold,

very, very cold. I'm staying at a small

hotel close to the airport. The hotel

is bright blue. There is a buffet din-

-ner every night, which is nice because

everyone looks forward to it.

WESTERN UNION

A N WILLIAMS
PRESIDENT

1204

The filing time shown in the date line on telegrams and day letters is STANDARD TIME at point of origin. Time of receipt is STANDARD TIME at point of destination

The hotel didn't have any real old stationary—
just these old telegram slips, which accordi—
ng to Mrs. Anguttivdluarssugssuak at the front
desk, can still be used through a wire machine
they have in the back room where the dogs sleep
sleep. I can't imagine what a wire is, but if
you're reading this, then it works.

WESTERN UNION

1204

It's strange writing to you like this, becau-
because we didn't know each other very long
did we? Plus, you can't reply.

While I never told you much about my life, I
also feel like I told you everything. Life
is slower now, somehow more real, but at the
same time less real. Also we are each other's
only link to R.

H.

HOTEL GLÄRNISCHHOF 8002 ZÜRICH
VORMALS EICHER

CLARIDENSTRASSE 30
TÉLÉPHONE (051) 25 48 33 TÉLÉGRAMMES: GLÄRNISCHHOF ZURICH

IÈRE CLASSE SITUATION TRANQUILLE AU CENTRE DE LA VILLE
CHAQUE CHAMBRE AVEC SALLE DE BAIN
DIR. HS. STAMPFLI

Dear George,

how are you? The last two weeks have been quite
uneventful. Spent most of the time flying around
the interior airports of Russia. I think I could
get used to cold weather. It's such a change
from Athens.

I'm in Switzerland now.
Not as much chocolate as you'd think.
I've been thinking a lot about what we were doing
with Professor Peterson. He's closed up the dig now
I'm sure--filled in the holes. I suspect all the pieces
have been catalogued by Giuseppe (whom you never met)
and put in some basement.
I wonder if you two are working together--maybe you
won't even get this because you're in North Africa or
somewhere. If you do see him--perhaps tell him I'm not
100%, but don't mention I'm flying around the world aimlessly
as he may worry.

                    Love

               Henry Bliss

Istanbul
Hilton ISTANBUL - TURKEY

GEORGE--HELLO

AS YOU CAN SEE I'M HAVING SOME PROBLEMS
WITH THIS MACHINE.

A couple of days ago (on a flight to Budapest)
a carton of homemade soup (mushroom) leaked
from its container and began dripping from the
overhead bin. The man sitting below the drips
had a deathly allergy to mushrooms and began
having a seizure,

A doctor on the airplane rushed over and began
pricking the man and cursing in Hungarian.

I'm starting to really wonder if you're
getting these letters.

Faithfully,

        H.

HOTEL
PHOENICIA
INTERCONTINENTAL
*

اوتيـل فـيـنيشـيـا
BEIRUT • LEBANON

CABLE ADDRESS: INHOTELCOR   TEL. 252900-TELEX NO 624

Dear George,

~~Please forgive me. I'm so sorry.~~ This is probably
my 20th letter to you and I'm suddenly worried
that you'd prefer that I wasn't writing to you.
What I mean to say is that I wish there was a
way for you to reply. I'm tired of talking to
myself.

I have a long flight to North America tomorrow,
so I'm really going to give it some thought.

      Your Friend

        H.B.

    p.s. How often do you think of Rebecca, George?
sometimes, when i leave my hotel room, I wonder if
I'm going to find that all the other guests have died.

GILCHER HOTEL

Danville, Kentucky

Hi George,

Isn't this your home state? If so
you were right. It's very pretty
and the people are sweet--like you.

I had biscuits and gravy this morning.
My waitress was called Misty.

Love
Henry

London Hilton   HYDe Park 8000

Good Evening George,

REBECCA

Tonight I told someone about~~Xmas~~.
It happened like this. Just as the flight
crew closed the doors on a flight from
Glasgow to London--a hairy man in shorts with
tattoos on his legs sat next to me and began
to shake. Then he began sweating so heavily
that the sweat literally dripped from his
forehead onto my legs.

The man was soon soaking wet.

T- Stifling a sob, the hairy man admitted how
he'd never flown before and was afraid the

cont..

London Hilton   HYDe Park 8OOO

airplane would crash and he'dbe killed.

So, strangely, I held his hand for the
whole flight, but covered it up with a ~~blankey~~
blankęt so no one could see.

An hour from landing, I told him about
REBECCA
~~xxxxxxxxx~~ He was very sympathetic. He said
I should try and get over it. I told him it's
a memory I can't shelve, so it just stays out.

He said that reminded him of a plate
that didn't fit with h is mother's bone china
dining room set, and although they never used
the plate, it was too unique and beautiful
to throw away and so they ~~dispal~~ displayed it.

H.B.

BY APPOINTMENT TO
HRH THE PRINCE OF WALES
SUPPLIERS OF BANQUETING
AND CATERING SERVICES
THE RITZ LONDON

THE RITZ LONDON

Hello George,

I've moved hotels as the waiters here were very
nice to me, and all had double breasted white
jackets, which I felt you would appreciate.

I've been thinking about Rebecca's sister and
grandfather. I wonder if they even knew?

I don't know how we would find them--because I
can't remember the name of her village.

Think about what I should do.
Also--I wish I'd kept one of her drawings. She
was such a gifted artist.

I don't suppose you have one?

Yours Always

Henry

PALACE HOTEL
COPENHAGEN

TELEGRAMS: PALACEHOTEL
PHONE: CENTRAL 4050
TELEX: 2493 · GIRO 62840

Hi George,

Something strange and upsetting happened
yesterday. Less than a minute before
landing in Denmark, a very old man a few
seats away from me announced very loudly
that he needed to use the bathroom. A
few seconds later, the airplane landed and
the putrid smell from the old am man's seat
made a woman vomit. The old man began
to sob, and everybody (except me) looked
at him. As he ws led off the aircraft by
a stewardess, he turned to the woman who
vomited and said:

   "One day you'll be like this."

            Hen ry.

After almost a year in the air, the communication problem was solved. From a catalog in your seat pocket en route to Shanghai, you read about (and then purchased) two mini-satellite fax machines. Both were sent to your hotel upon landing. After making a note of both fax numbers, you asked the hotel concierge to send the other machine (with your fax number written on the box) to George's address in Sicily.

Two weeks later in the Hotel Amsterdam, your fax machine started buzzing. Green lights flashed. You found a blank piece of paper in a desk drawer and fed it into the machine as demonstrated by a beaver on page 732 of the instruction book.

迷你衛星傳真機

Dear Henry

Are you reading this? Does this little machine work? Something tells me it's a gimmick. Will you please fax me back if it does? If you are reading this, then I can finally breathe a sigh of relief because we can talk again.

I also wanted to ask why you are flying around the world endlessly. I know it's how you are coping with what happened—the same way I drank to blur my childhood. Please come to Sicily and stay with me. I'll make a home here for you. I know it won't be like before, but at least you'll have a friend. I won't write anymore until I know this little gadget works. Professor Peterson keeps writing to me wanting to know where you are.

I miss our hospital book club.

Love,

George

P.S. If you ARE reading this—thanks for the mini-satellite fax machine, and I'm still not drinking in case you were wondering.

The PANTLIND

GRAND RAPIDS 2, MICHIGAN

Dear Geo rge:

Did you get my peply to your FAX yesterday
from Amsterdam? What a relief to hear from
you.
Now in Michigan. I think like me, it was
once grand and hopeful. But now people sleep
under cardboard boxes in the streets at night.

Ton ight, when I went into the hotel ballroom
for supper, I felt suddenly, and especially sad
for everyt ing t at happened. It's like we
all lived in this paradise without realizing
we did.

        Death makes everyt ing seem so real.

I have to stop writing now, the fire alarm is
going off and tnere's sm

HOTEL PFISTER

RAY SMITH, President.   RAY SMITH JR., Manager.

MILWAUKEE 2, WIS.

cont... FROM WISCONSIN--AMERICA'S DAIRYLAND

What I mean to say is that I've really felt hopeless this
past week, like I'm just going through the motions of
living. I can't think of anything happening that would
interest me as much as just thinking about Rebecca, nd
and what it would have been like to have a family with
her.

I'm relieved you're still not drinking,-I was wondering
about that. It's nice of the professor to be worried. He's
really been like a father to me--but I'm realizing I know
hardly anything about him. Has he really spent the ya majority
of his life in the middle of nowhere?

Write soon, dear George,
HENRY

p.s. There was fire in my last hotel--and so I went back
to the airport and took a flight to MILWAUKEE.,

迷你衛星傳真機

Dear Henry,

Try and look forward to something positive in the future.

What I mean to say is, give yourself something to look forward to. You've got to go on, we've got most of our lives still ahead of us. I've been going to church, which I know sounds stupid, but just being there with a giant wooden corpse nailed to a cross helps. I don't even understand what the priest is saying.

I'm learning to deal with this. I've also met someone who is helping.

Always yours,

George

Dear George:

I hope you get his because my mini-satellite-fax-ma
-machine is running o ut of something called MAXI-TONER.

Is yours?

This typewriter also needs some main tenance.

I'm glad you've met someone. You seem happy, George.
I imagi ne this person is a woman? If so she's lucky
because you're a deeply wonderful man.

Don't worry about me. I'm a bit drunk tonight.
Ive always wanted youtobe happy--you know that don't you?   *SAKI*

Even from the beginning when I realized that~youwereals
you were also in love with Rebecca.

LOVE HENRY

GRAND HOTEL DEL MARE
BORDIGHERA

Dear George,

A few days ago I sat next to some blind girl
on a flight from Havaˣna, Cuba. For the first
hour in the air, she made thousands of tiny lines
on a piece of paper. I thought this was interesting,
but after a while fell asleep.

When the airplane touched down, I woke up.

We reached the gate after a quick taxi. Then the
blind girl gave me the piece of paper with her
lines on. I though it was odd, but tnanked her.
I offered to help her off. She smiled and I saw
that sh e was xxxxxxxx pretty. She said tnat a
                          after
stewardess always comes ~~afere~~ everyone else has gone.

                                CONT...

GRAND HOTEL DEL MARE
BORDIGHERA

CONT...

In the terminal I bought a sandwich and espresso.
Then I found a place to sit for a few hours.
I opened the piece of paper he blind girl had
given me. It was the drawing of a hand.
The thousandsof tiny lines she had been making
had become a ~~close~~ perfect copy of my left hand.

Every line, every ridge, and every scar was
represented with uncanny accuracy.

Then I recalled how when she squeezed past me
in to her seat--she accidentally put her hand
down on top of mine- mine. Her hand was soft,
supple, and warm.

When I finished my sandwich, I looked at my real
han d, and realized it would never be as good as
her drawing of it. The blind girl had dark red
hair. Flying around the world is keeping me alive
at this point because I feel like I'm making
progress.

Love   H.B.

迷你衛星傳真機

BRITISH MUSEUM

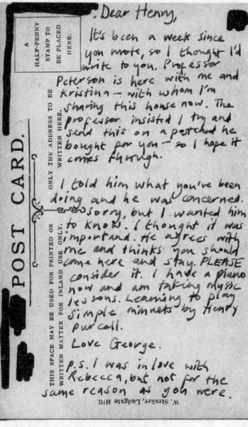

A HALF-PENNY STAMP TO BE PLACED HERE.

POST CARD.

ONLY THE ADDRESS TO BE WRITTEN HERE.

THIS SPACE MAY BE USED FOR PRINTED OR WRITTEN MATTER FOR INLAND USE ONLY.

Dear Henry,

It's been a week since you wrote, so I thought I'd write to you. Professor Peterson is here with me and Kristina — with whom I'm sharing this house now. The professor insisted I try and send this on a postcard he bought for you — so I hope it comes through.

I told him what you've been doing and he was concerned. Sorry, but I wanted him to know. I thought it was important. He agrees with me and thinks you should come here and stay. PLEASE consider it. I have a piano now and am taking music lessons. Learning to play simple minuets by Henry Purcell.

Love George.

P.S. I was in love with Rebecca, but not for the same reason as you were.

W. Straker, Ludgate Hill.

Dear George, Kristina, and Professor Peterson:

I've grown quite fond of life up here. Not sure what I'd do
on the ground anymore. Things are so peaceful ~~up here—especi~~
especially at night. Professor: please do not ~~wowy~~ worry.
I miss you, and the work we did on that boiling rock

LOVE

HENRY

ROOSEVELT
A THOMPSON HOTEL

7000 Hollywood Blvd Los Angeles CA 90028 T 323.466.7000 F 323.462.8056 Res. 800 950 7667 thompsonhotels.com

FORTY-ONE

Sometime during the second year of flying around the world, you happened to glance idly out the window to see that you'd been rerouted over Athens toward your destination in the United Arab Emirates.

You bit your lip so hard it bled.

One of the flight crew noticed a man bleeding in his seat. She brought you some water and asked if you needed anything from the medicine cabinet.

"There's a medicine cabinet?"

"Oh yes," the stewardess said.

She gave you Band-Aids and a sedative—which took effect almost immediately. In the dream that ensued, you were underwater, beneath the crisp cloak of the Aegean Sea, swimming and holding your breath for an impossibly long time.

Rebecca's body was up ahead tangled in sea grass. As you swam toward it, the current dragged it free. It bobbed against reefs, parted shoals of mackerel, slid along the rotted decks of sunken trading vessels. And her hair, like a slow fire, trailing with the current.

Then one of her shoes came off and spiraled away on its own as if making a break for it. You remembered the places the shoe had been. You remembered her shoes in the morning beside the bed, her size, 37.

When you woke up, women in burkas were foraging in the overhead bins for their possessions.

A baby was screaming.

Why hadn't she turned and swum toward you?

Hundreds of miles away in Greece, it was morning. Oranges stud the trees, even in winter. You imagined lines of cars at lights. Taxis on the main avenues around Omonia Square. Old women in black sitting on the steps of the church, their hard shoes bent to one side. You imagined your old apartment. A desk and the reflection of passing birds.

The square beneath your balcony. Athens at dawn, a cool blue breath.

Lingering stars.

At sunrise, the city blushes. Stone statues glow pink with life for a few minutes, and then fade back to plain white with no memory of their momentary passion.

You were the last person off the plane. In the terminal, you found a place to have some coffee. The women at the next table were laughing at something in a magazine.

You wrote Rebecca's name on a napkin and left it.

Despite two more cups of Arabic coffee, the sedative kept trying to pull you under. You had to get back on a plane. You dragged your body to the nearest ticket counter and asked to buy passage on the next flight. In a sleepy daze you watched the man swipe your passport.

"Go straight to gate 205," he said. "The plane is being held for you."

You took the documents without looking at them, passed through security, and boarded. As soon as your seat belt was buckled, you fell back asleep.

A few hours later, circling Athens, and you didn't even know.

FORTY-TWO

You sat very calmly in the airport for an hour in utter disbelief.

You were spared any buildup because you didn't know where you were until you were actually in the terminal.

But the terminal was different. It was another airport—one you had never seen.

You considered faxing George, but he would want to meet you. This was something you had to face yourself.

For years you flew around the world only to come back to where you started, more alone than ever.

The trunk of the taxi wouldn't close properly.

The roads into Athens were not the ones you remembered. There were large shops with big windows looking down onto the highway, billboards with spotlights, places to pull over and smoke or drink coffee.

The new airport sparkled.

Slightly unsure, you asked the driver where you were. He looked at you in his mirror.

"Athens," he said nonchalantly. "Greece."

You asked him to take you to a nice hotel.

"Nice?" he said.

"Nice."

"Very nice?" He was talking to you in his mirror.

"Just nice,"

"Okay," he said. "A just nice hotel."

"Thanks."

"But not a very nice one—because my brother's wife's uncle is the manager of a very nice one."

After passing under several tunnels and then through a toll-booth, the driver asked where you grew up. For a moment you hesitated.

"Athens."

"Here?"

"Yes."

"Your parents are Greek?"

Then suddenly you remembered that you are an archaeologist—more than that, you know all about bones, about the dead, about burial rites and traditions. That you have education, a PhD. You went to university. You met a girl.

"I was in love with someone here."

The driver swerved into the other lane.

"A girl here in Athens?"

"Yes, a girl here in Athens."

"Is that why you look nervous?" the driver said and laughed.

"I look nervous?"

The driver considered you in his mirror for a moment.

"And very thin," he said, picking something from his teeth.

After about fifteen kilometers, he started talking again. He asked if you knew her address. You shook your head.

"Family name?"

And then you realized that despite the new airport, the tollbooths, the shops, and the smooth roads, you were back in Athens. You were back in the place where your life had begun and where it had ended.

"If you think of it," the driver insisted, "call me, because I have a friend who can help you find her."

You want him to stop talking.

"She was a Greek girl?"

"French."

"Oh," the taxi driver said. "Then it's impossible."

You didn't recognize anything until you got into the city itself. And then the Athens Hilton—the glass sculpture of a running man, then Syntagma Square, the Hotel Grand Bretagne; memories flooded back but were somehow unconnected to everything around you. And there was something different about the city—as though it had forgotten you.

When you arrived at the hotel, the driver asked for the amount on the meter—plus the toll he paid at the booth. You didn't understand. You thought it was a trick. And you asked him really, how much did he want. Then the concierge came out, looked at the meter, added the toll himself, and asked if you wanted it added to your room.

Both men stared at you.

The new Athens had caught you off guard.

You gave the driver a 50 percent tip.

"Like the old Athens," you said in broken Greek, and the concierge and driver both laughed a little.

"If she was Greek I could have helped you," the driver said, getting back into the car. The concierge picked up your heavy briefcase and held the door.

At the check-in desk, there was a small basket of green apples on the counter. You asked for a room and the receptionist typed something into a computer.

"How long would you like to stay in Athens?" she said. Her fingernails were false and made a clicking sound when she touched anything.

"I don't know."

"A week?"

"Maybe only a few hours."

"A few hours? We have a two-night minimum," she said.

"Okay."

"Have you been to Athens before?"

"I don't know."

The receptionist laughed.

"You don't know?"

"I mean, it's all changed."

"Yes, of course," she said.

"Or I have."

"The room is very small," she said, "but there's a nice balcony if you're not afraid of heights."

FORTY-THREE

When you woke up it was raining.

You heard laughing from the hallway, then the jingle of a room service trolley. Someone was having dinner.

You opened the balcony doors.

In another building across from your hotel, you saw two girls smoking and talking. White underwear was drying on a line.

You drew a hot bath. It was too hot, so you put your clothes back on and looked for the coffee machine. You couldn't find one and went downstairs to the lobby.

A man and a child shared the elevator with you. They each had a towel. You stared at the child and then stared at the buttons. You were unsure which pain is worse—the shock of what happened or the ache for what never will.

After sitting down, a muscular bartender with white hair brought you an espresso. He gave a nod but didn't linger. You followed him with your eyes to the bar, where he put on a pair of glasses and looked older.

You stared out the window in silence. Then the bartender came over with a little cake. He was still wearing his glasses. He stood beside you for a minute.

You'll never know why he brought you the cake, but it made you feel better.

It was Sunday night and felt like a Sunday.

About two years ago, not far from there, you wanted to kill yourself.

When you went back upstairs to your room, your bath was cold and there was no more hot water. You took your clothes off and lay naked in bed. You wondered what George was doing. He was living with someone—an Italian woman. He was afraid to tell you things because he was worried you would be upset.

But you gave up the idea of feeling anything new when you left Athens two years ago.

You fell asleep without realizing.

And then another day.

You woke up and sat at the desk.

It had a glass top.

You looked at Henry Bliss in the mirror.

There were seven drawers in the desk and all were empty. A leaflet for afternoon tea had been slipped under your door. You glanced out through the balcony doors, and faintly sketched in the glass was a tired, thin man wearing threadbare pajamas and sitting alone.

It looked like more rain was coming.

Your child would now have been older than your brother ever was.

In the sky beyond your window: a thumbprint of birds, a few lonely shrubs on some distant balcony, and a confusion of TV aerials and satellite dishes stretching as far as you could see.

You walked over to your case and took out the typewriter. You set it on the desk and threaded a piece of hotel stationery through the drum. George would be worried.

Something in the room smelled faintly of flowers. Perhaps chamomile. You always kept some in the cupboard above the cooker back then. Sometimes you put some in a pan and poured boiling water over it.

Rebecca used to drink it at the table. You watched with the joy of knowing she would spend the night.

In your briefcase were things you had written down. Seeing them on paper was terrifying, but it freed you from what you were unable to admit.

You remember what George said once about language, about words and sentences—like Pompei, a world intact, but abandoned. You scramble down the words like ropes, he said. You dangle from sentences. You drop from letters into pools of what happened.

Language is like drinking from one's own reflection in still water. We only take from it what we are at that time.

Heavy rain beat upon your balcony doors.

You were back in Athens.

For two years you had been without a home, wandering the earth like Odysseus.

The neighborhood where your hotel was didn't seem like it was in the city where you once lived. It was the highest building in the Plaka—rising up from a narrow street that resounded violently with the acceleration of taxis.

Two years had passed. Your hotel could have been anywhere. The balcony could have led to any view. Outside, it could have been a desert, or heavy snow.

The hotel you were staying in was once very chic. In the 1970s you imagined beautiful couples gliding through the lobby, en route to the casinos of Monte Carlo, Nice, Cannes. On the roof they danced below the Acropolis in polyester gowns. They would all be old now, or dead.

Your hotel room felt safe. Or maybe it was all that rain. It was quiet too. And the rain was unceasing. All the dust was washing away. The scrubby trees in the park outside the hotel were bristling with moisture.

You went downstairs and asked the receptionist for a sedative. She directed you to a pharmacy on the corner.

It was cheerful and very clean.

You also bought toothpaste.

It had been just over two years since Rebecca died. You had seen the world, but learned nothing.

FORTY-FOUR

It was dusk of the following day when you woke up. The sky was orange. After drinking from the faucet in the bathroom, you felt a sudden madness. You dressed and left the hotel in a hurry, knowing exactly where you wanted to go.

You considered walking but it seemed like a bad idea. You sensed that you wouldn't make it—or it would get too dark and you'd be lost in the ruins.

Instinctively you found the Monastiraki metro station, but everything was different there too. Signs in English and the platforms were clean. There were even automatic ticket machines. A magazine kiosk in the center of the station had Internet access. Half of the magazines were in English.

You stepped through the orange doors of the train in the direction of Kifissia. There was an empty seat but you didn't sit down.

A young couple boarded a few stops later at Omonia. They kissed in front of everyone. His face was thin and red. She had gold hoop earrings. He was almost two feet taller than her. When they stopped kissing, he caressed her hair. People watched without watching.

Soon, you would arrive at her door.

As the train neared her station you thought of that woman dead with the glass in her face—lines of blood running down like red coral, the bricks of the fallen wall like loaves of bread.

Sitting in the Athens airport terminal, you knew you would go there. It's why you stayed. Going back to where everything happened would bring you closer to her.

You imagined her at the door, walking up steps or sitting on the wall with a book. Life would fill in the details of sound, texture, and light. We have the power to conjure presence but not life.

And your heart thumped with the anticipation of what wouldn't happen.

The subway train slowed as it approached her station, but didn't stop. People looked at each other.

Nobody knew why the train wasn't stopping.

You flew through the doors at the next station breathing hard. Then you walked quickly in the direction you came from. A vendor outside the station was selling pink plastic hairdryers. A dozen small girls were pleading with their mothers. The vendor was drying plums in a towel. A group of cats foraged in an open trash can.

You got closer and closer to her apartment—but not in the way you had anticipated. You were returning from a new direction. There was a broken tree branch in the road. Children were jumping on it—trying to tear it from the trunk. You walked parallel to the train tracks for another ten minutes until you saw a building with the sign SANTE written in blue. By then you knew where you were. It was time to hold your breath and dive.

A scooter ripped past. For a moment you imagined that you were going to find out that she was alive—that for two years she had been mourning *your* death. You wondered if ghosts return to the places they went before they died. Do they sit beside fountains and remember? Do they perch unseen at the edges of cribs, staring down at the sleeping creatures they can never know?

Ancient Greek tombstones were carved in the shape of a last action. A mother handing over her infant to someone living. A father waving good-bye to his living sons. A woman reaching out to her husband who has been waiting in the afterlife—he stands at her approach.

You imagined Rebecca carved into a square of stone.

She was holding hands with you and with George, but she had no face—for the face is a memory one cannot will in its entirety.

Then suddenly you were on her street. You looked up, and in all the madness of grief, you expected to see her on the balcony waiting for you.

FORTY-FIVE

Her building was gone. Every last trace of it erased. In its place, a block of condos with narrow windows, fifteen stories high. The balconies had black railings. The fabric awnings matched the color of the steel. There were no tattered, threadbare sheets blowing off rusted balconies in the late-day sun. No sleeping dogs in the doorway. And the dead and dying flowers had been replaced by tidy rows of hard green plastic shrubs.

There was parking underneath. A sign said so. The front door looked heavy. A camera and video monitor saved people a trip to the balcony.

You had expected to still see the tents, pieces of rubble, abandoned vehicles, the glow of small fires.

Then you looked down at your feet and noticed ants everywhere.

They were crawling up your legs. You stepped away and brushed them off. Then you left.

Everything had changed except you.

You passed the taverna where smoking men once played backgammon. In its place was a sleek, modern café with a dozen flat-screen televisions. Old men sat on stools doing scratch-cards and watching numbers change on an electronic board. Teenagers sat before plastic tables pressing buttons on mobile phones. The old marble counter had been replaced with a round glass kiosk from which a face looked out. The old men drank coffee out of plastic cups. Dusty strip lighting had been replaced with the bright buzz of new strip lighting.

You continued walking. The moon was weak and flat.

There was graffiti scrawled on a low wall crumbling dangerously at the top. You walked over and laid a palm on it. From within, the faint thud of a city you once loved.

You stopped outside a restaurant Rebecca once took you to.

Through the window you noticed the main seating area seemed to be shut down. Chairs were stacked upon the tables. Tools and debris lay on fabric sheets in corners where you and Rebecca once sat on straw chairs and talked late into the night. She liked to smoke your cigarettes. There were dumpsters along her street then, and dogs sleeping under them. Stray cats balanced at the edges of bins left open. They stepped carefully, without sound.

The man inside, next to the revolving meat, eyed you with suspicion. You entered and asked for a souvlaka. He tilted his head and took a pita from the stack. He turned his body to the meat and carved a few pieces. Then he wrapped the meat with french fries and yogurt in the pita and handed it to you in a paper cone.

You asked if you could sit down. He nodded in the Greek way that means no.

You hesitated.

"Look," he said, pointing with his knife to the mountain of boxes, old computers, and plastic containers that littered the place where you once were in love.

You ate standing up beside the door. People pushed past you. The sandwich was sweet and barely warm. Each mouthful was a painful effort. After, you bought cigarettes from a kiosk and walked back to her apartment. You smoked one after another on the steps, even though you hadn't smoked for two years. You lay down and cried noiselessly into your hand.

It was dark when your eyes opened. You had been asleep. Someone was poking you. Two policemen. One with a truncheon said something. The other laughed. He then asked you in English what you were doing.

"I was asleep," you said.

"Do you live here?" the one with the truncheon said, using it to point at the balconies.

"I did once."

They exchanged a few words and then listened to something on their radios. They seemed less interested in you now.

The one without the truncheon took out a pad of paper. "Do you have an apartment or hotel here in Athens?"

You nodded.

"Do you have any identification papers?"

"At my hotel."

"Then let's go."

They picked you up and led you off to a small blue police

car. They put you in the backseat and then got into the front. They both lit cigarettes and talked quickly in a Greek you didn't understand.

The one with the truncheon was driving. The other one looked at you in his mirror.

"There's someone you wanted to see?"

"Yes," you said. The cigarettes made you feel sick.

They were both looking at you, suddenly unsure of how to proceed.

"Who?" the driver said. His contempt had changed to genuine curiosity.

"A girl who lived there."

"Wasn't she home?"

"She doesn't live there anymore."

They nodded.

"I just miss her, is all."

"Greek girls are hard to love," the driver said, "especially for foreigners."

One of them offered you a cigarette. You smoked it and felt worse.

When you got to the hotel, they told you to get out.

"What about my identification papers?"

"Forget it."

You locked your hotel room door and shed your clothes. Then you sat naked in the bathtub. You turned on the taps, but they spat only lukewarm water. Then the water turned cold. A rash of spots appeared on your legs and stomach.

You reached up and turned everything off. Then you sat in a few inches of cold water, shivering. The strip lighting brought out red veins in your face. Your hands were dark from the sun. There was dirt under your nails. You wanted to get out but couldn't move.

Then a steady feeling that your stomach was rising into your throat. Your hands shook. A blazing hotness. You rose from the freezing water but slipped and fell hard on the marble tiles. Then you vomited with a long wretched growl.

The floor was covered. Your arms were covered.

The smell was like a bitter fire. You vomited again. You felt pieces in your nose. Your throat was burning.

Your body was rejecting the city that conceived you.

Your life now would be in how you wished to imagine it.

The past must be created as something new.

END OF BOOK TWO

Alone, most strangely, I live on.

—Rupert Brooke

BOOK THREE

FORTY-SIX

When you awake, you know that you have to leave but don't know where to go.

Eighteen hours have passed, and you're tired of being asleep.

You've almost run out of money and you have no one to ask for help.

You sit up in bed. You drink all the water from the minibar and then eat the almonds and the pistachios, throwing the shells into an empty glass. You can smell vomit.

You look at your briefcase and your dusty suit on the floor. Then you realize that the worst has already happened.

You clean up the vomit in the bathroom. Then you shower. Your nose has formed neat scabs on the inside.

You shave with the plastic razor and for some reason start thinking about some museum that George talked about when he came to visit you in hospital. It was a museum of wonder, he said, a museum of lost things, a museum that wasn't planned, but built slowly from the discovery of beautiful pieces recovered from the sea.

You want to see it. Then you will decide what to do with your life.

You imagine the faces of the fishermen as they free a piece of marble from the nets.

You slip from the hotel into bright light. Athens has changed again.

The streets, once cracked and sinister, are now swept with warmth. You can feel it settling on your arms and face.

A sense of poise.

Tourists are smiling at you.

Vendors call gaily from their stalls, and you begin to understand, with a sense of relief, that overnight you have become a visitor.

Athens is embracing you for the first time, like a kind, rich woman who has failed to recognize her own child from the broken days of her youth.

You take the metro from Monastiraki; this time you are going in the opposite direction. It's quicker than you remember, and cleaner.

The station at Piraeus has a roof now. The platform is swept. A uniformed railway employee answers questions and asks people with luggage where they are going. Tourists will remember Athens as a place where people were helpful.

You alight, stepping over the gap between the platform and the train. A stray dog wanders in to greet you.

You walk out from the station into the main square. It's very busy. North African men are selling pocketbooks on the street.

The pocketbooks sit on a bedsheet, their handles wrapped in plastic.

You buy a coffee and some heavy cake from a café. As you eat, a woman in black comes by with a cup, but you look away. She sighs loudly and walks off. You remember George. He'll be frantic, but this is something you must do alone.

You ask two old men on a bench where the museum is. They don't speak English and just nod their heads. Then you ask in broken Greek and get the same response.

A woman on the church steps doesn't know either. She's typing something on her phone but doesn't know where the letters are. Her finger circles the keypad as though she is casting a spell.

A man on an upside-down bucket is selling small tubes of glue from a folding table. On the table are things glued together.

He doesn't know where the museum is but asks if anything you have is broken.

"Everything," you say in Greek. He puts a tube of glue in your hands. You hold out a few coins, but he pushes them away.

You wander through a bustling market. Enormous fish laid out on ice. Some have twisted bodies. Smaller fish are being scooped into cones of paper.

Then you see animals hanging over bright red spotlights behind glass cases, their entrails unfolded for inspection.

Greek men shout at you to come over. A very short man sings as you pass. You turn toward his voice, and he takes your hand and leads you to his fish. He has very small feet.

You stand and look at his fish lined up on the ice. He smiles and smiles until you point to a small fish and say, "Okay."

He wraps it up for you and then, winking, throws in a baby octopus. You pay and ask him where the museum is.

He's never heard of it, but the fish come from his brother.

You keep walking, deeper and deeper into the chaos of the Athenian port. You ask a dozen people—even taxi drivers—how to get to the museum, but no one has ever heard of a museum for lost things.

You turn to walk back the way you came, still carrying a meal you can't eat. But you no longer recognize the streets you came down. You stand still, while everything around you is moving.

You sit in the shade at the edge of a park; a handsome man with sunglasses suddenly appears. He asks gently in Greek if you're lost. He has perfect fingernails and smooth hands. He is about to get on a large BMW motorcycle that's parked next to your bench. His suit is a deep gray and his graying hair combed perfectly to one side.

You explain that you're looking for the museum of lost things.

"The museum of Piraeus?"

You nod weakly.

"Turn around," he says.

Behind you is a small sign with an arrow pointing to a long white building. It says MUSEUM in Greek.

Then he gets on his motorcycle. You watch him drive away—wishing he had stayed. You think of George. He doesn't even know you're here. He's somewhere in Sicily, drinking coffee on his balcony, in love again, sweeping up the dust that blows around the city.

FORTY-SEVEN

A smoking woman with long nails asks if you want to leave your bag at the desk. When you say no, she asks what's in it.

"One small fish and an octopus."

She looks at you strangely.

"I don't even have a kitchen at my hotel," you add.

"Then why did you buy it?"

"Because I felt sorry for the fish man."

She says something to the security guard in Greek and then laughs. But he shrugs and looks at you, not with amusement but with respect—as though he were once a struggling fish man.

The first floor has sculptures that were pulled from the sea. You can tell because the stone resembles a hard gray sponge.

Some cases hold just limbs. Some are green with moss.

Then you wander through a room of gravestones that were discovered at a marine dump by an Albanian laborer. The stones have scenes carved into them.

The final moments of a life imagined by the tired carver.

The dead stare at the living in the full knowledge they have lost their lives. The faces are not detailed because the Greeks understood that one person's experience is everyone's.

We all sit down to the same meal, but at different times.

Carved upon one of the graves, a woman called Eirene from the city of Byzantium has died in childbirth. In the relief, her infant daughter is held by the relative who will raise her. Eirene reaches out her hand to touch her child for the first and last time.

In another carving, a man called Andron shakes the hand of a son already dead, and with his other hand touches the cheek of a son who is still living.

The security guard from the front desk is following you at a distance. You are the only visitor in the museum.

Upstairs is a room with three towering bronze statues. They have greened with age—though details are still visible. Each god has an outstretched hand. You sit and look at them for a long time.

You can't decide if the hands are giving or taking away.

After you vomited in the bathroom last night in the hotel, you cried for several hours on the floor—but then somehow awoke in a different city. Overnight, the set upon which you had played out your small tragedy was taken down and replaced with new scenery.

In the next room is a frieze that leaves you gasping.

· · ·

A fragment of your life has been cast in marble before your very eyes.

A young woman on a bed has died. She is watched by two men and a child. Asklepios, the Greek god of medicine, stands above the woman with his hands on her neck and back. He is bringing her back to life. The two men and the child watch.

Asklepios's own mother died while he was still in her womb. But Asklepios's father fought the flames of his wife's funeral pyre with a knife between his teeth. Then he sliced open her stomach and ripped out his unborn son.

Growing up, the boy realized he had the ability to heal. His power grew until one day he could bring the dead back to life. For this, Zeus destroyed him with a thunderbolt.

You think of your own father. You imagine the swell of your mother's womb, the stirring waters as you leave one world for another.

It seems pointless imagining what your brother would be like, because he died when he was a baby.

Things in your mind are shuffling into order.

And you realize that you've finally grown up. That youth has finished. In its place you have knowledge, which you must learn to carry. You must also learn to accept that death is the most sophisticated form of beauty, and the most difficult to accept.

From this moment on, you will always be conscious of what you are doing. And any future feeling, whether joy or grief or excitement or regret, will come now with an awareness of its own end—with shadows you never noticed in youth. Variation of feeling will become depth of feeling. And you will appreciate tiny things—and step with the confidence of someone over-joyed to know he is doomed.

You leave the museum and walk slowly up the road with your bag of fish. Cars parked with their bumpers touching. You pass a butcher and then a hairdresser. The women are sitting in chairs smoking.

A father carries his son on his shoulders. The father has a cigarette in his mouth and the boy is laughing. He holds his fa-ther's hair in clumps. They pass like a small locomotive.

You think of your own parents now.

Sitting in their chairs watching television. You haven't seen them for so long.

You've sent postcards, called them occasionally from Tokyo or London or Beirut. They think you're traveling for work.

You always tell them you're fine.

They tell their friends you're fine. "Up to his neck in Greece," your father says.

At the end of the street is a yellow telephone booth.

The phone is blue like the sea. You stand inside the booth.

A sticker on the handset says:

Πρέπει να είστε η αλλαγή που επιθυμείτε να δείτεστον κόσμο

You will never know what it means.

·   ·   ·

You decide to make a call. You're tired, but the promise of a new life is still with you. It's the feeling that you can take anything, or that you can accept anything—or that if everything you thought and think turns out to be a lie you wouldn't be upset or surprised or unable to go on.

You dial the operator. Then you key in your parents' telephone number in England. The operator tells you to hold on. It rings.

The operator comes back on.

After some confusion, they accept the charges.

FORTY-EIGHT

DAD: 7501478?

HENRY: Hi, Dad.

DAD: Henry?

HENRY: Hello.

Silence.

DAD: How are you, son? We haven't heard from you in ages.

HENRY: I know.

Dad shouts in the background, "It's Henry, dear."

DAD: Everything okay?

Silence.

HENRY: Not really.

Silence.

DAD: Well, I'm sure it will work itself out.

Silence.

DAD: Henry?

DAD (*talking to someone in background*): Turn down the telly a
minute, dear.

HENRY: It's good to hear your voice. Is Mum there?

DAD: She's here. What going on? Is everything okay?

HENRY: Is she okay?

DAD: She's watching *EastEnders*. Are you all right? She says hello.

Silence.

DAD: How's the digging?

Silence.

DAD: Henry?

HENRY: I haven't been working.

DAD (*suspicious*): Taking a break?

HENRY: I've been on a break, yes.

Silence.

DAD (*worried*): Oh.

Silence.

DAD: We haven't heard from you in about two months— your mother was getting worried. Last time you called was from Bulgaria—a dig was it?

Silence.

DAD: Henry? You all right?

HENRY: Actually, no.

DAD (*concerned*): What's happened?

Silence.

DAD: Henry?

HENRY: Someone I loved very much has died.

Silence.

DAD (*in a quiet, frightened voice*): What?

Silence.

DAD: Who?

HENRY: You didn't know her.

DAD: Someone you knew there?

HENRY: Yes, she was French.

DAD: And she died?

HENRY: Yes

DAD: How did she die?

Silence

DAD: Was it sudden?

HENRY: She was crushed to death.

Dad relays the story to Mum in a whisper. Mum gasps and grabs the phone.

DAD (*in background*): Harriet!

MUM: Henry?

HENRY: Mum?

Silence.

HENRY: How was *EastEnders*?

MUM: It's still on. Who is dead?

HENRY: A friend. In the earthquake.

Silence.

MUM: Two years ago?

HENRY: About that.

MUM: Why are you telling us now?

Silence.

HENRY: I don't know

MUM: Has something else happened?

HENRY: Isn't that enough?

DAD (*speaking in background*): He never said anything before.

MUM: You never said anything before.

HENRY: I know.

MUM: You should have told us. We're your parents.

Silence.

DAD (*coming back on the phone*): Henry, why didn't you say something?

HENRY: I don't know.

DAD: We thought you were working away happily with the professor.

HENRY: I was. Or at least I thought I was.

DAD: What did he say about this?

HENRY: I haven't seen him.

DAD: What do you mean?

Silence.

DAD (*with grave concern*): Is *he* dead too, Henry?

HENRY: I don't think so.

DAD: You don't think so? Henry, what's going on?

HENRY: He's not dead—I just haven't seen him.

DAD: Where are you?

HENRY: In a phone booth in Piraeus.

MUM (*speaking in background*): Where is he now?

DAD (*in background*): In a phone booth somewhere.

MUM (*in background*): What's he doing there?

DAD: What are you doing there? Where are you?

HENRY: I came to the museum. I'm in Athens.

DAD: Who is supervising the dig?

HENRY: I haven't been to the dig for a while.

DAD: Why not?

HENRY: I've been traveling.

DAD: Yes, we know that bit, traveling for work.

Silence.

HENRY: I don't know what to do now with my life, but I'm over the worst.

DAD: We haven't seen you in years, son.

MUM (*in background*): Years.

DAD: Years, Henry.

HENRY: I know.

DAD: Do you have any money?

HENRY: No.

DAD: Are you still in your flat?

HENRY: No.

DAD: Where are you?

HENRY: A hotel.

MUM (*speaking in background*): What happened to the flat?

DAD: What happened to the flat?

HENRY: Someone else lives there.

DAD: Henry, what's really going on?

HENRY: Since Rebecca died, I've been wandering around.

DAD (*in background*): Some girl called Rebecca died.

MUM (*in background*): His girlfriend?

DAD (*in background*): How should I know, Harriet?

DAD: Have you been working?

HENRY: No, just thinking.

DAD: About what?

HENRY: Rebecca. And my brother.

Silence.

DAD: Henry.

HENRY: I've thought about it a lot.

Silence.

HENRY: Dad?

Silence.

HENRY: I feel okay about things now.

DAD: I see.

Mum, in background, wants to know what he's talking about. Dad says he'll tell her after.

DAD: How long do you need to get everything together?

HENRY: About fifteen minutes.

DAD: Fifteen days?

HENRY: Yes.

DAD: Send us your details a couple of days before you come, and we'll pick you up from the airport.

Silence.

DAD: Call us anytime, son.

HENRY: Thanks.

DAD: Your mother and I had no idea that someone had died.

Mum grabs phone again.

DAD (*in background*): Harriet!

MUM: So who was Rebecca? You never mentioned her before.

HENRY: Someone I met.

MUM: A girl?

Silence.

HENRY: Yes.

MUM: A girlfriend?

Silence.

HENRY: I've just been drifting.

MUM: Well, we've missed you.

HENRY: Really?

MUM: But you've been living your own life. We didn't want to
interfere.

HENRY: I feel like I've come off course.

MUM (*in background to Dad*): He feels like he's been blown off
course.

Dad takes the phone.

DAD: Come home, son.

HENRY: Thanks.

DAD: Call us from the hotel with your details.

Silence.

DAD: We had no idea your girlfriend had died and that you'd
stopped working. Come home for a bit. And if you don't
want to work for a while, you have your grandmother's
inheritance to fall back on.

FORTY-NINE

Next to the telephone booth is a Yamaha scooter with a ripped seat. In a nearby building someone is drilling. Buses hiss past. The light turns green, and old people drive too long in first gear. People leave the bank in a steady drip, then linger to gossip outside.

A child is styling her hair with a purple plastic hairdryer. Sheets of plywood long forgotten rot against the metal wall of a kiosk. The sidewalk is gray and dusty. The road barriers are twisted where struck by vehicles. A woman is hanging a sign in the shop opposite. It says, MEGA BAZAAR.

Another child with a plastic hairdryer. A man in slippers smokes and reads the paper standing up. A teenager on a scooter. Her T-shirt says, I LOVE YOU, BUT. In the distance, a bare scorched mountain.

Another child with a plastic hairdryer.

Men in old polo shirts spinning beads over their hands. The men hover around you. They have nothing to do and want to talk. It passes the time. Gives them something to think about later at the kitchen table with the lights on.

You have felt alone too.

Standing at the intersection of Leoforos Iroon Polytechniou and Charilaou Trikoupi, you decide that to overcome loneliness you must conquer your fear. Once it was fear of rejection; now it is fear of the past.

When Athens was under Turkish rule, Piraeus was empty, uninhabited, a blowing stretch of dusty land, dotted with ruins at the edge of a city. Even the name had been forgotten. But slowly it rose again from the ashes and filled with people, cars, boats, bicycles; bustling markets of fish and meat; hard lemons and their green drying leaves; old men with newspapers; and the occasional table of plastic hairdryers with little hands reaching.

FIFTY

It's quite clear how your life will continue from this point on. So predictable, in fact, that you envision it from a street corner in Athens.

You imagine setting the bag of fish down somewhere near the phone booth and then going home to Britain.

There you will survey the artifacts of your childhood and decide on a new course for your life.

You can already feel it happening.

Months of quiet despair.

Then applying for jobs at museum offices in London.

You'll have to get a flat.

Dad will take your stuff in the Land Rover.

Mum will fill a box of cans from the kitchen cupboard, a few of which will be out of date.

Dad looking for coins to put in the parking meter. People walk by and see a car full of things to be unloaded. You'll have to get used to the city again—get used to being watched again.

Then dinner in the empty flat from a nearby takeaway with your parents. The smell of fresh paint.

Your father's usual enthusiasm. Your fishing rod in the corner for good measure.

You will work quietly in your first year and make some friends.

At night you will mostly come home and watch films on television. On warm afternoons you'll go to the pub with colleagues and watch wasps linger over the glasses.

People at work will see you as a shy young man of about thirty.

Someone will have a secret crush on you.

Nobody will know that you're really an old man, a ruined man with a sadness so deep it's like unbreakable strength. And when someone comes to you with bad news—their grandparent, an aunt with cancer, a cousin suddenly one morning in a car—you'll have to pretend any reaction beyond indifference.

You will eventually meet a girl in London—probably someone called Chloe or Emma—maybe at a summer pub or waiting for the bathroom at Foyles Bookshop on Charing Cross Road. She will introduce herself. A bit older than you. It's too late to be shy. You will talk about this and that. She will love books— went to Cambridge, but so many years ago now. She's lonely. She'll sense your depth without knowing you. It will get late without either of you realizing. You'll offer to walk her somewhere. She'll stop at Marks and Spencer for her dinner. You will watch her pick things from the shelves and put them into her basket. You will carry her basket. She will ask if you've eaten, and you'll say no. You will make love to her before dinner and then after. It will be the first of many nights. The mothers will want to know everything quickly. Houses will have to be tidied up. You'll be welcomed by her group of friends, who are witty and sweet but talk about you when they're drunk.

Soon enough you'll be visiting her parents the day after Christmas. You will laugh at her father's jokes, look at pictures of her as a child as they sigh; everything is happening so quickly. Her younger brother will smoke dope in his room and give you some. He'll tell you that you're cool and then ask what London is like—maybe even admit to you he's gay, even if he isn't.

She will kiss her parents good night as you wave to them sheepishly from the doorway. Then in the car she'll tell you the nice things her father said. You'll both laugh.

For her—it's the love affair you've already had.

In five years you will have your first child, a girl. You will love her immediately. She will giggle at bright colors and movement, random things too—like bread falling off the counter. Later, she will run from you naked—refusing to get dressed. She will cry when you drop her off at school, then cry when you pick her up. She will scream for you in the night and not know why. You will get promoted and oversee a big exhibition that makes the papers. You will recognize a few of Chloe or Emma's friends from the society pages in *Tatler*. You will choose Chloe or Emma's Christmas presents carefully from Liberty of London.

Also: romantic weekends in the Cotswolds or a long week-end in New York.

Years later, you'll have a fling with someone much younger, but it will only deepen your devotion to Chloe or Emma as you realize what a friend she's become over the years.

George will have started drinking again and die of something alcohol-related in a place like Malta or Corsica. You won't even know. His apartment will be cleared by the landlady's son, and his books and manuscripts sent to the dump.

Then one day, your teenage daughter on a long car trip will lean forward between the seats and ask if you remember falling in love for the first time.

Chloe or Emma will reach over and squeeze your hand—her greatest moment of vulnerability and she doesn't even know.

FIFTY-ONE

A few hours after you return to your hotel from the museum in Piraeus, the police show up again. The receptionist calls you to come down.

When the elevator doors open the police have already gone.

The receptionist hands you a book with most of the pages ripped out.

"What's this?"

"I don't know," the receptionist says and then tells you what the police told her. The neighbor who called them later realized she had seen you before—visiting the girl who once lived there. And that perhaps you were looking for the book she had found.

"But how did she get it?"

"I don't know," the receptionist says.

You open the book in the elevator. There's writing inside. It's in French. It looks like the hand of a teenage girl.

You run a bath and take the book in with you.

Standing naked between the clear water and the mirror, you recognize the handwriting. You sit on the side of the bathtub. It's definitely hers, you're sure of it.

The book smells like wood. There is dust in all the pages.

There are no dates, only entries—small paragraphs of text scribbled across three pages.

It's slow reading. Some words you don't know. You need a French dictionary.

After your bath, you thread paper into your typewriter and write out the parts you can read. You look up at the clock's quiet announcement of 4:16.

Everything you thought you knew about Rebecca has been called into question by these pages, these few sentences in a diary.

You feel deceived by fragments of a language you can barely read.

The truth seems simple and cruel: she hadn't trusted you enough to tell you the secret these pages expose. And now, your memory of her—like some portrait of a child, unaffected by time and death, has suddenly aged before your eyes and succumbed to ruin.

The memory you had been living to preserve is a fake.

And your greatest joy, your defining moment of victory, and your savage, unending grief have been the result of nothing more than an affair—a childish, Greek affair.

START

Every morning I awake in pieces--broken from the day before
and the day before that. Each small piece gets smaller with each day.

I spend every hour doing something for the baby, washing, cooking,
playing, watching, always watching--and the moment you dont't watch,
something happens--a fall f you dont see.

I'm too exhausted to do anyt ing for myself. My hair is limp.
I can't do anything with it. Everything depresses me more than
ever.

For the first time in my life--I know exactly my future.
Maybe I should tell the father. A few minutes in his truck and a
life id created. Mayve- May be he deams of being a father? I
doubt it. He(s probbly some mit who does this to all weean, women.

I'm doinge exactly as my mother did.

Everything I ever wanted is impossible.

I can imagine my screaming ball of flesh decades from now
at a party in Paris. MY mother, MY mother she will say--SHE
always wanted to do something interesting--maybe become an
artist. I did once.

And l'll still be here in Linières-Bouton, a village nobody
has ever heard of--working at the station cafe. The truck

18-20 N. NIKODIMOU STR. • PLAKA DISTRICT • 105 57 ATHENS/GREECE
TEL.: +30 210 3370000 • FAX: +30 210 3241875 • E-mail: salesepath@electrahotels.gr
URL: www.electrahotels.gr, www.electra-hotels.com

cont...

...drivers will still smile--but out of sympathy. My face and body
will have sunk.

      What am I going to do?

I can feel my body changing. She sucks and sucks. I love her eyes.
It's not all bad. I write the worst here. If I had a husband, he'd
be in trouble because I think men are pigs. They are pigs. No one
will marry me now. I am washed up. The best I can hope for is a
few nights.

      She's napping now.
      I wonder what she thinks about.

      I hate her.
      Actually, I love her and that's why I hate her.

She naps a-lot- very much. Every time I go outside and smoke, smoke,
smoke like mad. I wonder what my mother would do if she knew she was
a grandmother-l---l-. I'dlove to see the look on her face. I should
find a way to tell her friends--if she has any, bitch.

Grandfather is now away with his boules club. They are in Nice, fancy.
I wonder why he didn't call his daughter and tell her to come back to
us ?
I think he's afraid of women. Shit, why can't I meeta m n who is afraid
of women? -y-y- Most men are cowards. Women are not--look at mother, she

18-20 N. NIKODIMOU STR. • PLAKA DISTRICT • 105 57 ATHENS/GREECE
TEL.: +30 210 3370000 • FAX: +30 210 3241875 • E-mail: salesepath@electrahotels.gr
URL: www.electrahotels.gr, www.electra-hotels.com

ELECTRA PALACE HOTEL - ATHENS
★ ★ ★ ★ ★
Member of the Electra Hotels & Resorts

...was courageous. If only I had the courage to run away. I love
m y little ___?___ , but I need to get sorted out and then I could
come back and we would all be happier because I'd be happy.

De failures raise failures?

Maybe I should go away, maybe to Paris.

Fuck. I am so fat now, mostly above my thighs. When I war the
apron at work, my waist andlegs look like a single tree trunk. But
inside the fat me is the thin me who seduces men with her conversation
on Sartre, Camus, Genet--while they look at my tits. All I can say
now is that I'm alive. And my ankles look OK again. I should go
to Tours this weekend, the cinema, take come coffee somewhere, mn
maybe flirt with some guys. Maybe I could go see my sister. Last night
afetr I fed baby, I watched TV, a film about three men who go back to
to Medieval times. Grandfather Bll asleep in his chair. Baby and I have
slept in his big bed since ~~xxxxxx~~ being born. Their time machine breaks and they
are stuck in the wrong time,. After the film I looked at my face in the
mirror above the sink. Then I cried. Then a yogurt. Then I checked on
baby and wsovercome with lovep--rounded cheeks, tiny lips, so sweet. Like
cherries. I decided to work on my future. I would make a list, but when
I got back to bed, all I wrote was stupid and I wondered if I have any other
future than a fat single mother. Then I fed baby with duty. I hate myself
for hating this. I want to abandon the person I love most in the world.
WILL I EVER BE A LOVING MOTHER??? its something I never had. In a way my
mother and I are closer than we've ever been before, ever. Finally I
understand now she felt and why she ~~abandonedus~~. anandoned us. I think

END

FIFTY-TWO

It has to be Rebecca's journal because you recognize the handwriting and it mentions Linières-Bouton, the name of her village you couldn't remember.

She had a child.

You say it to yourself a hundred times.

It was her second pregnancy. You feel the betrayal in your body like a weight.

You wonder if the child knows what happened to her mother. You wonder if it's even possible. But details reveal so many similarities to Rebecca's actual life, it has to be hers, even if she made it up. It's strange how after someone dies, we sometimes learn things about them we didn't know when they were living. But for those left behind, even the smallest new detail is heavy enough to smash what is left of the heart.

And where is this first child? A date scribbled onto the page suggests they were written two years before Rebecca came to

Athens. But wasn't she a stewardess with Air France? Or was that just a lie to cover up what she'd done?

Perhaps at this very moment, there's some little person sitting up in bed—wondering if today will be the day the doorbell rings.

If not for the poise of the new Henry Bliss in the new Athens, this news would have obliterated what was left of you.

You sit in bed with the journal, and then fall asleep around dawn.

On the afternoon of the next day, you go up to the roof for a swim.

It's hot by the pool and some hotel guests have pulled their sun loungers into the shade. The journal is downstairs on the bed. Perhaps she was afraid you would not love her if she told you. You could have become a father to two children within the year. You could have become the family Rebecca never had.

You'll never feel the comfort of resolution now, and your Greek love affair will be playing itself out inside you forever—silently spinning around your heart like a web with no beginning or end.

All you can think of now is the child.

A fragment of Rebecca that's living.

What is this child like?

You know that Rebecca had a sister. Perhaps the child is with her?

You spend the entire afternoon by the pool.

You swim for a while and then go back to your seat. The waiter brings you ice-cold orange juice. You roll the glass on your chest because it feels good. The other guests are Polish couples and slightly older than you. The women talk in the pool while the men drink beer and laugh. They must be on vacation and having a good time.

By the late afternoon, you're tired and want to look at the journal again.

As you wait for the elevator, you notice a marble relief attached to the wall. You step closer to inspect it, holding the towel around your neck the way George used to. This marble relief is a copy of the relief from the museum, the one with Asklepios raising a woman from the dead as the two men and the child watch.

You ignore the elevator and study it, marveling at the coincidence of its presence in your hotel.

The small marble child is watching the resurrection of her mother as two men stand on either side. The child's mouth is open in awe. She is standing on tiptoe. Asklepios is exchanging his life for hers.

The child's hands are clasped.

The woman is coming back to life.

You imagine her eyes impossibly wide.

Screams of joy.

Screams of fear.

Her heart is pumping again—her lips go from gray to burgundy.

In an instant, her body is light and supple.

But the dead don't come back to life. They sit frozen in our minds, finally free, capable of everything and nothing in a paradise where they can do no wrong.

When the towel falls from around your neck and the elevator returns full of people, it's suddenly clear what you must do. Even if it's only anger driving you, you envision yourself in France looking for Rebecca's child, scouring bakeries, schoolyards, coin-operated rides outside supermarkets, swings and slides, public pools, the empty fields where children play games.

You wish you'd saved a few of Rebecca's things. You wonder if George has any. You rush back to your room and turn on your mini-satellite fax machine. It beeps, rattles, and then spews out messages. After five pages of worry from George, you press reset and take the machine over to the desk.

You reach for a leaf of hotel stationery and begin composing a fax.

Two hours later when you return from dinner you notice your telephone light blinking. You pick up the handle and press the square button.

It's a voice message from George. He says he can't believe it. Then he doesn't say anything. Then he wonders if it's true, and if it's even Rebecca's journal in the first place. He still doesn't have a telephone but will call back from the place on the corner.

You compose a fax, telling him that the journal refers to the village and her grandfather and her sister—and that it has to be her and not to call because you're leaving for France immediately.

George replies within seconds.

He wants you to come to Sicily and discuss it.

He's very worried about you.

He can't believe it, he writes. He wants you to fax proof.

You write that it's all in a journal and can't be faxed, but that it's true and that all the time you knew Rebecca, she had a child in France that she'd run away from.

George faxes back to say that he still can't believe it. That there must be a mistake.

He also tells you that he was married last month. You fax back asking why you weren't invited to the wedding. George replies that he thought it might upset you.

You reply that it would not have. You explain that you want him to be happy. He writes back that he is and he wishes you were and is there really a "phantom child" of Rebecca or are you having an anxiety attack?

Both his parents are coming to Sicily to meet his new wife.

You think of your own parents. Your mother will be washing her hands in the kitchen sink, looking at the tray of violet flowers she has yet to plant.

Your father is drinking coffee and reading the *Radio Times*.

You sign off with George and then telephone them from the hotel.

You tell them you have just enough money to get home but have one more thing to do before you return for good.

Your father says he can't wait to see you, and that there are about two dozen letters for you from the International Mini-Satellite Fax Corporation in Shanghai, and they look quite urgent.

·　　　·　　　·

As you close your case and check the room you notice something happening in an apartment across the courtyard. A child's birthday party. The adults are wearing paper hats. You open the door and the distant sound of party music fills your room.

You continue searching, and then look again, drawn by the sound of applause. Somebody opens the balcony door. It's a man. He's wearing a white shirt that is too big for him. He sees you looking and you realize that it's your neighbor, the one who left the fish—the one who boiled towels from the hospice—the one Rebecca sketched before coming over.

He smiles at you and then bends to pick up a small boy at his feet. He says something and the boy waves to you. Then they turn away and fall back into their lives. You wonder how long it takes to be happy again.

You keep watching.

The cake arrives.

Wishes are cast like nets.

FIFTY-THREE

None of the drivers want to go to the airport because it's fifteen minutes before midnight and the rate doubles after. This is the old Athens. You say it's an emergency, but no one cares. It's not their emergency.

You look around for the x95 bus that used to leave for the airport every hour. But there are so many buses now.

And then a driver gets out of his taxi and shouts that he'll take you.

Like most Greek cab drivers, he doesn't wear a seat belt. He is driving faster than everyone else on the road, as though he senses your urgent desire to escape. There is bouzouki on the radio. You are flying through Athens. The car vibrates as you roar past the Athens Hilton at 150 kilometers an hour. Then a red light and the car shudders violently, skidding to a line of scooters. Old Athens has come back to kill you—to hold you in its memory like a fly in amber.

And then traffic thins out as the highway branches into several lanes. Lines of flower shops, cell phone shops, bakeries with their doors open, sex shops, hardware stores with mops hanging in the window like funny heads, concrete apartment blocks, offices, parking lots, factories, bridges, warehouses with bright signs.

Once you enter the airport, you don't need to turn around. The blinking city in the distance no longer belongs to you.

For on some noisy street of cooking and kiosks and children out late, there is another Henry Bliss—another dreamer in the last days of youth—somewhere between enthusiasm and disaster, not yet in the shadow of paradise, not yet in the bounty of its ruins.

FIFTY-FOUR

Circling Paris at dawn.

A measured spin.

Waiting for the right moment to descend.

You wonder who is watching—whose eyes you have crossed. Perhaps someone through an early window is distracted by a distant smudge, a dot of beating hearts in the sky.

Below your seat, morning has uncloaked millions of different lives. As you swoop down over the Seine, you hear a couple arguing but still holding their cups of coffee . . . cars reversing out of garages into small clouds. You see men with brooms in empty classrooms . . . the bright window of a bread shop and its tired girl . . . a child with messy hair hiding under the covers . . .

Another day has come.

The engines are slowing. Wheels underneath unfolding with a yawn. The stewardess buckles into her seat. Her hair is tied above her neck. She is staring at you.

You are in Paris.

A single city with a thousand names—it stretches over miles and miles engulfing villages and towns in one slow breath.

A city dissected by water.

People walk along its edges, full of thoughts.

The heart of the city is a church, a place where wishes are scattered by tolling bells.

And the parks are quartered by trees and ancient statues of vague proclamation.

You spend the morning in the business section of the Air France lounge printing off maps, hotels, and addresses. An Indian woman in an apron brings you curry sandwiches and glasses of tonic.

Then you stand in line at the rental car desk for an hour.

The woman looks flustered. She has one car left when it's your turn—an executive sedan. She hands you the keys and a piece of paper to initial. It's impossibly expensive—but your credit card, as if sensing the urgency of your quest goes through without complaining.

On the contract is the number of the parking space where the car is. The key is a small black cube with four rings on it.

When you go outside, you see three damaged Fiats and what looks like a spaceship.

You put your briefcase in the backseat and start the engine by slipping the key into the dashboard. Everything comes to life. A monitor flips out. A prompter on the screen asks you in French to input your name and then set the language. You don't understand how to do this and so you write Henry and then press enter without reading the instructions.

The side mirrors fold out by themselves like ears. You wonder how you're going to go unnoticed in a tiny French village with a car that has a top speed of 200 mph.

You turn on the navigation system and key in the name of her village—but somehow you set the car into a language you don't understand.

After adjusting your seat, the car says:

آمل ان يكون نهارك سعيداً. أين تريد أن تذهب؟

The navigation system is also a map. You decide to follow the arrow on the monitor.

Navigating the roads outside Paris is fairly easy.

There are billboards everywhere for milk or chocolate or socks.

When traffic stops in a five-lane tunnel, you look into the car next to you and see five children in the backseat of a battered Citroën. Their faces are gaunt and handsome. An Ethiopian family. You smile at them. One waves back. You wish you knew his name.

Two hours south of Paris, you stop to fill up with diesel. Then as you pull away, the car says something else:

لقد ملأت السيارة بوقود الديزل، لديك 800 ميل قبل أن تفرغ، هنري.

"Sorry," you say to the monitor. "But I don't understand anything you're trying to tell me."

Then you say, "Reset, reset," in a French accent.

لم أفهم الطلب يا هنري. أرجوك أن تعيده وسيسعدني أن أنفذ طلبك.

"Reset."

الصوتية، أرجو أن تضع السيارة في حالة الوقوف ثم أن تنظر إلى

كتاب المعلومات الخاص بالسيارةللحصول على قائمة الأوامر

"Okay."

عفواً، أرجوك التكرار.

"Goddamn it."

ألغ.

After two more hours you stop at some roadside services to use the restroom. Families sit on the grass chewing baguette sandwiches. It's quite windy.

There is a restaurant inside a bridge that connects one side of the A11 motorway to the other side. People going in opposite directions sit beside each other and eat.

In theory it's a brilliant concept. The bridge has glass sides. But the salad you ordered gave up long ago. Leaves hang off the plate as if drowned. After, you sit outside and listen to the sound of laughter. There are children climbing all over the swings, some hang off shouting.

None of them know each other in real life.

You look around at the world—at all the strangers and all the cars lined up and packed up with tents and coolers and bicycles and sleeping bags. It's wonderful. And your journey is one of many.

And there is no real life, except what we imagine.

Maybe the little Rebecca you so desperately wish to find watched you circle the city from a concrete tower of small rooms and boiling pots. It's impossible to know if you will ever find her.

You drive another hundred miles, then stop at a gas station. The hand dryer comes on by itself. There is also a vending machine for balls of toothpaste that you are supposed to chew and then spit out. You buy five to give yourself something to do in the car.

You learn quickly that the toothpaste balls are a big mistake. You put two in at once and within a few minutes, a dense cloud of minty foam is flowing from your mouth and into your lap. You open the window and spit everything out. Then you scoop a few handfuls of foam out the window. You haven't seen any other cars for some time.

After another hour of silent driving, the car starts talking again:

إن واجهت تأخيرا كبيراً، أتريدني أن أجد لك طريقاً آخر؟ أستطيع أن

أن أجد لك مطاعم ممتازة قريبة من مكانك اقتراب في إشغال الطريق،

افعل ذلك، هنري. هل أنت جائع أو ربما عطشان؟ بإمكاني

"Thank you for saying that, car—you're right, it has been very hard for me over these past two years."

عفواً

"I still don't know, but at least I'm trying."

عفواً لم أفهم

And then finally you reach your exit for the road to Linières-Bouton.

It is very late in the afternoon. You've passed several rivers. The headlights have come on by themselves. You are on a narrow road, the sort that was designed for horses and people waving—not supercharged German automobiles.

You drive for another hour, slowing down for very long

curves and speeding up for hilly straights. There are no other vehicles but for the occasional tractor, throwing up dust as it grinds home through afternoon fields.

You enter Rebecca's village at dusk.

You plan to sleep in the backseat of the car, which is large enough for two.

You drive slowly past a small church and a *boulangerie* with the shades pulled down.

The village of Linières-Bouton is nothing more than an open mouth of crooked houses, a few blowing trees, a slow high river, and a café–post office.

Old people in gardens wave to you. They are picking things for supper.

Their lives are slow and calm.

Nothing but the quiet fantasy of guessing what comes next.

Long walks through changing fields, and that softly falling question: where are the hearts that once loved us?

There are early lights on in some of the houses. Others look abandoned—their shutters closed like blank pages for night to fill.

You cross a railroad track overgrown where it extends past the road. Then you notice how it ends abruptly at the edge of someone's garden.

Then 1930s advertising in fraying sheets on the side of an obsolete barn.

Little Rebecca might be at home in any one of these houses.

She has inherited her mother's ability to wait.

You imagine a girl at the edge of hayfields, thinking about her mother in the last golden moments of day. You see her small shoes—dirtied at the toe from running. In the morning they sweep the grass with dew.

You know you must be tired because these thoughts make you stop the car and open the window.

You haven't smoked much in the last few years but wish you had a cigarette now.

You feel your own pain shrink in the presence of this child's.

Such relief in humility.

You think of George, how difficult his life has been. You want to drive to his boarding school in America and eat ice cream sitting on the wall with him. You want to give him a scarf and gloves, his first Latin dictionary, a winter coat.

And then you toy with the fantasy that if there is a child you could become its father.

When you touched down in Paris, you sent George a quick fax to tell him what was going on. He wrote that he was coming—but you told him to stay in Sicily with his parents and wife and keep swimming.

Another hour of driving around you decide to find an empty field outside town. As you pass a sign with a red stripe that says you're leaving the village two bloodhounds run out and stand in front of the car. You brake hard. Their eyes, like marbles, are held steady by the Audi's blue headlights.

The dogs won't move.

Then the car says something to you.

هناك عائقان في الطريق، أحذر، هنري.

"Yeah, I see them—thanks, car."

When you get out to shoo them away, you notice a poster stapled to a telephone pole.

A circus tonight at 9:00 p.m. in a village called Noyant.

The poster has a clown smiling and a lion standing up on its back legs as if asking for a cookie.

You glance at your watch.

The show will begin in ten minutes. Every child in the area will be there. All you have to do is look for an approximately four-year-old girl and an old man—Rebecca's grandfather—or a woman who could be Rebecca's sister. You feel a burst of adrenaline.

Cows bolt as you swish by.

You arrive in the village of Noyant a few minutes later and park outside a small supermarket.

Circus signs point toward the grounds of a church.

The tent up ahead is a blue and yellow miniature version of a big-top. Its sides are tied with long ropes and staked with wood.

Outside the small big-top is a miniature pony, a baby goat, and a large Alsatian tied with a rope. You can hear grass being ripped by the two small mouths as you pass. The dog wags his tail and looks at you but does not stand up.

Beside the tent is a red van.

As you near the tent entrance, you notice several children hanging about. They stop talking and look at you. Your first instinct is to turn and walk away, but then you would appear even more suspicious. You have no choice but to keep walking and say hello. One of the children asks you in French if you're here for the circus. You say you are. It seems to be the correct answer because the other children cheer among themselves.

You explain in French that your father was in the circus and you were passing and decided to see it, to remind you of old times.

The children nod but don't seem to believe you.

Then one of them asks if your father was a clown.

You shake your head.

A ringmaster then?

One of the children, a little girl, explains that the circus will not perform for fewer than fifteen people. She is too old to be Rebecca's child. You smile politely.

You are the twelfth person, another child adds—which means only three more people are needed to start the performance.

Circus music plays torturously on a loop through loudspeakers.

Children hold hands and dance.

The parents talk in a circle by the wall. Some of the women smoke. It's a warm night. The air smells faintly of hay. The children's faces are soft like cheese.

After a few minutes, the ringmaster appears from the trailer and checks his watch. He shakes his head at the children. They raise their arms to protest, and just when it seems that all is lost—three figures appear in the distance. A toddler out for an evening walk with his parents. He is wearing only a T-shirt, a diaper, and little shoes. His parents are talking and haven't noticed the small big-top. The children start shouting at the toddler. Everyone is watching. As the child spies the small big-top, he stops and looks curiously toward it. Then he notices the group of children calling him over.

His parents call after him. They jog to catch him. The children explain that a circus has come to town. The couple are German and don't seem to understand. Then the ringmaster counts the crowd and blasts an air horn.

The German family is swept into the tent with everyone else. The toddler is sitting with the other children. His parents watch anxiously from among the local parents.

But no sign of a small girl or an old man.

You are about to sneak away when a boy dressed in a clown costume approaches and asks how many tickets. You laugh. He smiles and asks again. He is about thirteen. You say that you were only looking. He explains that you must buy a ticket for the show to proceed—that you are the fifteenth person.

You give him some money, and he rips a stub from a roll of mint green tickets. Then he hectors you inside with an air horn.

As you enter the small big-top, you notice a wooden sign advertising the circus. It has been propped up against a First World War memorial, beside the names of those who fell long ago in a cold place of terror.

FIFTY-FIVE

The ringmaster and his son begin by doing handstands. The music is much louder inside the little big-top. Everyone is watching them balance. The ringmaster's arms tremble and his face turns red.

When the applause thins, the music becomes a drum roll and the circus duo leave the tent. In a few seconds the ringmaster and his son return with clubs of fire juggled by the ringmaster who almost sets fire to himself when a club lands on his shoulder. The son watches and claps in time.

When the clubs burn out, the ringmaster leaves the tent again. The air smells of sulfur and hay. The tension mounts—and then suddenly an old man holding a cabbage appears from under a tent flap. Everyone laughs and the children shout his name. He raises his arms as if to say, "Where am I?" Then he holds up the tent flap he came through to reveal his garden gate.

Then the ringmaster returns with flaming hoops and a dog. He is startled to see an old man with a cabbage standing in the ring. His son starts drumming again, and the old man disappears back through the flap into the safety of his vegetable garden.

Both father and son spin the hoops with long sticks. The tent fills with even more smoke.

A few of the children start coughing.

The German toddler is crying and wants his parents.

In all the confusion, a small girl enters the little big-top and sits next to you. Her teeth are very white and her hair is unbrushed. She's wearing striped purple pajamas and sandals. You look down at her and she gives you a smile so false it's funny and you laugh. Her little face turns back to the action inside the ring. You look around for her parents, and then a man enters and sits down next to her. He is in his late forties, dressed in an old T-shirt and blue jeans. A few of the other parents wave to him.

He is wearing tortoiseshell glasses and is unshaved.

And then Rebecca walks in.

The little girl beside you signals to her. The ringmaster seems to notice her because she's beautiful. The man with the tortoiseshell glasses moves over and she sits down.

You cannot move any part of your body.

Her hair is much longer than you remember, but the same deep red that lightens in sun. She is wearing clothes you have never seen. Same freckles though—and each one exacts a breath from you.

The circus performers are riding tiny bicycles and carrying enormous cups on their heads.

Your eyes shoot backward as though your body is forcing you into sleep. Then your head starts to boil and you are sweating. Your stomach is churning. You are forced to turn away because your body is falling to pieces. And then thousands of remembered moments—like birds flapping their wings inside your skull.

The severed hand.

Dots of blood on the canvas.

Her body falling silently to the water.

You hover between the living and the dead.

But the dead cannot live again.

They cannot see, they cannot hear, they cannot breathe, they cannot talk. Their minds are empty, and they cannot have any thoughts.

Two clowns are standing in front of you, prodding your chest with a long sponge finger. The music is drowning everything, your eyes are rolling around and you can't see anything. The smaller clown is trying to drag you out into the ring. People are shouting.

Rebecca is looking at you. She's laughing and waving you out into the ring with the hands she once pressed against your bare chest.

Then you stand up, scream her name, and fall into a circle of waiting darkness at your feet.

FIFTY-SIX

Delphine jumps back in fright when the grown-up's eyes open quickly.

He is no longer where he fell.

She has been dabbing his head with a cloth soaked in witch hazel. The scent makes her nose twitch. The visitor is very still under heavy sheets but looks at her. Then when he looks at Mama, he tries to get up. Delphine steps back even farther. Then suddenly Sebastian is upon him.

"It's not Rebecca," he says to the stranger. "It's her sister, it's Rebecca's sister, Natalie."

The man lies down again, breathing hard as if he had just run somewhere fast but did it without moving his legs. Delphine looks for the drawing she made of him. Perhaps it will cheer him up.

Behind the bed is a picture of her, and another picture of Sebastian and Mama.

"Rebecca's sister is a twin?" he says as though he's trying to believe it.

"Oh, yes," Delphine wants to say. "A twin—oh yes—except that she is in heaven, with the angels and Napoleon."

The sheets were yesterday blowing on the line—blowing like sails little Delphine ran through on the grassy deck of her ship bound for circus island. The sheets puffed and glowed with noon.

And then it was lunchtime. Sigh. Time to stop and eat.

The strange man is looking at Mama again.

Delphine watches his eyes because grown-ups play games of secrets.

Like little white animals the man's eyes switch between old portraits that Sebastian found in the basement—and the face of Mama which is so still (like forgotten bath water) that it could be its own portrait if it wasn't connected to a body and the world.

The man looks afraid.

Perhaps he thinks we have kidnapped him?

What if we have, by accident? Would we all go to prison? Probably not before lunch though.

The radiator starts clanging and soon it will be hot, and the room full of hiss, like some little girl dreaming of snakes.

Delphine likes to pick the paint that peels in the corners where it gets damp, even though she knows it's naughty.

She hides the tiny paint people in a box that once held bon-bons and still smells like them (as if the box is remembering his lost friends).

Then she is distracted by the hanging chandelier.

All those cobwebs.

Maybe the visitor will think it's a beehive. Delphine wonders if that's where honey comes from and that it's high up so she won't get stinged.

She was stinged in the summer. Her arm has a mark that's too small to see, but it's there.

Then without thinking she steps toward the stranger and lifts her bare arm.

"I was stinged here," she says.

"You were stinged?" the man says with a lulling sweetness.

Delphine nods, "Yes, right here—do you believe me?"

"You speak English," the stranger says. "Just like Rebecca."

"Yes, I speak English," Delphine says. Then she points with

her elbow to the man sitting at the foot of the stranger's bed. "But Sebastian taught me, not my aunt."

The stranger is being very nice—maybe he prefers children to adults.

Tucked up in the white sheets reminds Delphine of her baby, her very own child, in the mouse village of secret plops in the hedge that stretches up bursting with birds who fly out chirp chirp chirp chirp chirp chirp—scaring everyone, especially the plastic mice who pretend tremble. Birds just don't know where they're going.

The man's eyes are big and sad.

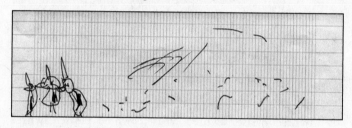

Plastic mice and their poisoning plops.

Delphine wonders if she is going to say: "I'll be your mother, little lost boy."

Then suddenly *he* says something to Mama.

"What's happening?"

Then he says:

"Where am I?"

Mama doesn't answer but glances at Sebastian.

"Our house," Sebastian says. "Her name is Natalie, I'm Sebastian, and this is our daughter Delphine," Sebastian says.

"Natalie?" The man says, exasperated, "Delphine?"

Will he cry?

Will he cry?

Sometimes grown-ups cry.

Sebastian steps over to the strange man's bedside. "Yes, Natalie. She is Rebecca's twin sister."

Sebastian's accent is sharp and heavy, East London, he told her once.

"Twin? Her twin?"

"You called her Rebecca," Sebastian says to the visitor. "That's why we brought you here."

The stranger closes his eyes.

"Who are you?"

"Henry Bliss," he says.

Delphine giggles but everyone ignores her. She is repeating his name in her head. She can't stop herself:

"Awnree please, awnree please, awnree please, awnree please."

She giggles again.

Sebastian turns to her with his finger held up to his lip, which means "I'm not mad but shush down now."

"What's happened?"

"You fainted," Mama says.

The man stares at her.

Delphine steps under her mother's arms and folds them over her little body.

"You knew my sister?" Mama says.

"She never mentioned that you were a twin. How could I not have known that?"

Delphine wonders who he is talking to. Should she say yes or no or *oui* or *non*? And then words just fall out of her small mouth.

"Maybe she forgot."

They all look at her without laughing.

Then the radiator starts banging again. There is no talking for a few moments, and then the radiator stops and Sebastian asks the stranger another question.

"But you knew she had a sister?"

"Of course," Henry Bliss replies.

Mama and Sebastian glance at one another quickly as if to pass a secret without saying it.

"Seems odd you didn't know she had a twin," Sebastian says.

"Do you know what happened to her?" Mama asks slowly. Her face is shaking.

"Yes," the stranger says very quickly. "Do you?"

Sebastian nods. "We got a letter from the French embassy in Greece. She had registered with them when she went to live there—all French nationals have to."

"When did you know her?" Mama asks.

"When?"

"Yes."

"In Athens."

"You weren't with her then?" Mama says.

Delphine looks at her mother to explain it all carefully, but her mother is purposefully ignoring her as if to say "Don't ask now because even though I'm not talking, it's still interrupting."

Henry Bliss doesn't answer.

"As I said, we brought you here," Sebastian said quietly, "because you said the name Rebecca before you fainted."

Delphine imagines Mama and Sebastian's questions softly raining down upon his head like pillow feathers.

"Were you in Athens for the earthquake?" Mama asks softly.

Delphine feels her mother's whole body behind her.

Her eyes have begun to take in light.

"I couldn't get to her in time . . ."

"In time?" Sebastian asks without moving his head. His eyes study the stranger carefully, as though waiting for the right moment to pounce on the truth.

"Before her building collapsed."

Mama starts crying.

"How long did you know her, Henry?" Sebastian says, but gently.

"Long enough to love her."

Then Mama runs out, but Delphine is rooted to the spot.

Sebastian sighs and puts his hands in his pockets. After a long silence, he says: "If you're up to it, Henry—why don't you get dressed and come down for lunch. Delphine will get you a towel and there's a bath down the hall."

"How long was I sleeping?"

"Almost fourteen hours. We even had the local doctor examine you while you were passed out."

"What did he say?"

"He said you probably needed a good kip and that you should probably drink more water, but all French doctors say that."

Delphine rushes off to find the towel.

"Why did you come here, Henry? To tell us?"

Henry sighs and turns to the window.

Outside it's very green. The whistling of birds across the panes, a song only slightly muted by the uneven squares of glass.

"To see——" Henry says.

"Go on," Sebastian says.

"To see, if she had a family. Where is her grandfather?"

"He died about a year and a half ago. Natalie was living in Paris. It was before I met her actually."

Then banging from upstairs.

"It's Delphine," Sebastian says chuckling. "The towels must be on a high shelf and she's trying to get them. Let's take a walk after lunch, Henry Bliss."

"Okay."

"Be nice to get out in the fresh air."

FIFTY-SEVEN

You sit opposite Natalie and sip green soup. There is a clock ticking loudly from the mantelpiece, as if counting down to something. Natalie keeps looking at you. Her beauty is breathtaking. She's a little bigger than her sister, or an older version, but the eyes and cheekbones are the same. She holds her spoon with the same delicacy, between finger and thumb. You want to set your spoon in the bowl and grovel at her feet. You have to keep telling yourself that it's not her, it's not Rebecca, and that you must go on. You feel the sudden urge to leave, to stand up and run out. Watching Natalie eat is a strange form of torture, as it reminds you how wonderful your life will never be.

On the table is a shopping list. The handwriting is almost identical to the handwriting in the diary, but they were twins after all. It could still be Rebecca's child.

Then Sebastian asks where you are from, and you're telling him when suddenly Delphine bursts in wearing a bathing suit and ballet slippers. She's also carrying a plastic whale.

"Delphine, go upstairs and change," her mother says.

Sebastian smiles and puts down his spoon.

"Am I fancy enough for the circus?" Delphine says, looking at you.

Then Delphine begins to dance.

"Delphine!" her mother cries, and the little girl dances out of the kitchen and up the stairs. Sebastian laughs and Natalie glares at him.

"*Qu'est-ce que tu fais, Sebastian?*"

He nods and then gets up.

"Your soup is getting cold, circus girl!" he shouts up the stairs. "*Vite, vite.*"

Then Sebastian looks at you. "Funny, eh? Kids."

"You got any brothers or sisters, Henry?"

You set down your spoon.

"I had a brother," you say. "But he died when he was a baby."

"Sorry," Sebastian says.

When Delphine comes down Sebastian is washing lettuce.

"The soup is cold now," her mother says.

"I had to pee."

After lunch, Natalie stacks plates in the sink. Sebastian takes a pack of cigarettes from the drawer. Delphine sees them.

"*Non, non, non, non,* Sebastian! No smoking, remember?"

"In the house, Delphine—no smoking in the house."

"You shouldn't smoke, Sebastian!—it could make you die."

"Let's take a walk," he says, touching your arm. "I'll show you around."

Sebastian steps into a pair of Wellington boots and hands you a heavy black walking stick with a silver owl at the top.

"Found this in the house when I was renovating."

Delphine wants to come but her mother takes her upstairs.

You step out the front door into a country lane. The hedge-rows rise up on each side. Blackberries stud the leaves and branches. There are birds flying high above you.

"So you were Rebecca's boyfriend in Athens?" Sebastian says.

"Yes, exactly."

"Natalie still gets upset about it."

You nod in understanding, then walk in silence for a kilo-meter or so.

"Forgive me for asking this," Sebastian says. "But is there an-other reason you came here?"

A few white cows on the hillside eat their way across pas-ture. The air smells of grass and manure.

"To see if she had family."

"Not to fall in love with her all over again?"

You say nothing because it's true. Then your mouth is full of words, and impulsively you confess to Sebastian that Rebecca was pregnant.

He stops walking and touches your arm.

"With your child?"

You nod.

He seems more disturbed than you would have thought.

Neither of you move.

After a few moments, Sebastian seems like he wants to ask you something, but then shakes his head.

"What's done is done," he says. "I'm glad you told me—it won't go any further, I promise."

You walk for a long time without speaking.

The road gets very narrow. Sebastian explains that it was built for horses and small traps. Then he points out a truck stop café where Natalie and Rebecca worked when they were teenagers.

You remember the journal but say nothing. You don't know what to think and consider that you will never know whose child Delphine really is—that you'll never know whose feelings they were. To find out could cost the happiness of a little girl who is loved and knows nothing of the tragedy that defines you.

"When I arrived here," Sebastian explains, "the village was almost deserted. There was no work for the young, really, and so the elderly either died alone in the village or moved to nursing homes in the cities, closer to their kids."

"But how did you end up here?"

"By literally crashing into it—into a stone wall, actually."

Sebastian stops walking and drinks in the air with long, deep breaths.

"Earlier that day," he went on, "I had taken drugs in a quiet corner of Gare du Nord in Paris, and then, in a sort of calm stupor, I climbed into a Mercedes that some foolish twat had left running outside the station.

"Does that surprise you?" Sebastian asks.

"A little," you say.

He is walking quickly now. You walk alongside him, listening, searching his story for a wisdom you can relate to.

"I drove and drove, not knowing where I was going, but just driving. Then I must have turned off the highway and begun driving through the countryside around here. And then at some point, I crashed into a wall in the village."

"A few hours later at dawn I awoke covered in glass and partially crushed by the stones that had fallen through the windshield. And if you think all that is far-fetched, then listen to this, Henry. I stepped from the car and fell in love."

Sebastian stops walking again and spreads his arms.

"With all this dereliction, I found myself enchanted."

Sebastian is much older than you thought.

He has a brother with Down syndrome that he wants to move in with them eventually. Then you both come upon an abandoned barn. The walls are slanted gray stone with hanging moss.

Sebastian leans on a gate and lights a cigarette.

Chickens dot the yard, pecking around a battered Mercedes they're using as a coup. All the windows are missing. The front end is also completely smashed in. A sign on the top says:

TAXI

PARISIEN

Sebastian laughs.

"The shiny paint gives it away," you tell him.

"Chicken shit will take care of that pretty soon," he laughs. "That part of my life is long gone."

Sebastian walks you around the barn, pointing out birds' nests, beehives, low bushy green squares covered with wire that mark the beginning of his organic vegetable business.

"Anyway, to cut a long story short, I bought a derelict house for €15,000, did it up, and then opened a little café, which I only do now in the summer—Delphine is the waitress, if you can imagine that—I have an old espresso machine and of course Coca-Cola and fizzy drinks for the kids. And I met Natalie when one day she came into my café when she was down from the Paris suburbs with Delphine, trying to sell her grandfather's house. But the house couldn't be sold."

"Why?"

"Mold—it's close to a lake and somehow the water has seeped underneath and the whole place is fucked. But it's a big part of her life, you know—it's where she and her sister grew up, so even though it's a wreck, it would upset her to get rid of it completely—so it's just standing. I'll take you to see it if you want."

You nod, but then you think you wouldn't like to see it.

As you step through tall grass toward a gate, you decide to burn the journal. You're still not sure who wrote it. You'll never be sure and don't care anymore.

Delphine is a happy child—and truth is just a lie that everyone believes.

Sebastian holds the gate open and tells you about the British Spitfire plane he found in the woods behind the house. He said that it was hidden there by the Résistance during the war after it crash-landed in a muddy field. Once his organic vegetable business is in full swing, he's going to buy the parts for it and get it airborne, teach Delphine how to fly, he says.

After crossing a few grassy meadows, you see Sebastian's tall house in the distance. The shutters are painted white. Clouds drift beyond the roof.

"Did the house come with the café?" you ask him.

"That's a secret," he laughs. "We didn't buy it from anyone—we just live in it."

"Do you know who it belongs to?"

"I do," Sebastian says. "A family that left after the war for Paris because they were collaborators."

"Do you know anything about Rebecca's mother?"

"I do, as a matter of fact," Sebastian says.

"Is she in Paris?"

"Yes. How did you know that?"

"Rebecca told me."

"Natalie doesn't know," Sebastian admits.

"Know what?"

"That I went to see her."

"Is it true she abandoned her children?"

"It is—and it's lucky for them she did."

"Why?"

"She's got something—a mental thing—same as what her mother had."

"Rebecca's grandmother?"

"Yeah—she killed herself in the lake when Rebecca's mother was a little girl."

FIFTY-EIGHT

The next morning, you wake and go downstairs. It's getting cold. Fall is coming. A bright nest of fire crackles and spits in the stone fireplace. Sebastian is outside splitting wood with a long-handled axe.

A cat stops eating and looks up at you. Before you can pet it, you hear purring.

You decide to take a walk before breakfast, to stretch your legs and feel the morning wash through you.

You don't want to see Natalie anymore. She's a stranger dressed in the clothes of someone you once loved. It's impossible to love someone after they've died. And that's why it hurts so much.

Maybe tomorrow you'll go back to Wales.

You step into your shoes and leave quietly by the back door. You turn the handle very gently. The morning air is cold. A shallow mist lingers low across the fields.

You pass Sebastian's vegetable patch and climb over a gate into empty pasture.

Then you hear, "Oh, Henry!"

You look over a short hedge.

"It's Delphine!" says a young voice.

"Yes, I recognize you."

You climb over a gate and join her on the other side.

"I have a surprise for you," she says.

"Really?"

"Yes, really."

"Why are you awake so early, Delphine?"

"Oh, I like to get up early," she says. "So does Sebastian, but Mama sleeps all morning and sometimes keeps him in bed, which is so boring."

She pulls a piece of baguette from her pocket and hands it to you.

"Breakfast," she says.

"Can we share it?" you say.

"No, that's yours—I have these," she says, taking a handful of blueberries from her pocket. Delphine is wrapped in a double-breasted black wool coat, mittens, and a woolen hat. However, underneath the coat she is still wearing pajamas, which she's tucked into her Wellingtons. The pajamas have cartoon frogs on them.

"Have you come to let all the frogs go?"

"Frogs?"

"On your pajamas."

Delphine looks down at her leg.

"No, I need those."

She points at holes in the mud she has carved out with a spoon. "Do you like mice?"

"I love mice," you say.

"Well, Sebastian doesn't, which is why I've made them a home here."

"In the mud?"

"It's where they're happiest."

Delphine leans down and takes one of the plastic mice from its hiding place. It's about the size of your thumb. It has a brown face with a painted-on shirt and tie.

"Does he like it here?"

"It's his home—give me your hand."

You let her take it.

"Can I put your hand in his den?"

"If you'd like."

"You don't mind?"

"No, I don't mind."

"What about mouse plops?"

"Mouse plops?" you say.

"What if there are mouse plops?"

"From him?" you add, pointing at the plastic mouse.

"And his kids."

"It's okay," you say.

"Sebastian said they're bad. I got in trouble. He yelled."

"Mouse plops?"

"Yes, if you touch them—they're poisoning, Sebastian said."

"There are plops in here?"

"Give me your hand, Awnree. Please."

She grips your hand again and guides it down to the tiny hollow in the mud. She puts your hand in and steps back.

"Can you feel them?"

"Who?"

"Not who—the plops."

"Delphine," you say, turning to her, "there are no plops in here."

"No mouse's plops?" she says.

"Can I see that mouse?" you say.

Delphine hands you the mouse. You turn it over and sniff his bottom.

"Delphine, this sort of mouse doesn't plop—and so there are no plops in there."

A look of wild joy on her face.

"Want to play?"

"I'm going for a walk."

"Where are you going?"

"I really don't know."

"Want a blueberry?"

"Okay."

She takes one out of her pocket and gives it to you.

"These mice don't even make plops!" She laughs. Then she takes out another blueberry and eats it herself.

You thank her for the blueberry when her face suddenly darkens. She sticks her fingers into her mouth as if she's trying to make herself sick.

Her eyes bulge with terror and confusion.

Her mouth opens and closes—as if she is singing, but no sound comes out.

You grab her shoulders.

"What's wrong?" you say sternly, shaking her. "Delphine! What's wrong!"

The lines of muscle in her neck are visible.

Her tongue is lolling in and out of her mouth.

You frantically position your clenched fists under her ribcage. Her small body lifts easily and she flies forward— dropping the plastic mouse clenched between her fingers. Her hat and one of her gloves comes off. You position her again— then violently thrust under her ribcage.

Her face is purple.

Her body flies up like a doll, but whatever you're doing is not working.

Then another thrust, and something shoots from her mouth. She is suddenly on the ground, coughing, retching—taking very deep breaths. She spies her mouse in the grass and slowly reaches for him. Then she lies on the ground with her eyes open wide.

You pull her toward you and hold on tight. You rock her gently.

She is touching the outside of her throat.

At that moment it starts to rain.

She looks at you and smiles.

"We'll get wet," she says.

Then, she pushes off and stands looking at you, not saying thank you, but there's something in her eyes that tells you she understands what happened. Water is running down her face, and you don't realize it immediately, but she's crying.

You watch her disappear toward the house, then get up very slowly. You are covered in mud.

Crows bark in the trees.

Every fiber in your body tingles. You are in the place that was meant for you. Everything had to be arranged like this to get you here.

And you were ready.

It's something you feel, like a weight in both hands; it's the faith that embodies God but incorporates logic.

And there are hands we live between that open and close.

Once aligned there is nothing to fear.

And the tapping of rain in the fields is the tapping of footsteps passing.

You are breathing again. You are with form.

FIFTY-NINE

When you go back to the house to find your car keys, Delphine
is in the garden throwing handfuls of blueberries from a bowl.
Sebastian is trying to take the bowl, but she's screaming and
screaming. Natalie is laughing from an upstairs window. Birds
are swooping into the narrow spears of grass as blueberries fly
from small, determined hands. Hands that are forever yours.

You grab your keys and hurry back outside in the direction
of the village.

There is mud splattered along one side of the Audi where
cars and tractors have passed in the rain. You grab the journal
off the backseat and stuff it into the glove box, and then lock it.
You switch on your mini-satellite fax machine and it immediately starts buzzing and flashing with messages. You hold down
the reset button. The machine stills. You rip a piece of paper
from the journal but can't find a pen. Then you notice the typewriter sitting on the backseat.

DEAR GEORGE

YOU WERE RIGHT ABOUT WHAT YOU
SAID ON THE BOAT TO AEGINA.

THERE ARE NO MISTAKES

COMING TO SEE YOU IN SICILY
AFTER I'VE SAID A FEW GOODBYES
HERE IN LINIERES-~~BOUTE~~ BOUTON

SHOULD ARRIVE TOMORROW.

MEET ME IN THE MAIN SQUARE OF
YOUR VILLAGE IN THE AFTERNOON.

I LOV E AND MISS YOU

    HENRY

P.S. I'M LEAVING THE TYPEWRITER HERE.
    IT WILL ONLY WRITE IN CAPS NOW,
~~AS*IF*TO*SAY*~~ SO I FEEL LIKE I'M SHOUTING

When you turn the car on, the voice says:

آمل ان يكون نهارك سعيداً. أين تريد أن تذهب؟

You lean down and kiss the screen.

SIXTY

Heavy clouds drifting.

You circle like Daedalus, the doomed father of Icarus.

And then you realize it's not cloud, but smoke from an ancient fire.

Your plane cuts the silent plume of Mount Etna. From the mouth of a volcano a white scarf is unfurling.

By the time Daedalus arrived in Sicily, his child had already fallen into the sea. You look down and imagine two feathered wings, each the length of an arm.

The city of Catania.

It shimmers from above like coins in the rocks.

Waiting for your suitcase everyone stares at one another.

A child is watching you as the belt shudders forward. She is inching toward it. She wants to touch. Her father puts down his cell phone and calls out to her.

"Valeria! Valeria!"

She pretends not to hear.

She is wearing eyeglasses and HELLO KITTY earrings.

Her shoes have glitter in the straps. She is here for the summer in the place where her father was a boy. Her doll will be given new clothes by a grandmother in black. She'll try certain foods for the first time and like them. Everyone will clap because it's the food of her people. She looks at you without smiling and tries to guess which suitcase is yours.

Without speaking you have become friends. You are talking with your eyes. You will never get to know one another. You will never even share a coffee or a fire or a book about the sea or any other moment, except the one right now that is this moment.

And then you realize that you are thinking the way you used to.

When you were Valeria's age, you had the flint in your hands.

Your mind is unreeling all the history you can fathom.

Dinosaurs pull leaves from the tree above the shed. The sky echoes with the leathery snap of pterodactyl.

You run toward the house.

Your parents are watching television.

The excitement is pouring from you.

Your pants are wet because you waited to pee.

You hold up the rock.

It's the greatest moment of your life. You smile at the little girl and her father.

Dreamers conquered the world long ago.

SIXTY-ONE

You are in a small Sicilian taxi. The interior is dusty—a bag of flour burst open.

The past is a mess of lines, like a sketch seen from afar.

Our perception of the future is the past in disguise.

The driver is taking you to Noto.

The driver taps the steering wheel and whistles softly through his teeth.

Our greatest power in subtle, momentary gestures.

For a land of rolling yellow fields, clear seas, and heavy baked rock—Sicily's human history is a violent one. Myths of dismemberment, towns growing from slits where limbs were swallowed by the earth, countless invaders, earthquakes, volcanoes, and battles—those early lessons in human anatomy.

You see water in the distance, a blue unblinking eye peeking over the hills.

To Sicilians you are another invader. You have come to learn—to take away knowledge. Like Odysseus, you are a single soul with the burden of ages.

Sicily was a gateway to the underworld. It was where Orpheus came to find Eurydice.

You have been dropped in the main square.

There are trees everywhere.

People huddle in their shadows.

We see in others what we want and what we fear.

Close to the square there is a fountain of many streams. A cage of water. To get there, you must perish in the heat.

People wander through the park. There are stone heads on blocks. Their features have worn away. But even the faceless dead of these stone men have shadows as real as anyone living. Like the Sicilian people themselves, the statues defy their historical disfigurement with a dignity foreigners will never understand.

You will one day dissolve in the earth or in fire.

And the trees are bursting with life, but their leaves are frayed at the edges.

You are sitting on a bench in Sicily, in the town of Noto, where George lives.

Once destroyed by an earthquake and then rebuilt.

After every chapter of devastation, there is rebuilding.

It happens without thought.

It happens even when there is no guarantee it won't happen again.

Humans may come and go—but the thread of hope is like a rope we pull ourselves up with.

And the sky is an open mouth. The streets of Noto are busy. People drain into the piazzas from the alleys—they negotiate their town in measured steps like hands on a clock. Their lives are the same but always different.

In a square cornered by a baroque church and a *gelateria*, you can see someone you know sitting on a bench and your body breaks with joy. He has been waiting for you.

He is wearing the clothes you last remember him in: linen trousers and a white shirt with a tie in a Windsor knot. Blue blazer, despite the heat.

He sees you and rushes over.

You both stand and look—two people separated only by the girth of everything they have to say.

Then he is upon you, all arms.

He is the first person you have hugged in years. Sicilians may not be particularly welcoming—but public shows of emotion are met with passionate approval.

You hold one another and recreate an ancient tableaux.

You look for shadows but see only the stone beneath, worn by centuries of footfall, centuries of pursuit and aspiration, centuries of worry that came to nothing.

He is certainly more handsome. His face is in two halves now, darker and more chiseled. When your bodies separate, you sit down on a bench.

There is a resolve in his voice you have never heard before. And then bells of the church come to life and shower you with hollow tones.

Three hours later you are sitting in his kitchen. The table is light blue. His café-style chairs are bright red. He is stuffing two fish—*spigola*—with dried oregano and salt. The fish in his hand is a silver muscle, a flash of life.

You start telling him about all the flights you took. The fish makes a wet sound when he sets it on the wooden cutting board. There is blood on his hand.

You are drinking fizzy water from a tall glass with white lines. There is a pair of scales on the fridge. There is also a calendar on the wall. There are several cats in the apartment. They are thin and their fur is coarse and uneven. They are the strays of the town. George tells you that he feeds them regularly.

On the walk back to his apartment from the square, you asked about the professor and his work in Turkey. You listened attentively. You can't wait to see him. George carried your case and gave every beggar a coin. And he moved with the air of someone who is happy.

"Sicily is the gateway to the underworld," he said.

You know he can sense the emotional void inside you—for his new love echoes in your abandoned house.

He is working now as a professor. He teaches American exchange students. He has aged, you can see that, and he is still sober—which is a relief.

George tells you more about his wife. She is not here tonight, he says. She is with her mother. But tomorrow her brothers will bring her home from her village of Francofonte. She is excited to meet you. He can't stop telling you how beautiful she is.

He has fallen too, but in the opposite way.

SIXTY-TWO

Like the armies that once landed here in wooden ships, you had been prepared to invade George's world with the endless narrative of journey.

But when you feel the lines of words poised and ready to fall in breathlike blows from you mouth, you feel only the soothing emptiness of this hot island, this "hollow ball of fire," and the words age in your mouth and turn to crumbs and then ash.

Perhaps in dreams these words will come to life again— once they are splashed with sleep.

George leaves the table once during dinner to get a plate for bones.

After you have eaten, you wipe your hands with the halves of lemons. On a tall wooden sideboard with glass doors, there is a photo of a sad old man. George sees you looking.

"My father remarried."

"Your father?"

"To a woman from Nigeria. They were just here—my mother came too with her boyfriend, same one she's had for years."

George has become everything that he was capable of, while you have been ravaged.

Later you wander the streets outside his apartment talking.

You tell him everything.

George asks where the journal is.

"It's in my case."

He wants to see it.

"You don't think the child should have it?" he says.

"No. Do you?"

"No. What good would it do?"

"I was going to burn it, but I thought we could leave it in the sea."

"We can," George says. "If that's what you want."

Then you eat *granita di caffè* from plastic cups.

He orders two bottles of water. Sobriety suits him. There is an effortless elegance in him the locals admire. He tells you he's building a library for his department. He asks if you can help fill it, if you can find things to go in it. He tells you he wants knowledge to be given to others. You think he will soon become a father.

He is full of the breath that brings life to empty places.

You are hatching from the past.

Glimpses of light, of feelings, thoughts, and ideas, wait to be discovered again.

No . . . not discovered, but appreciated.

The time of discovery has finished for you.

Your life now is the appreciation of all that is good—all that is worth living for. And you embrace life and its inevitable end like hands joined in prayer.

Your stillness is no longer despair but patience.

Your grief is something to be admired—the pain of severance. A scar where something used to be.

To love again, you must not discard what has happened to you, but take from it the strength you'll need to carry on.

END OF BOOK THREE

Love is most nearly itself
When here and now cease to matter.

—T. S. Eliot

BOOK FOUR

SIXTY-THREE

Henry Bliss finally woke up in the late morning.

He opened his eyes and for a moment was unable to place himself. Then he remembered that he was in Sicily, in a small town.

Through the old lace curtains above his bed, morning seemed especially clear.

Then the sound of George laughing.

Then talking.

As Henry dressed, he noticed that George had left a shirt and tie out for him on the inside door handle.

Henry knotted a four-in-hand and hurried into the living room.

George replaced the telephone handset.

"That was my wife," he said. "Are you hungry?"

Under a plastic umbrella, George and Henry ate Sicilian hamburgers of horsemeat with ketchup and mayonnaise from a burger van.

They talked in depth about Professor Peterson and his new project in Turkey—and then about how George and his wife, Kristina, were planning to visit him there for Christmas.

Then suddenly, the sound of a cannon firing. Henry jumped in his seat. George chewed. It was another wedding, he explained. There was one almost every day in the summer. Another deafening boom resounded through the town.

George described his own wedding. The brass band that followed them through the piazza. The trailing families, then tourists at the rear, enchanted by the public custom of a Sicilian marriage.

A few birds passed over their heads, perching finally on a headless statue at the edge of the square.

Then George asked Henry why he had really come to Sicily.

Henry's gaze rolled over the uneven terra-cotta roofs.

"I suppose I don't know. I wanted to see you, of course—but I don't know why beyond that. It was saving Delphine from choking that finally got me here. But I don't know why."

"Sometimes it takes a while," George said. Then he admitted that his love for Rebecca was different than Henry's—a truth he realized only after he met Kristina.

"Back then, I just wanted someone I could care about—and who cared about me—isn't that silly?"

"Not if you've never had it, George."

George smiled. "Well, I've got it now and more. Are you happy for me?"

"Blissful," Henry said.

"Why don't you stay a month then?"

"Why?"

"Because it's probably the last time you'll ever have the freedom to stay somewhere for a month on a total whim."

Henry nodded appreciatively. He would have to call his parents. They would protest and he would have to convince them he's feeling better or has found work.

"How did you meet your wife, George?"

"She drove over my foot here in the piazza."

"Is that how you meet everyone, George? They run you over."

George laughed. "You'll see."

Then a man came over with a small Tupperware box. He shook the box and George dropped a coin into it. And then another cannon shot boomed through the town, and the sky was a tangle of birds—like seeds thrown against blue porcelain.

The street was beginning to fill up.

"Let's go to a café in the very center of town for coffee. It's where I told Kristina we'd meet her."

George stood up and waved to the tall man clearing tables. He was wearing a plastic apron and had a long nose. The man shouted something and waved them off.

"He's been here for decades," George said. "He does a roaring trade, but will never open an actual shop. It's just not the way they do things here."

In the distance, down the Via Luca, a brass band played.

Henry laughed. "Is it the same one that played at your wedding?"

"It is," George said. "It's like so much here—unsophisticated but sincere."

They walked in silence for a little while, and then George said, "I know what you're thinking."

Henry turned and looked curiously at his friend.

"You're wondering how I can live here," George admitted.

Henry smiled. "I don't think I want to know."

"You couldn't live here, could you?"

"No, I couldn't," Henry said. "But I didn't know why until I saw you."

"Oh?" George remarked.

"Because I need more than love."

George smiled. "Is it that obvious?"

The brass band in the distance was getting closer. A teenager with one arm passed quickly at a trot, beating his only fist in the air to the blasting trumpets.

George stopped walking. The brass band was suddenly upon them, going in the opposite direction.

The off-key trumpet players were at the back, and the procession was trailed by babies being pushed in strollers, a suited man walking alone with flowers, friends, family, endless cousins, a gang of young children—two of whom were dressed for a mock wedding—and then finally, two carabinieri in blue uniforms, trailed by a clothes rack on wheels with rows of inflatable Spider-Man helium balloons.

George led Henry to a café in the center of the village, and they sat down.

Before the waiter came to take their order, several children who had been sitting quietly on the steps stood up and called over to George, who pretended to ignore them.

"I think those children are calling you," Henry said.

"Try and ignore them," George whispered.

"They look persistent."

"Don't make eye contact. If you do then we're finished."

"I think I already have because they're coming over."

"Oh dear."

They came over in a small pack, saying "Ciao, ciao, ciao, ciao, ciao, ciao" in a church voice to the tourists they brushed past at the rickety tables set up on the cobbles in front of the café.

They surrounded George and Henry like a band of outlaws.

"*Questo è il mio amico Henry,*" George said, presenting his friend. The children smiled respectfully.

Then one of the smaller children said, "Welcome, old man!"

George reluctantly raised his hand to the waiter, and the children cheered. The waiter cheered too, and the children ran off into the café and emerged a few minutes later—each with a cone of gelato.

"Just when I think I've lost them," George said. "They pop up somewhere."

"Who?"

"Those little bastards," he said pointing. They see him gesture in their direction, but their mouths are too full to say *grazie*, so they wave the same way George waves when saying good-bye to people.

"You're going to be an amazing father one day, George."

George shrugged. It was a new habit of his that Henry noticed was particular to the Sicilians.

And then the brass band appeared again—this time going in the other direction, and fighting with a larger crowd of people.

Henry noticed a woman in a wheelchair behind George's chair, about to get swallowed up by the procession.

"Excuse me for a moment," Henry said.

The woman smiled when she saw him.

"Thanks so much," she said in a heavy Italian accent.

The wheelchair handles were made of ostrich leather. The chair was a handsome dark green.

"You speak English?" Henry said.

"Of course I do."

"Sorry," Henry said, not really knowing why.

"I'm the one who is sorry," she remarked, "for not being here to meet you yesterday."

"Kristina?"

"Oh, Henry. Isn't that why you came over?"

"No."

"George was right then," she said. "I *am* going to have a crush on you."

SIXTY-FOUR

After some fresh coffee, Kristina said she wanted to cool down in the sea.

"Wait until you see our car," George said, signaling to the waiter.

"My husband loves his car more than he loves his wife."

"This must be some car," Henry said. Then he took out some bills.

"I have a tab," George said. "Keep your money."

"Don't argue with him," Kristina said. "For someone who grew up rich, he's very generous."

"Well, thank you, Signora Cavendish," George said, slightly embarrassed.

"I just meant to say that you're kind."

"I know," he assured her with a wink. "Let's not argue in front of Henry."

Henry took the handles of her chair. The lanes of the town were warm.

George carried her up the stairs to the front door. She talked to Henry the whole time. George looked tired but didn't say anything. They all freshened up, and in an hour were outside again. George wheeled his wife toward a row of garages that faced their 1930s apartment building.

"For my wedding present," George said, "I finally took my father up on his guilty need to buy me things."

George fiddled with a rusty padlock and then slid open the garage door. The front end of a deep green automobile glinted where the sunlight reached inside the open door. Henry brushed his fingers along the headlight.

"It's not an E-type, is it?" Henry said.

"But that's not why it's special," George added. "Of course, 1966 E-type Jaguars are unique—but this is truly a one-of-a-kind, modified by Jaguar at the factory to accommodate Kristina's chair."

"A bespoke E-type? You've certainly gone up in the world, George."

"They changed my chair too," Kristina said, "to bolt in next to my husband."

Henry and Kristina waited outside the garage as George started the engine and slowly pulled forward into the light. The hood was enormously long.

In George's absence, Henry and Kristina looked at one another with a simple, unspoken appreciation for the parts they had played in the life of a man they both loved.

The engine fired and spat.

George got out and unfolded a ramp. Kristina positioned herself at the foot of it and George pushed her up. Then he clamped the chair to chrome bars that held the chair in place.

"Amazing," Henry said. "It's so quick."

Henry clambered into the very small backseat behind Kristina as she brushed strands of blond hair from her face. Then she helped George find his sunglasses.

Like many vintage automobiles, the seats carried the particular odor of leather, oil, and wood that had been cooking under glass for decades. The streets they negotiated were only wide enough for traffic to proceed one way. People waved from chairs set in doorways. The car was very loud.

"They all know me," George shouted above the engine. "She has a peculiar throatiness, doesn't she?"

"She?" Kristina shouted.

"His other wife," Henry pointed out.

As they neared a tunnel, two cars swerved around them, narrowly avoiding a head-on collision with an oncoming truck. Vespa scooters overtook on the inside, raising small clouds of dust. Their passengers bounced along unperturbed.

"If you consider that the driving is largely unregulated—it's actually civil," George shouted above the engine.

Behind them a small Fiat roared at its engine's full capacity— inches away from the antique Jaguar. Henry turned around to see a middle-aged man with a perfectly calm face, close enough for Henry to tell that he needed a shave. The man nodded hello. Henry waved.

"The Italians don't really like to be alone—even when they're driving," shouted George. "And I love that about them."

"He's always talking about 'the Italians,'" Kristina said.

"What do you do for work?" Henry shouted to her.

"Cardiologist," she shouted back.

"That's interesting."

"Yes," she said. "I love it. I work mostly in hospice."

George turned down a small, dusty road that didn't seem to lead anywhere. Flowering oleander that lined the narrow lane was coated with white dust. As the road condition deteriorated, George slowed to a crawl.

"When I was at boarding school," he said, "I never dreamed I'd be driving an English E-type with my two best friends somewhere in the Mediterranean." He turned and looked at Henry. "And so happy after everything we've been through."

"You've come a long way since then," Henry said.

Kristina nodded. "Yes, he has—I'm very proud of him."

Henry smiled, wondering how much George had told her.

The road ended in a mess of cars parked crookedly against a stone wall. Henry could neither see the water nor hear it.

A scatter of children climbed the wall and then set off along a narrow path with bags and chairs.

It had been many years since Henry had walked on sand.

George parked at a distance from the other cars. Henry asked Kristina if they wanted to be parents, but then quickly regretted it—suddenly conscious that somehow it was beyond her physically.

George pulled up the handbrake. "If it happens it happens."

Then he took up his wife's hand.

"I'm just happy we're together. That's the main thing. That's enough for me."

"We don't know yet if I can," Kristina admitted, turning to George. "But we hope, don't we?"

"Would you raise them in Italy?"

"Right here in Noto," George said firmly.

The sunlight was very bright, and fell evenly upon the ground, washing everything with a bright glaze. The path to the beach looked narrow and rocky.

"How far is it?" Henry asked. George was unbolting his wife's chair.

"About a five-minute walk," he said without looking up. "Not too far—would you grab the bag of towels in the trunk?"

Henry nodded. He sensed a tension in George's voice and again regretted bringing up the idea of children.

"We have grapes somewhere in a brown paper bag," Kristina said.

Kristina unbuckled from her seat as George unfolded the ramp and lined up the wheels of her chair with two grooves in the door frame. When she was out of the car, George folded everything back up and bent down to lift her. She kissed him once and then reached her arms around his neck.

"Do me a favor, Henry, and put her chair in the car, would you?" George asked.

"You're going to carry her all the way?" Henry said.

"I am," George replied. "I always do—it saves me from having to join a gym."

"Stop it," Kristina said. "And concentrate—I don't want to be dropped."

"Stop what?" George answered with an exaggerated innocence.

"Stop teasing."

"Who am I teasing?"

"Me."

"I love carrying you," he insisted.

"No, you don't."

"Yes, I do."

"Why?"

She turned to Henry. "This will be good."

Henry put down the heavy canvas bag of beach towels.

"It's simple," George said. "I need to be needed."

Kristina glanced up at Henry.

"It's actually true," she said. "It's his only flaw."

When they were halfway, George stopped to maneuver Kristina onto his back. He stepped carefully past low thick plants and the occasional jutting rock. The sky was a heavy blue, and the sun weighed down mercilessly upon them.

When they arrived at the beach, people were camped in groups—huddling in the shade under cotton umbrellas. The water was very still and of a light brown tint. Children splashed laughing. Old men slept under wide-brim hats.

In the distance, rocks rose up against the horizon. Some people had swum out to them with snorkels. Kristina said the plants that grew on the rocks attracted fish and other forms of life.

After George drove the umbrella into the sand, they lay on brown towels and ate grapes. Kristina was wearing an orange bathing suit, with a towel folded over her legs.

"I still can't bring myself to go out there," George said.

Kristina touched Henry's arm.

"We're so glad you came," she said.

"She's right, Henry, we don't have to talk about it," George sighed. "I'm sorry for bringing it up."

Henry lifted a corner of the towel to dry his eyes.

"I'm glad you said it, actually," Henry admitted. "I'm glad you said it because I was terrified you were going to ask me to go swimming." After saying this he cried a bit more, and then he laughed.

Before leaving, Henry watched George carry his wife to the water. She screamed as they entered the sea. It must have been cold on her legs. George didn't flinch. He bore her weight with the poise of the truly devoted.

It was very hot on the sand. People strolled by looking at Henry, not rudely, but as if they wondered who he was.

Henry carried Kristina on his back to the car. George trailed with the bag of towels making comments about an ancient ruin in the distance.

They slept away what remained of the afternoon.

At dusk, George entered Henry's room with a glass of water.

"We like to dress up for dinner, Henry, if you don't mind— just for fun, you understand."

"Dress up? Like in animal costumes?"

"No." He grinned. "Kristina is wearing a dress and I put on a tie—it's very Italian."

"I'm not sure I have—"

"Borrow something else of mine—though my shirts might be too big for you. I can't believe you've traveled with only these things for two years—it's almost religious."

"Don't worry," Henry said. "I have plenty of other baggage."

Over dinner, they opened the doors to the long balcony that ran along the edge of the apartment.

The sound of life from the street below filled the house.

Insects chirped and hissed from tall palms nodding over the piazza.

They talked about many things. Kristina explained how the heart works, the miracle of electricity and valves, chambers, arteries, and veins.

George gulped glasses of cold water. Then Kristina wheeled herself to the sideboard for the wedding album.

It was still quite hot and they were all sweating.

"So what's next, Henry?"

"I don't know. I'm broke."

"I can lend you some money. But on the condition you stay with us for a while."

Henry nodded. "I actually think I'd like that."

"Bravo!" Kristina exclaimed from across the room. "I'd love it too."

"Stop eavesdropping, you," George said.

"George and I sometimes listen to music in the evenings," Kristina said, holding up a compact disc case, "Beethoven's *Pastoral*?"

They relocated to the balcony.

The high, crisp notes swept out into the dusk, igniting the great horizon beyond.

Night came with many stars.

And then one afternoon, without telling anyone, Henry went swimming. Weightless steps carried him forward until salt water came up to his chin.

He let his mouth fill, determined to take in some part of that other world.

He felt his body rise and fall with the current.

He floated upright in perfect silence, drifting farther out.

And then the water was suddenly dark.

The sensation of cold.

The sensation of change.

The sensation of sensation.

END OF BOOK FOUR

NINE YEARS LATER

PARIS, FRANCE

Instead of going straight home from the shop with his small bag of groceries, Henry decides to stroll through the courtyards of the Louvre Museum.

It is midsummer, and everything around him is glowing.

Henry has worked at the Louvre for seven years. He is a curator. He reconstructs scenes from the past to illustrate their beauty and significance.

His latest show includes pieces on loan from the Museum of Piraeus.

Professor Peterson is helping to prepare the book that will accompany the exhibition. Henry has known the professor now for more than thirty years.

Thankfully, the book they are working on for the exhibition is taking months to put together. The professor is staying with the Malraux family on the other side of Paris. They have a grand piano in their apartment. They also have a driver with photographs of his children on the dashboard. Céleste and Bernard are their names.

Professor Peterson likes to work late in the archives when evenings are warm like this. He likes to open windows and stare out into the many courtyards around the Louvre.

He drinks sherry by first wetting his lips.

His eyes are attracted to people who move slowly.

He walks with a cane and has trouble hearing.

George is still living in Sicily.

He has two young children.

He says it was hard but they did it.

Italian is their first language and they all have strong Sicilian accents.

When Henry visits in the winter, the children climb all over him. Their mother shouts at them to stop, but everyone is laughing.

The house is marked with the lines and scuffs from her wheelchair. Stray cats still wait outside the door for scraps. It's always hot, and something is cooking.

Henry's friends from the museum have already left Paris for their summer homes in Burgundy or the Loire Valley. Henry will soon join them for long dinners, the soft fumes of wine, warm gushing rivers, long dreaming nights in heavy sheets, falling asleep under trees, afternoon baths, the joy of friendship.

The stones crunch beneath Henry's shoes. Inside his shopping bag is a clay pot of yogurt, an orange, an apple, and a bottle of water. The plastic handles weigh in heavy lines upon his fingers. He likes to feel its swing as he walks—like a pendulum, timing his journey across the open squares of the museum, from which stone watchmen, carved high into the walls, peer blindly down at the tourists and their silver boxes of lightning.

A young couple have shed their backpacks to make ripples in the black waters of a fountain. A homeless man talks to himself about something important.

Henry walks slowly. His hair is graying, and he likes a glass of wine before bed.

Sometimes he walks home along the River Seine and, remembering his old friend in Sicily, drops a coin into any hand that reaches out for one.

Sometimes he thinks of her, of them. Of what could have been.

Sometimes it's all he thinks about.

But he doesn't stop walking anymore.

He doesn't stop to look around.

He keeps going.

He can feel the weight of their lives in a single step forward.

And he is enchanted by the beauty of small things: hot coffee, wind through an open window, the tapping of rain, a passing bicycle, the desolation of snow on a winter's day.

On his slow walk on this brightest of nights, Henry Bliss passes high windows that reveal the museum in fractional glances; the sleeve of a Napoleonic uniform in oil, a white marble shoulder, the head of a lion sewn into a tapestry.

He approaches the steps that lead to the dim archway between courtyards—a narrow echoing chamber through which everyone must pass to reach the vast relief of occupied space.

Setting his foot upon the first stone, motion draws him.

Someone has fallen.

A woman is lying on the ground.

The people around gasp, but stand at a distance—their heads move with dismay and indecision.

Henry drops his bag and breaks through the crowd.

He's soon on his knees with his palms out.

He touches her; cradles her head and cushions it with his hands against the sharp stones of the courtyard.

She stares at him without blinking.

It's the story he will one day tell his daughter:

A camera in pieces.

He takes all her weight and the heaviness to come.

He raises her back into the world.

Her arms push on his, but he lifts her with his eyes.

ACKNOWLEDGMENTS

The author wishes to acknowledge the following:

Les Arts Florissants, Amy Baker, Erica Barmash, the O'Brien Family, Joshua Bodwell, Bryan Le Boeuf, Dr. A. S. and Mrs. J. E. Booy, Darren and Raha Booy, Douglas and Aneta Borroughs Esq., Milan Bozic, Ken Browar, David Bruson, Gabriel Byrne, Tricia Callahan, Billy O'Callaghan, Pamela Carlson, Jessica Chen *for Chinese translation*, the Connelly Family, Mary Beth Constant, Joan Copeland, Christine Corday, Christina Daigneault Esq. *of Orchard Strategies*, Ryan Davies, Emily Dixon, the *East Hampton Star*, Dr. Laura Falesi *for help with archaeology*, Peggy Flaum, Tom Ford, Dr. G. Frazzetto, the Frazzetto family *in Sicily*, the Gaddis Family, Valentino, Dr. Bruce Gelb, Dr. Greg Gulbransen, Jen Hart, Dr. Maryhelen Hendricks *at SVA*, Dolores Henry, Gregory Henry, the Hermès Group, Nancy Horner, Sebastian Horsley, Mr. Howard, Jaguar Automobiles, Dr. M. Kempner, Alan Kleinberg, Hilary Knight, Agnes Korbani *for Arabic translation*, the Ladies' Village

Improvement Society of East Hampton, Bénédicte Le Lay *for help with French translation*, the Lotos Club, Peng Lun, Madeleine *for her remarkable drawings*, Alain Malraux, Lisa Mamo, Michael and Delphine Matkin, McNally Jackson Booksellers, Dr. Edmund Miller, Dr. Bob Milgrom *at SVA*, Cal Morgan, Samuel Morris III, Bill Murray, Dr. William Neal of Campbellsville University, Neil Olson, New & Lingwood, Lukas Ortiz, Cristina Palomba, Robert and Babette Pereno, Professor William and Mary Peterson, Simon and Tam Petherick, Francine Prose, Jonathan Rabinowitz, Stephanie Reed *for help with archaeology and linguistics*, Rob, Alberto Rojas, Hala Schlub, Ivan Shaw, Anthony Sperduti *at Partners & Spade*, Philip G. Spitzer, Virginia Stanley, Jeremy Strong, Lorilee Van Booy, Jan T. Vilcek, Marcia Vilcek, and Rick A. Kinsel *of the Vilcek Foundation*, Fred Volkmer, Catrin Brace and Judith Kampfner of the Welsh Assembly Government, and Dr. Barbara Wersba.

Very special thanks to Rich Green, Carrie Howland, Michael Signorelli, and Poppy de Villeneuve, and extra special thanks for poetic brilliance and friendship to Lucas A. Hunt.

And enormous thanks to Carrie Kania—whose editorial brilliance, unequaled sense of humor, generosity, addiction to style, and deep friendship helped make this book possible.

Books by Simon Van Booy

LOVE BEGINS IN WINTER
Five Stories
ISBN 978-0-06-166147-1 (paperback)

"Incurable romantics will savor Simon Van Booy's tender, Maupassant-like fables . . ."
—*The New York Times*

THE SECRET LIVES OF PEOPLE IN LOVE
Stories
ISBN 978-0-06-176612-1 (paperback)

"Breathtaking . . . chillingly beautiful, like postcards from Eden."

—*Los Angeles Times*

Why?
Each volume consists of famous excerpts and passages from philosophical, biblical, and literary sources with an introduction and commentary by Simon Van Booy.

Why We Need Love
ISBN: 978-0-06-184554-3
(paperback)

Why Our Decisions Don't Matter
ISBN: 978-0-06-184555-0
(paperback)

Why We Fight
ISBN: 978-0-06-184556-7
(paperback)

"[They] have an instinctive appeal . . . the three smartly designed paperbacks address their themes directly."

—*The Economist*

Available wherever books are sold, or call 1-800-331-3761 to order.